"I don't have to explain my motives or my feelings, not to you or anyone else."

Sam stood, her heart racing, her palms damp. The defensiveness of her tone made her shudder. Or was that Aidan's effect on her?

He continued to close in, smoothly, soundlessly. The predator preparing to pounce on its prey, she thought, firming up her resolve. She was nobody's prey.

"You're too complicated for me, Aidan. You have angst and ghosts and danger swirling around you. I have goals and a strong desire for simplicity in my personal life. We don't go together."

Aidan narrowed his eyes. "You're not afraid of me, are you?" He'd told her once that she should be. And yet...

"No," she said, swallowing the sudden knot of panic in her throat. "Of myself."

ABOUT THE AUTHOR

Jenna Ryan loves creating dark-haired heroes, heroines with strength and good murder mysteries. Ever since she was young, she has had an extremely active imagination. She considered various careers over the years and dabbled in several of them, until one day about nine years ago when her sister Kathy suggested that she put her imagination to work and write a book. She enjoys working with intriguing characters and feels she is at her best writing romantic suspense. When people ask her how she writes, she tells them by instinct. Clearly it's worked since she's received numerous awards from *Romantic Times*. She lives in Canada and travels as much as she can when she's not writing.

Books by Jenna Ryan

HARLEQUIN INTRIGUE

The Woman in Black

Jenna Ryan

Harlequin Books

TORONTO • NEW YORK • LONDON
AMSTERDAM • PARIS • SYDNEY • HAMBURG
STOCKHOLM • ATHENS • TOKYO • MILAN
MADRID • WARSAW • BUDAPEST • AUCKLAND

For Shauna:
Kind Fate brought you to us,
Cruel Fate took you away.
We'll miss you, Shauna, always,
Until our dying day.
(Love you, even in Heaven, Baby)

ISBN 0-373-22450-8

THE WOMAN IN BLACK

Copyright © 1998 by Jacqueline Goff

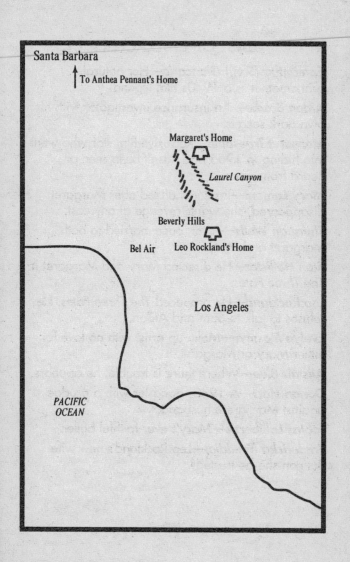

Santa Barbara

↑ To Anthea Pennant's Home

Margaret's Home

Laurel Canyon

Beverly Hills

Bel Air   Leo Rockland's Home

Los Angeles

*PACIFIC
OCEAN*

CAST OF CHARACTERS

Samantha (Sam) Giancarlo—Her natural grandmother is a 1940s film legend.

Aidan Brodie—An insurance investigator with his own dark secrets.

Margaret Truesdale—Reclusive film star who went into hiding in 1953 and hasn't been seen or heard from since.

Mary Lamont—Institutionalized after Margaret disappeared, she wants revenge at any cost.

Thurman Wells—Actor, once married to both Margaret and Mary.

Stan Hollister—He directed Mary and Margaret in *The Three Fates.*

Leo Rockland—He produced *The Three Fates.* He refuses to talk to Sam and Aidan.

Evelyn Mesmyr—Make-up artist with no love for either Mary or Margaret.

Alistair Blue—Where there is trouble, he appears.

Dorian Hart—A 1940s gangster with a grudge against Margaret's husband.

Tobias Lallibertie—Mary's ever-faithful butler.

Fredericka (Freddie)—Leo Rockland's new wife. But can she be trusted?

Prologue

September 17, 1953

Thunder rolled like a giant bowling ball through the blackened skies above the Hollywood Hills. Forked lightning split that blackness into two jagged pieces. Heaven, thought a grimly satisfied Mary Lamont, appeared as displeased at the current state of affairs as she was.

Turning from the lead-paned window of her elegant home, she let the sheer silk curtain flutter back into place. Rain pelted the outer walls, as livid a barrage as the one inside her head. How dare the studio fire her! They couldn't complete the movie without her.

"*The Three Fates,* my size seven foot," she snarled at the parrot that watched her warily from its gilt perch. "More like *One Fate and Two Fools,* if you ask me." Which no one had, of course.

A crash of thunder momentarily overrode the insistent knock that echoed across the marbled foyer.

"Go away," she shouted at the double doors. "There's no one here but us has-beens. Go back to your precious Margaret Truesdale and let me wither away like the Fate I would have played if…" She couldn't choke the rest out. She drew deeply on her cigarette holder and tossed her chestnut hair instead.

"Let me in, Mary." Thurman Wells's voice rose above the storm.

Not his usual dulcet tones tonight, Mary thought smugly and congratulated herself for affecting that much at least.

"Go away," she ordered again. "I've nothing to say to you."

Trailing smoke behind her like a royal mantle, she started up the winding staircase. Let Tobias deal with the rabble. That's what butlers were for. To put out the garbage and bring her a hot toddy after the power lines went down, which they undoubtedly would with all this high wind and rain.

The radio announcer's voice floated eerily down the stairwell from her bedroom. "Suspense," he said, then paused for dramatic effect. "Tonight, Roma Wine brings you—"

The actor's name and story title were lost in another resounding clap of thunder. Probably no one with talent. Who wanted to do radio anymore? Not her, no sirree. She was a film star, a glorious shining point of light in the cinema firmament, or however that ditsy blonde had put it in the big-money musical whose premier she'd attended last year.

A funny glittering haze assailed her as she thought back. It seemed a stretch to remember last week let alone last year. Why, she couldn't even recall what she'd done today. Except that she'd been fired, of course. That she recalled with crystal clarity. She was out on her ear. Oh, and there'd been that big furor about Margaret, as well. Perfect, beautiful, talented Margaret Truesdale. Just thinking her name, Mary was tempted to throw up.

"Mary!"

Partway up the lavish stairwell, she spun to face the man who'd barked at her. He stood like a dark-haired dog, a Lab, suited and chapeaued, dripping all over her polished marble floor.

"What?" she barked back. She didn't bother to ask how he'd gotten in. Ex-husbands produced copies of the keys they'd supposedly relinquished upon divorce like magicians pulled rabbits from top hats. She'd have Tobias change the locks first thing tomorrow.

Thurman glared at her as only he could. Elegant annoyance was stamped all over his handsome face. Poor old Clark. He'd never made female hearts go pit-a-pat like Thurman.

"What do you mean, what?" he demanded. It was almost a growl. Mary resisted the urge to spit at him. "You attacked the script writer, for God's sake. What on earth were you hoping to accomplish?"

She regarded him as a queen might an ignorant peasant. A veil of smoke hid his shrewd blue eyes from sight. "Nothing else seemed to be working," she replied offhandedly. She flexed her scarlet fingernails like a cat retracting its claws. "I only gouged him a little. Hardly more than a scratch. I suppose he went crying straight to Leo."

"You're lucky he didn't go crying straight to the cops. He wanted to."

"But you talked him out of it," she purred, descending slowly. "I can always count on you, can't I, darling?"

"Stan stopped him."

"Really?" She reached the bottom, walked to a mahogany table and began to wind up one of her three dozen precious Italian music boxes. Strains of Chopin's "Polonaise" tinkled lightly through the foyer. Too bad about that annoying thunder. "Stan did that for me? What does a mere director care about such matters? I'd have thought as producer, Leo—"

"You're no longer studio property, Mary," Thurman interrupted. Headlights glanced off the stained-glass panels beside the front doors. He turned to look, then scowled back at her. "You really botched things this time. Harassing studio executives, causing public scenes, then that attack today—and always, *always* your consuming hatred of Margaret."

Mary flung her smoldering cigarette and ebony holder to the floor. "Don't speak that name in my presence," she shrieked. Clapping her hands to her ears, she tried to block the memory of it. "She's nothing. She's no one!"

"She's gone," Thurman said. His eyes narrowed. "You know she is. You were at the studio when Leo broke the news."

Gone? Mary's scrunched eye muscles relaxed. Yes, of course, she *was* gone, wasn't she? Like Garbo. They'd made the announcement yesterday on the set. Margaret Truesdale had disappeared, no explanation, no warning, nothing. She'd simply vanished from Hollywood.

The soothing "Polonaise" worked its way into her fevered mind. "Gone," she said softly, wonderingly. "That's right. I'm the star now. Anthea's not good enough, any fool can see that. It'll be *The Two Fates* now. All that moron writer has to do is fix the script and—"

"The film's been shelved, Mary," Thurman said. Glancing behind him, he made a subtle motion with his head.

"Shelved!" Violent emotions flooded in, fury followed by spite, then confusion. Her fists balled at her sides. She saw nothing except Margaret's face, taunting, always taunting. She shook the confusion off. "That's ridiculous, Thurman. It's impossible! We're more than three-quarters of the way through the picture. You said it yourself, Margaret's gone…"

"But not forgotten," Thurman said quietly.

His wistful tone had a similar effect of acid splashed on an open wound. A snarl emerged from Mary's throat. Her muscles bunched. Aware only of her target, she lunged straight for Thurman Wells's lying throat.

She had no idea what happened next, why her flight was halted with a neck-wrenching abruptness that caused her teeth to sink into her tongue. It was as if she'd hit a wall, except that only her limbs seemed affected. Her feet, though still thrashing wildly, covered no ground.

She felt her sleeve go up, then something pricked her arm. It stung so she tugged away. "Who the hell are you?" she demanded rudely of the man in white who was holding her. "I gave you no leave to touch my person."

"She played Mary Queen of Scots once," Thurman explained tiredly. "Relax, Mary. These men are here to help you. We all are."

She lashed out, kicking and swearing. "Traitor!" Her foot struck the mahogany table. Her favorite music box would have shattered if Thurman hadn't reacted swiftly and grabbed it in midair. Her next kick, deliciously vicious, caught him in the stomach. He grimaced but made no sound.

"Take her away," he instructed the white-coated men. Three of them, Mary noted, one with a very mean-looking needle in his hand.

She felt woozy already, thick-headed. "Damn you, Thurman," she raged dully. "I'll kill you for this. I'll…" Another voice reached her ears. Margaret's voice, coming from upstairs. From her bedroom!

"Oh, God," Thurman murmured. "Wouldn't you know it. I'll get the radio. You take her out. She has to be committed tonight, that's the deal. Otherwise…"

Groggily, Mary raised her limp head. "Otherwise what? And what's that witch doing in my house?"

"It's the radio, Mary," Thurman explained. "Otherwise, the man you attacked will press charges."

"Temperamental jerk," she slurred. Her chest heaved as Margaret's voice droned on upstairs. She managed to catch Thurman's eye. "I'll get her," she vowed, breathing heavily. "I'll find her if it's the last thing I do." The men dragged her forward. "Do you hear me, Thurman?" Her voice rose to a shriek above Margaret's, the thunder and the delicate strains of the "Polonaise." "If it's the last thing I ever do, I'll find Margaret Truesdale. And when I do, I'll kill her. I'll kill her!"

Chapter One

November 5, 1996

Sam didn't like unknown commodities. Mysteries, yes, but not this overblown cloak-and-dagger stuff.

"Go to the old woman's house and see what she's got," her editor at the Los Angeles *Break,* one of the city's smallest and least known newspapers, had instructed gruffly. "She didn't give her name, but apparently she did the Garbo thing forty-some years back. Maybe there's a story in it."

Sam liked her time-worn editor and so accepted the assignment without a fuss.

A cool autumn wind ruffled her long black hair as she started up the winding drive. The house before her looked vaguely imposing with the late afternoon sun silhouetting it from behind. Mauve and umber clouds stretching wispy fingers across the sky over the gabled roof, accentuated the strong feeling that she'd somehow stepped through a time hole into a bygone era. Something about this sequestered house in Laurel Canyon made her mind switch automatically to black and white. She half expected to look down and find her deep coral pantsuit had turned gray.

She should have changed, she realized belatedly. Sally had figured they'd be dealing with a cracked and faded movie queen. The word "elegant" hadn't entered the conversation. But elegant the mansion before her most certainly was.

She rang the doorbell then strained to hear the chime. Even muffled by a thick oak door it sounded musical, a bit overdone, but suitable for a movie star from another age.

She was repositioning her oversize leather shoulder bag when a lone eyeball appeared at the peephole.

"Ms. Giancarlo?" a man's proper British voice inquired.

"Samantha—Sam—I mean, yes." It was the house, she decided as a chain rattled on the other side. She wasn't a stutterer by nature.

This time an entire man greeted her. He was tall, as thin as a reed and balding slightly. Very erect and steady, though, for someone obviously well into his seventies.

"Please come in," he bade her politely. "Madame is in the parlor."

"It really is a time warp," Sam murmured.

Graying brows went up. "I beg your pardon?"

"Nothing. I say things out loud sometimes. It's a bad habit."

"I can imagine. Will you come this way?"

The man must be the butler Sally had mentioned. Theodore Something. Whatever his name, he suited the house to perfection. It wasn't often in Sam's experience that people fit their surroundings so well.

On the other hand, she didn't often see houses as lavishly laid out and decorated as this one appeared to be. Potted palms, fronds of pampas grass and even a miniature lemon tree dotted the entry hall, which in itself was not so much spacious as cleverly designed. The staircase was another matter, a grand affair, broad and carpeted with creamy pink plush. The hardwood floor and newel post were solid oak, the light fixtures Lalique, the portraits—well, she knew nothing about art, but they looked expensive, authentic even to her inexperienced eye.

And yet she perceived at once a false sense of airiness about the place, false because of the shadows that loomed high above her head in the sculpted nether regions of the plaster ceiling. One might see light at first glance, but there was darkness here, too, an overriding air of intrigue both past and present.

Sam peered at a collection of framed photographs above a long glass table. "That's Joan Crawford, isn't it?"

"Yes, it is. The madame knew her quite well."

"She knew a lot of people, if these pictures are any indication." Sam fixed him with an inquiring stare. "What's the madame's name? Theodore, isn't it?"

"Theo Larkin. Madame will answer your other questions in her own time and fashion." He beckoned for her to precede him. "The parlor is through here."

"I should have worn a dress," Sam said with a sigh.

Theo's placid expression didn't alter. "Madame is not a snob, if that's what you're thinking. Neither is she trapped— excuse me, I should say, living—in the past."

"Is there a difference?"

"A subtle one. We are all of us, in one way or another, trapped by our pasts."

An odd remark, not untrue, just a funny thing to say to a complete stranger. Unless, of course, he was preparing her for a confrontation with an eccentric harridan who would expect instant recognition followed by a gushing list of all the movie credits in her pre-and post-war repertoire. That being the case, Sam would take Sally apart for sticking her with this assignment.

The parlor turned out to be a comparatively small room. Plants and flowers abounded, though not so many that Sam felt stifled. The carpet here was Persian, exquisite except for a tiny scorch mark near the flowered sofa.

Madame or one of her cronies must have dropped a match or cigarette.

The subject of her interview was using both when Sam entered. She was also, Sam noticed, sitting in the least revealing spot in the room, opposite the shaded French doors in a high-backed chair with the light angled away from her carefully made-up face.

She was old, Sam could see that right off. She sensed a hard life, or perhaps "afterlife" was a better term. Some celebrities took the passing years in stride; others fought them to the bitter end. This woman looked to have fought and survived, little more.

Even expertly applied cosmetics and discreet lighting couldn't conceal the skin that sagged on her neck and chin. Her eyes were less visible behind tinted lenses, but her hands, rheumatic and mottled with age spots, gave much away. Her appearance spoke of hard times, determination and too much sun in the glamorous post-war days of the forties.

Without preface, the woman stated, "I was considered beautiful once. Sit there. That will be all, Theo. Bring coffee and rum in fifteen minutes."

Intrigued by a voice rusty from the affects of alcohol and smoke, Sam sat as directed. She chose the side of the sofa nearest her hostess, making no attempt to hide her curiosity. At closer range, the woman's eyes were brown, red-rimmed but sharp enough to be called biting.

"Well?" the madame demanded, inhaling deeply on her cigarette. "Do I pass inspection?"

"I was trying to see if...I'm sorry, I'm being rude. Curiosity's a failing of mine."

"You're in the billion-plus club in that regard."

Sam dug out her old-fashioned notepad and pen. "You don't pull any punches, do you?"

"Not many. Never have. Do you recognize me yet?"

The dreaded question. Sam searched for a believable excuse then submitted to honesty and shook her head. "Sorry. All my editor said was that I should come out here. No explanation, no background, only an address. I'd have gone to the archives except..."

"You weren't given a name." Another drag, another cloud of smoke veiling her faded features. "I'm an old woman, Ms.

Giancarlo. I don't expect you to recognize me. Did your editor mention that I requested you specifically?''

"Me?" A small frown marred Sam's forehead.

"No, I thought not. Odd, because it's usually men who omit details. I often think how much better this world would be if run by women. No matter, you're here, and you've no idea who I am. I shouldn't expect you to, really. How old are you? Twenty-five?"

"Thirty."

"You look younger. At any rate, my star disappeared from the Hollywood heavens more than a decade before you were born."

"So you are like Garbo, then."

"The comparison's been drawn. Theo, in particular, enjoys it. A good man is my Theo. Been with me forever. We'll probably die together."

Sam strove for a discreetly clearer view of the woman whom she judged to be about five foot five or six. She was very thin, verging on frail. Her black dress, sequined and long-sleeved, revealed little of her bony frame. Her hair was a silver-streaked crown, combed and sprayed into a modified version of a late forties style. The effect jarred but was not unpleasant.

Recalling her remark about dying in tandem with Theo, Sam arched dubious brows. "That's a morbid point of view, if you don't mind my saying so."

The woman shrugged. "Morbidity's relative when you reach my age. My health's only so-so, and I refuse to stop smoking. I'll go the way of my dear colleague, Bette Davis, eventually, though not, I hope, for a few more years. Ah, there you are, Theo. Prompt as always."

"Shall I pour, Madame?"

She waved him off with her cigarette. "I haven't gotten to the shock, yet. Leave it here. The steadier of us can pour later."

Sam eyed her warily. Patient to a point, she was tiring rapidly of this woman's blunt nondisclosures.

"Who are you?" she asked the moment Theo departed.

"You're a candid little thing."

At five foot seven Sam was neither little, nor a thing. But candid, yes, she tended to be that. "I'm a journalist," she said, preferring that to the less flattering "reporter." "It's my job to be candid."

"Bull. It's your job to be pigheaded. Mine is to be mysterious." A bony hand emerged from the dusty aureole of light. "Maybe you'll recognize my name when you hear it. Someone, my dear Samantha, has learned of my whereabouts and fully intends to kill me. I'm Margaret Truesdale."

MARGARET TRUESDALE.

Sam recognized the name instantly. Her mother was an old movie buff. According to her, Margaret Truesdale had been a star of the highest caliber in her day. Tough, fair, beautiful, only mildly temperamental and one of the best actresses the Hollywood studio system had ever produced. Her final movie, *The Three Fates,* had never been completed. Nor had any excerpts ever been shown. All copies of that film had vanished shortly after its leading lady. Studio executives apparently had no idea where the canisters had gotten to…unless, as a few of them had speculated, Margaret herself had stolen them.

Triumph flashed in Margaret's dark eyes as she regarded Sam. "You do know me, then. How wonderful."

"You disappeared," Sam said unnecessarily. "Why?"

Margaret leaned forward. "For reasons I am not prepared to disclose."

"Then why did you contact—"

"I'm getting to that." Margaret's finger stabbed the air in front of her. "For the moment, you must accept that my reasons for going into seclusion are private and personal. They have nothing to do with the fact that someone wants me dead."

"You're sure of that?"

"Certainly. I know who's behind it. Do you see that box in front of you on the table? It's a music box. Open the lid."

Sam hesitated, then complied. Delicate strains of Chopin's "Polanaise" filled the air.

"It's Italian," Margaret revealed, lighting another cigarette. "It appeared on my doorstep yesterday. It belonged to one of my co-stars in *The Three Fates*. I'll be honest and tell you that she and I were not friends. In fact, the term 'rivals' can't begin to convey the feeling of animosity that existed between us. We made numerous movies together, I in the starring role, she invariably in a secondary capacity. That's how it was in the beginning and how it remained until the bitter end."

"What was her name?" Sam asked, jotting notes.

"Mary Lamont. There was a third Fate, of course, but we had no quarrels. Only Mary and I were at constant odds."

"And you think—what? That Mary sent you this music box as some kind of warning? A death threat?"

"It would be Mary's style," Margaret said dryly. "She always had a flair for the melodramatic. It got the better of her more often than was healthy—her imagination, I mean. She was forever in trouble with the studio. She spent half of the last five years of her career on a psychiatrist's couch. In nineteen fifty-three, shortly after I left Hollywood, her ex-husband, Thurman, finally had her committed. According to my sources, she's been in and out of institutions ever since."

Sam winced at the thought. "I assume she's out now."

"Absolutely." Margaret tapped an ash into a silver bowl. "She escaped from Oakhaven last week. The story's been hushed up, as you can imagine, but the bald truth is she's out and she wants me dead. She's made no bones about that over the years. Her doctors will tell you. I'm her obsession. Her sole aim in life is to destroy me. Thus—" she indicated the music box "—her little gift. She wants me to know that she has found me at last. The rest..." Margaret gave a fatalistic shrug. "The rest is anyone's guess. All I'm sure of is that she will try to kill me. And she will go on trying until either she succeeds or she herself is dead.''

Sam had stopped writing long ago. ''You need the police, Ms. Truesdale, not a repor—a journalist.''

''It's Margaret, and there will be no police. I want no publicity. None. This must be a private investigation by someone I can trust completely. I'd ask Theo, but he's too old, his son's dead and his daughter's married to some fanatical religious man from New England.''

Uneasiness crawled over Sam's lightly tanned skin like a swarm of red ants. ''You need a detective agency.''

''I need you.''

Damn, she'd just known Margaret was going to say that. ''I don't do murder investigations,'' she said, flipping her notebook closed. ''Stories, yes, but I have no training in investigative work. I'll interview a murderer once he or she's behind bars, not before.''

Margaret emitted an unladylike snort and sat back. ''This from the young woman who sent a would-be mugger to hospital last year with three cracked ribs and very sore private parts? I'll bet you kept that baseball bat as a memento.''

How had she learned that? Sam shrugged. ''The guy tried to grab me when I was loading my gear into the trunk of my car after a game. I didn't think ramming the bat into his midsection would break ribs, but I guess he didn't tense properly. The rest was instinctive. It has nothing to do with—''

''You were adopted, weren't you?''

Sam stopped dead. ''How...''

''I checked. Do you know your real parents?''

Her equanimity, one of Sam's better qualities, slipped several notches. ''My real parents,'' she said coldly, ''are Carlos and Anna Giancarlo. I don't know or care who my birth parents were.''

''You never looked for them?''

''Until I was about seventeen, yes. Then I realized it didn't matter.''

"You simply gave your curiosity the boot, hmm?"

"I dealt with it. I can be strong-minded when I want to be."

"Of course you can. It runs in the family."

"What family?" Sam demanded.

"Mine. Yours." Margaret's chin angled upward in a direct challenge. "Ours."

"Don't be ridiculous. We're not related." Sam hesitated, her fingers freezing on the zipper of her shoulder bag. "Are we?"

Margaret let out a cackle that would have done Broom Hilda proud. "We most certainly are, young Samantha Giancarlo. I had one child in my life, a daughter. That daughter was your birth mother. By blood and birth and enough digging to have burrowed halfway to China by now, I'm your grandmother."

"You pour," Margaret instructed. "Put rum in mine. I'm not as steady-handed as I was once. I was involved in an accident many years ago."

Sam's head swam. She poured automatically, managing not to rattle the bone-china cup and saucer. Her grandmother? Margaret Truesdale? But if not the truth, then why would Margaret have brought her here? Asked Sally specifically to send her here?

"You're in shock," Margaret chortled with something akin to glee. She sobered at Sam's skeptical expression. "And you don't trust me. I have the necessary documents, all the genuine articles. Theo will bring them before you leave."

Unable to marshal her thoughts, Sam handed her the coffee. "When did you find out?"

"Three years ago."

"Why didn't you tell me?"

"Because as you said before, you already had a life. I saw no reason to intrude upon it. I, above all, understand the need for privacy. I respect it. I brought the subject up today for the simple, selfish reason that I require your help. You're the only person, aside from Theo, that I can turn to.''

Her gnarled fingers touched Sam's knee, sending an apprehensive shiver through her body. "Will you help me? I have nowhere else to go."

Sam knew herself well enough to understand that her conscience would shoot down any objection her mind might raise. Better to accept that she was going to help the woman and deal instead with the shock.

"I'll..." She cleared her throat. "Yes, all right. I will help you. If I can, that is."

"But first you want more information," Margaret finished for her. "In a nutshell, or the encyclopedic version?"

"A nutshell's fine for now. My mind's too numb to absorb the details."

Margaret stubbed out her cigarette and lit another. Resting her head against the chair back, she said, "Your mother's name was Delores. That's the name she grew up with, I didn't give it to her.

"The timing was bad—impossible, really. I was unwed and I owed my soul to the studio in any event. They decided I should go through with the pregnancy then give the child up for adoption. Naturally, I went along with them. That was an end to it for over twenty years. Then I got curious and did some digging. I discovered that, like me, Delores had become pregnant at a young age. And like me, she gave her child—you—up for adoption."

She raised a forestalling hand as Sam opened her mouth. "I don't know who your father is if that's your next question. Your mother never named him. From your coloring, however, I'd guess that he was Italian, as your adoptive parents must also be." Her eyes scanned Sam's slender features. "You're quite beautiful, my dear. Indeed, I might go so far as to say exquisite. I would have killed for skin like yours fifty years ago. Golden brown eyes—almond-shaped, black hair, skin like honey, and fine-boned to boot. I could circle that wrist of yours with one arthritic hand. But I'm getting off track, aren't I? Tell me, do you have children?''

"No.''

"Spoken in such a judgmental tone. You think Delores and I are heartless monsters, don't you?''

Sam was in no fit state to be tactful. "I think you at least were in a position to be stronger.''

"You don't know the studio system if you believe that.''

"Other women did it.''

"Ingrid, for example?''

"She coped.''

Margaret set her somewhat angular jaw. "So did I. You don't have all the facts, Samantha.''

Sam's saucer clattered onto the table. "That's because you won't give them to me.''

"You're snapping.''

"I'm upset. You've just turned a life I thought I knew upside down.''

Margaret gurgled a smoke-congested laugh. "Would you rather I'd kept the truth to myself? No, I thought not. You have my streak of curiosity, tempered perhaps by love and logic, but present inside you nonetheless.''

Finishing her coffee, she sent Sam a speculative look. "That's it, the nutshell version.'' Faintly bloodshot eyes shifted to the ornate music box. "As for the more dangerous matter, Mary must be caught. You will need to start your search immediately. I suggest you do it at her last known place of residence, the Oakhaven Sanatorium twenty miles farther into the Canyon.'' Her expression became grim. "I warn you, Samantha,'' she said gravely. "Mary is out for blood. My blood, but she'll kill anyone who gets in her way. She's insane. And she would derive extreme pleasure from murdering my one and only descendant.''

A ZOMBIE-LIKE STUPOR settled over Sam's mind for the next six hours. The first three were spent on a jam-packed Los Angeles freeway.

She didn't call her parents in Stockton when she got back; not a chance would she hurt them by explaining that her maternal grandmother had walked—no, be honest—bulldozed her way into her only granddaughter's life. This, Sam reflected, was her problem to handle, and handle it she would.

"You got guts, I'll give you that."

"Bag it, Guido." Sam swirled the dregs of her old friend and mentor's favorite red wine, family wine from his home fifty years ago in Truro, Italy. Guido Bocce was sixty-seven years old. He ran the newspaper archives, or news morgue as he jokingly called it, lived above an Italian grocery store and still called her Minx twenty years after their first meeting.

Now he gave her his best Gepetto smile—a not especially convincing thing, considering his scrawny build—fingered his shaggy white mustache and refilled her glass. "I'll see what I can turn up for you tomorrow," he promised, uncustomarily solemn. "I hope you're dealing with a crackpot, but I think you probably aren't."

Sam grunted. "If you mean Margaret, she's the genuine article. I saw the documents, Guido. I'm her granddaughter, all right. She even had a copy of the adoption papers."

Guido took a contemplative sip. "Too sweet," he said. "You're sure she's Margaret Truesdale?"

"Sure enough. I saw a picture in her front hall. A younger version, but I'd guess it's her."

"Did you see Betty Grable?"

"No. But Agnes Moorehead was there. I liked Endora."

"Your mom liked Samantha better."

"I know. Named for a television witch. Too bad I didn't inherit her television powers, as well." She drank for a moment in thoughtful silence. Then, holding the glass in front of her, she asked slowly, "Would you do it, Guido? Would you help her?"

"Yes, but then I'm a fan. And I'm older than you. Less to

lose if Mad Mary gets me in her sights. Did you ever see *Hush…Hush Sweet Charlotte*?''

''A long time ago. Was Mary Lamont in it?''

''No. She'd have been good in the lead, though. She'd have made a great crazy woman.''

Sam frowned. ''If she was such a basket case, why did the studio hire her?''

Guido sat back and considered. ''She could have been a great actress. That was the tragedy of it. She had the talent. It was the focus she got wrong. She hated Margaret more than she loved acting. If she could have forgotten that hatred even for a moment, one wonders what might have been.''

''I'm starting to wonder if I'm not the crazy one instead of her. I don't know the first thing about detective work. I'll start at Oakhaven, but after that, I have no idea.''

Guido pursed his lips. ''Could be I have an in at Oakhaven. I'll see what I can do. Margaret can't guess where Mary might be?''

Sam sighed. ''If she could, Mary wouldn't be there for long, would she? I wonder how she found Margaret?''

''I have a better question.'' Guido topped his own glass. ''What's Margaret Truesdale doing living so close by in Laurel Canyon?''

''She wasn't, not at first. She went to Europe when she dropped out of sight. She only came back this year—thinking it would be safe by now, I suppose. She's renting the canyon house. She must have figured Mary's obsession would have played itself out by now—assuming she knew how strong it was in the first place. She didn't say so, but I don't think she left Hollywood because of Mary Lamont.''

''I'm sure of it,'' Guido confirmed. ''Mary Lamont was fired from *The Three Fates*. At least the decision was made to fire her the same week that Margaret disappeared. Margaret was the star, undisputed. Mary was a problem and disposable in the eyes of the studio bigwigs.''

''Weird history,'' Sam noted. Finishing her wine, she

reached for her bag. "I'd better get going, Guido. I want to be at Oakhaven early tomorrow morning and my car's making funny thumping noises."

Guido prevented her from rising with a blue-veined hand pressed upon her slender, tanned wrist. "You'll be careful, won't you, Minx? I'll help all I can with Oakhaven and background material, but my bum knees won't allow me to do much else."

Smiling, Sam reached over and kissed his gaunt cheek. "I'll be extra careful," she promised. "Forewarned is forearmed, or whatever that stupid expression is. I'll look for Mary. I won't get in her way."

"Don't," Guido advised seriously. "She was volatile when they called her sane. I heard she gouged an orderly's eye out the first time she was committed."

With a shiver, Sam pulled back. "I have better reflexes than a seventy-seven-year-old woman, Guido."

He shook his head. "Madness has its own rules, little Minx. Mary Lamont is as unpredictable as an April day—and as dangerous as Sweet Charlotte's vicious sister *any* day of the week."

Chapter Two

John Christian looked exactly the way the head of a psychiatric institute should. He had a short, immaculate beard, a round face, dark-rimmed glasses, and a permanent expression of concern on his forty-five-year-old face. He reminded Aidan Brodie of an older Leonard Maltin and was, despite the white lab coat and ever-present platitudes, one of the most sincere and caring people he knew.

John toyed with a Cross pen as he settled Aidan into a seat across from him in his professionally decorated office. The effect was easy on the eye. The deep mushroom carpet, the cushy earth-toned furniture, the pastel landscapes, the potted plants on Grecian stands, even the big bay window behind him that looked out over acres of secluded woodland spoke of comfort and security. People paid through the nose to be sick here. It was pure dumb luck that John actually happened to care about his patients' well-being.

Stretching his long legs out in front of him, Aidan studied his old friend through half-lidded eyes. "You mentioned a favor," he prompted when John didn't speak.

"What? Oh, yes. Sorry, my mind's on—other things. Related problems. Can't let this debacle get out. Escaped patients. I should have seen it coming, Aidan. Insane does not preclude stupidity. I of all people know that."

Aidan's eyebrows came together. "Who are you talking about?"

"Mary Lamont. Ever heard of her?"

"Film star, circa nineteen forty."

"A bit later, but you're in the general area. And she wasn't quite a star, a fact which undoubtedly played into her, er, breakdown." The pen fell onto the blotter. Setting his elbows on the desk, John rubbed his forehead. "It's such a damned mess. I can't contact the police. The negative publicity would destroy us. But I can't let Mary wander around on her own, either. She's...too unstable."

Aidan caught the hesitation. "Unstable as in dangerous?"

"Extremely, but I didn't say that."

"How dangerous?"

"The truth? Deadly."

"To herself or someone else?"

"Someone else. An old rival." His eyes slid sideways to the fireplace. "She shouldn't have been here, Aidan. That's how bad she is. I admitted her as a personal favor—and, all right, I confess, a trunkload of much-needed cash. God, if the press gets wind of this, we'll lose our patients. We'll be ruined. As it is, we're in the red. Nonpayments, back payments, taxes. You wouldn't believe how many rich and famous people have guttersnipes for relatives."

"Mommie Dearest," Aidan murmured.

"That's one side of the story. As I've come to realize, there are two sides at least."

"Point taken. What do you want from me?"

"Your expertise."

A sigh welled up. Containing it, Aidan said patiently, "I'm an insurance investigator, John, not a private detective."

John's expression bordered on frantic. "I need you, Aidan. You're the only person I can trust. The job's not dissimilar to yours."

Aidan regarded him for a long moment, his features contemplative but otherwise unrevealing. "I have two weeks coming," he said finally. "I can take them now if it would help."

John looked as if the weight of the world had been lifted from his shoulders. "It would... Yes, what is it, Mr. Blue?" he asked in minor annoyance as the door behind Aidan clicked open. "I thought we'd concluded our business."

Aidan didn't turn. There was no need. He'd met Alistair Blue in the lobby. The man was young, with dark curly hair that was also long and scruffy, shocking blue eyes and an arrogant attitude that would have done a youthful Henry the Eighth proud.

"I saw her room," Alistair said cockily. "Her stuff's been packed away. I need to see that, too."

John shot Aidan an aggrieved look. "Have you two met? Yes? Good. Alistair's looking for Mary, too, Aidan. To make a long story short, he was sent here by Mary's ex-husband, Thurman Wells. We contacted Mr. Wells when she escaped in the hopes that she'd go to him. He was understandably upset, and so hired Mr. Blue here to try and locate her."

Still not turning, Aidan asked over his shoulder, "Are you a licensed investigator, Mr. Blue?"

"Not exactly." The insolent defensiveness in Alistair's voice was clear. At best he'd be twenty-four or five. "I've had training, if that's what you're asking."

"What kind of training?"

Only Alistair's cocksure attitude saved him. "Enough to do this job."

"Don't count on it," John muttered. Louder, he said, "Mary's belongings are her personal property. I'm afraid I can't help you, Mr. Blue."

"You'll help him, though, won't you?" Alistair accused from Aidan's side. Then he let out a long breath, jingled his keys and shrugged. "Oh, all right. We'll see who tracks her down first, Brodie."

"That we will," Aidan acknowledged.

A nurse tapped on the door. "Excuse me, Dr. Christian. There's a woman to see you. Samantha—" she checked the card in her hand "—Giancarlo." Her fingers came up to shield the side of her mouth. "She's a reporter."

John nodded. "That's right. We spoke yesterday. Send her in, please." Ignoring Alistair, he said to Aidan, "This woman, Samantha Giancarlo, is also interested in locating Mary. As it happens, I owe someone at the L.A. *Break* a favor. After all, we do have a lot of famous people here. Guido's a good man. He's kept my confidence before. He assured me that none of the information I provide to the young woman will appear in print."

Aidan looked at him. "What's she after if not a story?"

"Guido didn't say. All he told me was that she's tenacious. And," he added with a wry twist of his lips, "trustworthy. I hope he's telling the truth and she's not a lying journalist looking for a juicy story. Ah, good day, Ms. Giancarlo." He rose, a smile emphasizing the worry lines on his face. "I'm John Christian. That's Mr. Alistair Blue next to you, and this is Aidan Brodie. Aidan's an insurance investigator and a friend. Alistair is also here on Mary's behalf. You've come to me for the same reason, it seems."

Courtesy, hammered into him by his strict Irish mother, brought Aidan to his feet. Control, hard-won through street fights and geographic circumstance, allowed him to react with only vague surprise.

She was gorgeous, fine-boned and clear-skinned, beautiful far beyond current Hollywood standards. The Italian in her heritage was self-evident; the delicacy, he suspected, was entirely deceptive.

She wore black pants and a red blouse and held out a firm hand for all present to shake. Her hair, which resembled silk, fell thick and wavy around her shoulders. She could do professional shampoo ads with hair like that. Aidan wondered distantly why she'd chosen journalism instead.

The directness of her professional manner answered that question. "I'm sorry to intrude, Dr. Christian," she said firmly, "but I need some information about Mary Lamont. About her obsession, if you will."

"Obsession?" Aidan sent John a level sideways look.

"I was getting to it," John mumbled and indicated Alistair with a subtle head movement.

Alistair appeared uninterested in the woman's remark, although his eyes did an almost insultingly efficient job of ogling her.

"If you'll excuse us, Mr. Blue," John said pointedly.

"What? Oh, yeah. Sure." He swaggered toward the door. "Catch you later, Ms. Gian—er, Samantha."

Her smile was abstracted, a mere movement of her sexy lips. Aidan foresaw no end of problems if their paths crossed more than once, twice tops, on this case.

He didn't trust her, either. Reporters were notorious liars. Any means to get a story, ethical or un.

John ushered her to a chair, pulling it next to Aidan's and dusting off the padded seat. When he returned to his desk, he began shuffling through a stack of papers.

"Should put all of this on the computer," he mumbled while Samantha watched every nuance in his expression. "I know it's here. Helen Something. Murphy? Marlowe... Ah, here we are. Murdoch. Helen Murdoch. Mary said that name over and over again. Seemed to like the sound of it."

"Why?" Aidan and Sam asked as one.

Aidan glanced at her, but she was leaning forward, staring at John. "Is it one of her friends?" she inquired hopefully.

"Not that we're aware of, Ms. Giancarlo."

"Sam," she said automatically. "Who then?"

John scratched his nose, resettled his glasses, and shuffled some more. "Here it is again. Helen Murdoch. And here. She asked several of our other patients if they liked the name. At a guess, I'd speculate that she was plotting her escape and planned to 'become' Helen Murdoch when she got out."

Aidan surveyed Sam impassively enough but with an intensity she'd be hard-pressed to ignore. "What exactly is your interest in this case, Ms...."

"Sam," she supplied. Polite; not effusive, but he sensed she found it distasteful to be rude.

She regarded both men in turn. "I wish I could explain but I can't. Not yet. As I, and I'm sure Guido, told Dr. Christian, I'm not acting in a journalistic capacity." She spoke now to John. "You can check my credentials. I'm not a rag reporter. I've never hidden in a bush or a hotel parking lot in my life. I don't even cover 'star' stories as a rule."

Aidan kept his gaze fixed on her face—a fairly easy thing to do. "What do you cover, then?"

Her eyes flashed. In annoyance? "Human interest mostly. Elderly men and women who are not your typical grandmas and grandpas, weird inventions, that sort of thing."

Aidan continued to watch her. He'd been told he had a weighty stare; however, if Sam felt uncomfortable under scrutiny, she gave no indication.

John cleared his throat. "I think we're straying from the point here. We have an, er, somewhat disturbed woman on the loose. I don't want anyone hurt because of that."

"How did she escape?" Sam asked point-blank.

Perverse amusement tugged on the corners of Aidan's mouth.

John spread his fingers wide. "That's the sixty-four-thousand-dollar question. We still haven't figured it out. She must have had help."

"An ex-husband?" Sam theorized.

"Possibly, but not Thurman Wells. Come to think of it, I don't believe she was married to anyone else. I gather Thurman married her on the rebound from Margaret Truesdale. Er—" He glanced sheepishly at Aidan. "Margaret Truesdale was Mary's obsession. Do you know of her?"

"I think so."

"Mary hated her," Sam inserted. "Or so I was told."

Aidan's brows arched. "By whom?"

He shouldn't have made her smile. It took her features from ravishing to spellbinding.

"I'm not easily tricked, Mr. Brodie."

"Aidan."

She turned back to John. "Who else might have helped her?"

John's face screwed up. "There was a man who used to visit, but that was years ago. He stopped coming rather abruptly. We assumed he died. Mary seemed to think so. His name was Tobias Lallibertie. He worked for her in her heyday."

Aidan shifted position in the decidedly uncomfortable chair. "How long has Mary been here?"

"Five years. Before that—well, I'm not at liberty to disclose her medical history. Suffice it to say this was not her initial confinement, or even close to it."

"But she was free at intervals after the first time," Sam presumed.

"I'm afraid so."

"Often enough to set up a plan of revenge?"

"Possibly."

Eyes on the window, Aidan remarked, "She concocted at least one plan within these walls."

"Her escape." Sam's fingers curled as if they itched to be writing this down. John looked away, disconsolate.

Enough, Aidan decided, standing with an athletic grace that belied his six-foot, three-inch height. Deceptiveness was his middle name. Deceptiveness, pride, and an enigmatic facade. The combination worked, right down to the Irish honor that had developed of its own accord in his childhood and which he would not have traded for ten pots of leprechaun gold.

"I'll see what I can find, John," he promised, then gave Sam a courteous nod. "It was a pleasure meeting you." Trite but true. He turned to John. "Let me know if any new information turns up."

"It won't," the other man predicted with dismal finality.

"I was responsible for her welfare, and I screwed up. Royally. Try back issues of the L.A. *Times,* or those old *Look* and *Life* magazines. They might tell you something. Mary harped mainly on one subject, one person, during her stay here. But there must have been others besides Margaret Truesdale in her troubled life."

"There was Thurman Wells," Sam reminded him. She made no move to stand, Aidan noticed. Her feminine wiles would shift into overdrive the moment he left. Poor John, he'd have a hell of a time resisting that.

Thankfully, he wasn't John. Resistance was not a problem for him. His gaze slid one last time over Sam's face and body. At least, it hadn't been until now.

He should back off, tell John he was sorry, and go about his business. Old film stars weren't his style. Neither were beautiful reporters with mysterious intent.

"Watch your back," John cautioned in parting.

Aidan offered him a wry smile. "I always do, old friend."

Too bad in this case it wasn't his back that was in danger....

"I THOUGHT you'd be gone."

Sam paused at the top of the porch stairs. Aidan Brodie glanced up at her. He was crouched beside his right rear fender, doing something she couldn't see.

"One of the 'guests' decided to use my tire as a chalkboard," he said without rancor.

Did she detect a note of ironic amusement in his tone? She definitely heard an accent, a cross between Irish and Scottish, heavily tinged with American. Straightening, he tossed a grimy cloth into the back of his sixty-two Cadillac convertible. Black, as she would have expected for a man like him.

"Did you find out all you wanted to?" he asked.

His eyes were a faded shade of green, quite beautiful really, disarmingly intense and, she would bet, quick to perceive. Luckily Sam was no pushover. You couldn't be and deal with Sally Dice everyday.

"Not really," she answered, descending. "I got waylaid by a woman calling herself Miss Flora Bundy. She collects flowers and exotic feathers. It was like stepping into a scene from *The Uninvited*, the part where they all trooped out to that rest home run by a woman who was crazier than any of her patients."

"I met Miss Bundy." Aidan's lips quirked. "I saw *The Uninvited*, as well."

He was giving her very little expression-wise, beyond a certain humorous wariness. Unfortunately, he gave plenty in every other sense.

Sam could honestly say she'd never beheld a man like Aidan Brodie before, and so was understandably fascinated. He was tall, athletically lean, broad-shouldered but not bulky, quite remarkable to look at, yet not what she'd have called Hollywood handsome. No loss there. Ken dolls held no appeal for her.

She studied him unapologetically, aware that he knew what she was doing. Whether they endeavored to hide it or not, people always dissected other people's outer shells. It was human nature to be curious.

His hair was quite long, down to his shoulders in the back and almost as long on the sides, unstyled but more appealing loose than if he'd followed tacky trend and confined it in a ponytail. His features—well, now those she really couldn't describe. His nose was strong and fit his face perfectly. "Classic" might be the right word for it. His face was on the narrow side, his mouth sensual, his eyes more expressive than most men's. She wondered vaguely if he was married, then poked herself. It didn't matter one way or another. She had Andy, after all. He was nice and kind and thoughtful, a bit erratic, but fun for a night out. Too bad he was currently on assignment in Argentina.

Having lost the thread of their dubious conversation, she glanced up at the blackening sky. "Where did the sun go?" she exclaimed, surprised. "It was beautiful when I got here."

Aidan secured the top of his classic car. "You should take note of the weather reports, Sam. There's a storm heading down the coast from San Francisco."

Rain and wind didn't bother her. Navigating treacherous canyon roads in a sporty little car that was only functioning on two-thirds of its cylinders did.

"I'd better get going," she said, removing her keys from her leather bag. She faced him with no apparent glitch in her composure. "I'm sure we'll bump into each other from time to time, Aidan."

He took the hand she extended, holding it for a beat longer than was necessary. In that beat, his gaze caught and held hers. "John's a good friend of mine," he said quietly yet with an underlying warning that made the hair on the back of her neck prickle. He paused, then added a deliberately ambiguous, "Take care, Sam."

She pulled her hand free as swiftly as possible without appearing spooked. Sharp-tongued Margaret Truesdale had nothing on this man. She couldn't believe that even Mary Lamont would be more daunting. If soft-spoken threats were a specialty, they'd surely be his.

"Goodbye, Aidan," she returned with an arch of her delicate brow that was a complete pose. She needed to get away from him. No more chance meetings. None. He was too sexy and far too shrewd to suit her. She'd need to be on her guard with him constantly.

A low peal of thunder rolled threateningly across the sky. She raised her head. Angry black clouds bunched together like sullen allies.

Out of range of Aidan Brodie's powerful aura, Sam's nerves at once began to settle. She felt his gaze on her back, but didn't concern herself with it. Distance, that's what she needed to cope with him.

Tossing her bag onto the passenger seat, she slid into her five-month-old Mazda Miata. The engine started with a touch, paused, hiccuped and promptly died. "New car bugs, no problem," Andy, whose brother worked at the dealership, had assured her. Every vehicle, new or old, had them.

Five unsuccessful attempts later, Sam swore fluently and gave the steering wheel an irritable bang. Trust Andy's flashy brother to pick out the only lemon on the lot and sell it to her. Trust her to trust him enough to buy it. Guido was right. She had to get over the belief that people were basically good and should, for the most part, be given the benefit of the doubt.

The first big drops of rain splashed against the windshield. Sighing, Sam hunted out her seldom-used cellular phone. Not surprisingly, the batteries were dead.

"Problem?" Aidan called from his car parked directly ahead of hers on the drive.

"Yes," she yelled, then swiftly retracted the admission. "No."

He might not have seen her slap her cell phone onto the passenger seat. He couldn't have missed the sick engine. Flipping up the collar of his dark green jacket—it looked good with faded jeans and well-worn work boots—he jogged to the window.

"What's wrong?"

Frank to a fault, Sam eyed him doubtfully. "Are you mechanical?"

"Garden variety. I'm better with old cars. It doesn't sound like the battery."

"It isn't."

Again that cryptic near-smile. "Do you need a lift?"

Did she want to bother John Christian? Because she'd have to if she rejected Aidan's offer. Of course rejecting it would be the smart thing to do.

"Yes, please," she replied. "As long as you don't try to pump information out of me about the source of my interest in Mary Lamont."

Now he did smile, right up to his eyes. "I was raised a gentleman, Sam, by a strong Irish mother and proper Scottish father. I don't pump."

Right, and pigs flew. Only an idiot fool would buy that bit of blarney. On the other hand, she felt decidedly out of her depth with this case. If John's sense of the woman had any merit—and no doubt it did—Mary Lamont was an obsessive, unpredictable shrew, an almost-great actress with murder on her severely unbalanced mind. An exchange of information might not go amiss at that.

They ran to Aidan's vintage Caddy, wrestled the doors open and started off a mere ten seconds before the skies opened up.

Sam buckled in and peered at lowering storm clouds. "God must be on a rampage," she murmured.

"I beg your pardon?"

She bit lightly on her tongue. "Nothing. When we had big storms, my brother used to tell me that God was angry."

"And His anger caused the thunder?"

"No, moving His furniture made thunder. Anger came out as lightning and rain." She raked damp tendrils of hair from her cheeks and forehead. "You don't have brothers and sisters, do you?"

A canny brow went up. His eyebrows were as expressive as his eyes. "How do you figure that?"

"You don't babble. You seem very—" she searched for the word "—private. You don't get much privacy when you have three siblings especially when there are less than two years between oldest and youngest." Noting his sideways look, she said, "Adoption. Three of us were adopted, one was my parents' child."

He eased the car off the winding drive and onto the slippery canyon road. "Which one?"

Sam grinned. "One of my brothers. We don't know which. My parents never told us and none of us were old enough to remember our mother being pregnant. It could be Michael. He's the eldest. It's not Anna or me. We found our papers when we were young. Anyway, Anna's too Scandinavian fair. My parents came from Italy. It might be Danny. His eyes are blue, but that can happen with brown-eyed parents. How did we get on this subject anyway?''

Aidan shrugged. ''Probably me. I was making conversation. You're very beautiful. It's a distraction.''

Sam accepted the compliment with equanimity. ''Thanks, but I'd rather look like Anna. Do you remember Grace Kelly before she married Prince Rainier? That's Anna to a tee.''

The door was open now; they both knew it. Since she wasn't the one attempting to navigate a slick canyon road, Sam braved it first.

''John's right, you know. Mary has it in her mind to kill Margaret Truesdale. They were rivals from the start, but apparently all hell broke loose during a movie they made together called *The Three Fates.*''

Aidan's impassive gaze rose to the rearview mirror. ''And just how do you know that, Sam Giancarlo?''

Sam considered for a moment. She'd maintained her silence at Oakhaven, partly because she'd taken a strong dislike to Alistair Blue and partly because her instincts had advised caution. Now uncertainty overrode caution. She wasn't stupid by any means, but realistically she wouldn't recognize a proper investigation from a hole in the ground. And while she fumbled around, what was to stop Mary from going for Margaret's jugular?

The thought of blood spilled in the grisly fashion that a madwoman like Mary Lamont might envision brought a shudder to Sam's skin and a calm admission of truth to her lips.

''Margaret Truesdale is my natural grandmother.''

The car swerved sharply and she had to clutch the dashboard to avoid being flung against his arm. ''It isn't that big a jolt,'' she declared. ''What are you doing?'' This as the Caddy rocked to the right.

Eyes fixed on the wet road, Aidan demanded, ''Is there anyone behind us?''

Sam looked. ''No. Why?''

''Do you know this road?''

The next curve, taken on two wheels, threw her against the door. "It's twisty," she said, righting herself angrily. "Have you gone mad? There's no one behind us, Aidan, so if you're trying to outrun—"

The realization hit with the next bend and a glimpse of the speedometer, which read in excess of fifty miles per hour. Only a suicidal maniac would drive that fast in the rain. And Aidan Brodie was not suicidal.

Clawing the hair from her face, Sam stared through the windshield. On full, the wipers couldn't begin to keep the glass clear.

"You don't have brakes, do you?" she whispered in a terror-choked voice.

"Not unless they're hiding," Aidan replied, aggravatingly unruffled. "Unbuckle your seat belt, Sam, and get ready."

"Ready for what?" she demanded, her eyes fastened on the blurred road. "Aidan, I'm not..."

"Yes, you are," he said flatly. In a movement too swift for her to anticipate, he shot across the seat, grabbed her around the waist, and took her with him out the passenger door.

Chapter Three

They rolled and tumbled forever, over slippery rocks and flowers, through soggy bushes and along a mud embankment. Sam hit her head twice and her shoulder once, very hard. Aidan maintained his grip the entire time, which probably helped her but couldn't have done him much good.

In the back of her mind she heard a sound like an agonized crunch of metal far below. Her fingers clawed for something solid to grab, a vine, a twig, even a firmly planted rock. She found several but nothing that she could catch for more than a split second.

Visions of *North by Northwest*, doubtless fueled by the tone of the past two days, flitted through her head. This might not be Mount Rushmore, but it sure as hell felt close from her vantage point.

It took both of them to halt their fall; Aidan to dig in with his heels and Sam to grasp a sapling birch.

They must have gone down miles, she thought grimly, afraid to move for fear of losing her grip. Her body ached and she had sharp pains in her shoulders and knees.

"Are you steady?" Aidan asked. He sounded winded and hurt but not seriously so.

"More or less." She was panting, unable to catch her breath or still the trembling in her strained muscles. She recognized the signs. Shock wanted to settle in. She fought it, hauling herself upward with a determined grunt and every scrap of her remaining strength.

"There's a plateau of sorts," Aidan said from below. "Can you reach it?"

"I think so... Yes."

Her fingers curled around the rocky ledge. Although slick with mud and weeds, it held fast as she dragged her bruised body onto it.

Once there, she collapsed on the far side and prayed for Aidan to join her.

When she rolled over and scrambled back to the side, she spied his head. Relief swamped her. As he hoisted himself over the edge, she caught his sleeve, then winced and sat with a thump.

Aidan immediately frowned. "Are you all right?"

She touched her right ankle. "I think so."

"You don't sound convinced." Kneeling, he took her foot gently in his hands, removed her shoe and probed the bone with his long fingers.

Part of her wanted to pull away. Another larger part was too absorbed to move. He had a velvet touch, better than an anesthetic, but nowhere near as safe. Banking a shiver, she said softly, "It's fine, really, Aidan. I think...what?"

Aidan had glanced up. Sam brushed rain and hair from her eyes and followed his gaze to a point on the canyon floor. There sat his '62 Cadillac convertible, impossibly wedged between two oak trees. The entire driver's side was crumpled inward.

"Maybe it's not too bad," she began, then decided not to bother. The thing might not be totaled, but it was a mess. Pointless platitudes didn't strike her as something Aidan would welcome.

Her mind cleared as if washed clean by the driving rain. Thunder shook the ledge, or seemed to. A chill wind whipped through her soaked clothes and hair, but it wasn't entirely responsible for the chill that enveloped her.

"Was it deliberate?" She slid her shoe back on. She had to shout to be heard above the noise of the worsening storm.

His expression told her nothing. The aura, or whatever it was that radiated from him like heat from a fire, was another matter. His anger was palpable, controlled, but simmering.

"Yes." He answered calmly, his deep green eyes unwavering as they regarded the battered remains of his pride and joy. "The brakes were new. The line must have been cut."

"Alistair Blue?" Sam surmised.

"Or Mary."

"She wouldn't be hanging around Oakhaven, Aidan." A shiver borne entirely of the cold this time made her teeth chatter on his name. Without removing his gaze from the car, Aidan pulled off his jacket and wrapped it around her shoulders. She did her best to conceal it, but he must have noticed her start of pain.

"You are hurt." He sounded displeased. "Let's get out of here first, and point fingers later."

He would have stood except for Sam's hand that suddenly clamped down on his forearm, restraining him. Her voice was sharp. "What if he's up there, waiting for us?"

Climbing to his feet, Aidan eased her up. "In that case," he said, frighteningly matter-of-fact, "he'll have a few questions to answer—before he winds up a sorry neighbor to my car."

RAIN PELTED the sides of the phone booth outside the small canyon store in... Alistair didn't have a clue where he was. Some lost little community that Lucy and company had undoubtedly passed through en route to L.A.

Alistair loved Lucy, didn't think much of Uncle Milty but thought Jack Benny was a hoot. Of the person on the other end of the phone, he was presently thinking daggers.

"I told you to warn him off, not to harm him, Alistair," a crackling voice snapped. A pause, then, "Did he survive? Did you check to see?"

Alistair's gaze swept the mist-topped hills. Pretty, but he preferred the desert. "He had enough time to bail. I'm sure he did. Brodie's no amateur."

"What about the woman?"

"You wanted her brakes fixed, too?"

"I didn't want anybody's brakes fixed, you idiot. They have no part in any of this. Margaret's the key, not these tawdry secondary players. Do I make myself clear?"

"As mud," Alistair muttered.

"What did you say?"

"Must have been static. Do you want me to check it out?"

"If you wouldn't mind. Remember what I said."

"Yeah, I know. Eyes and ears open. Call if I see or hear anything remotely suspicious."

"I'm not saying you won't have to perform a few distasteful deeds," the voice continued. "But I decide how and when. This is a game of revenge, Alistair. A deadly game."

Some game, Alistair thought, batting at a wasp with his elbow. "Which one do you want me to tail?"

The protracted silence was punctuated by a loud burst of static and pelting rain. "The man for now, I think. Brodie, did you call him? I want to think about the young woman some more."

Who didn't? Alistair wiped the salivating corners of his mouth as he hung up. Put up or shut up, his grandfather had told him when he'd been a volatile teenager. He'd put up then and promptly been packed off to a juvenile camp for his efforts. For now he would shut up, stick his copy of *The Picture of Dorian Gray* in the VCR and think lewd thoughts of the delectable Sám Gian– Something. He'd think bloodier ones later of Aidan Brodie.

His lip curled in disdain. Who knew? Maybe he and Mary Lamont would turn out to have a common problem after all.

GUIDO'S ATTIC-STYLE office was hot and stuffy and cramped, overrun with filing cabinets, old boxes, a microfiche viewing screen, and somewhere on one of the cluttered shelves, a computer that was the dustiest thing in the room. He wore suspenders under an open black vest, a white shirt with the sleeves rolled up, and bifocal glasses, the old-fashioned kind with only half a lens. The dead files were his domain and even Sam wouldn't have dared to trespass without his permission.

"Here it is. You see?" Guido stabbed a calloused finger at a photo, presumably a publicity shot taken in the early fifties. "That's Margaret in the middle. Mary's on her right, Anthea her left. As you see, Anthea was a blonde, shorter and rounder than the other two. She got the nice-girl parts in every movie she made, except one. That exception was thanks to Margaret who put in a good word for her with the studio bigwigs."

"It says here that Anthea and Margaret were cousins." Sam, who'd been reading over his shoulder, indicated the appropriate line. "Did you know that?"

Guido's wrinkled face screwed up in concentration. "Come to think of it, I did. Funny thing, that. Anthea disappeared at the same time as Margaret. Must be a connection."

"I'll ask next time I see Margaret," Sam promised.

Guido went back to packing his pipe. "You sure Margaret was telling the truth about you being her granddaughter?"

"She had the papers, Guido, and I checked with the hospital. It was a private one. The studio preferred that for their stars."

"Discretion, Minx."

"Margaret was admitted March 11, 1948, for an undetermined female indisposition."

"They couldn't say pregnancy on-screen in those days."

"Apparently they had trouble saying it off-screen, as well. Anyway, the hospital should have the records on computer. I'll look into them, but I'm sure they'll bear out Margaret's story. I also put out feelers on the name Helen Murdoch, but so far nothing."

Guido puffed contemplatively, a frown deepening the ridge

between his eyes. "I don't like it, the brakes going like that. It must have been deliberate."

Sam disguised a shudder. "It was, Guido," she said gently. "Remember, I told you Aidan Brodie called me last night. His car's been pulled out. It's in pretty bad shape but the mechanic said the line had definitely been cut. Either it wasn't meant to look like an accident or the perpetrator was a rank amateur."

Which she doubted Alistair Blue was—assuming of course that he had actually done the deed. Two days after the fact, Sam was torn. What if Aidan had damaged the brakes himself? It was possible that he wanted her off the case. More than possible, it was probable.

He'd still been there when she'd left the institute. That had surprised her a little, though not sufficiently for her to question his offer of a ride. But what if he'd "fixed" her already malfunctioning car? What if he'd tampered with his own vehicle? An extremist would go that far; a seasoned driver might take the risk. But did either of those descriptions fit Aidan Brodie? She sighed and wished she knew more about him.

Gnawing on the stem of his pipe, Guido asked, "This accident happened when? Sunday?"

Sam nodded.

"That's two days ago. Anything since?"

"Nothing except my ankle hurts and my car's still not working right." Though for what reason she had yet to determine. "If it turns out to be a lemon, Guido, I'm going to strangle Andy when he gets back."

"He's not worth the effort," Guido said with an absent wave. "Strangle his idiot brother and tell Andy to find a vacant actress to wine and dine. You need a man with a mind. Now this Aidan Brodie…"

"Has nothing to do with our conversation," Sam maintained firmly.

"Humph. What's that?" He pointed at an old movie magazine she was thumbing through. Sam was seated cross-legged on the couch amid a sea of magazines and newspapers. Guido, perched on the arm, leaned over to examine the article in question. "It's Margaret, Mary and Anthea in *The Three Fates*."

Sam peered closer. "They're not in makeup," she said doubtfully. "How can you tell which movie it's from?"

"I read the caption."

"Oh." She wrinkled her nose. "I hate pat answers." She looked back at the photo. "They really were beautiful, weren't they?"

"Margaret was. Take another look at Mary. There's a hardness about her that stems from spite."

"Maybe, but her features are still good. And her hair would be if it weren't for the stupid styles back then. Chestnut brown with red highlights."

Guido's eyes twinkled. "I like brunettes myself."

Sam smiled, her first genuine smile since she and Aidan had shot off the canyon road. Her palms still went clammy when she recalled the incident. "Margaret's features are finer," she agreed. "But their look was similar otherwise. I suppose that's why Mary felt jilted by the studio. She had it all, right down to the talent, you said. She probably figured she should be getting starring roles."

"She had the look, all right. And yes, she was talented. But she didn't possess even a speck of Margaret's charisma. Take *The Three Fates*. Fates are witches, you know. At the outset, none of them were what you'd call white witches. It was natural that Mary should be cast as the most evil. Unfortunately, 'most evil' did not translate to 'lead.' That role required Margaret's talent, and her ability to bring the audience with her when she finally made the transition to good. It would have been a fascinating movie if it had been released. It's a shame there's nothing left."

"Are you talking about the original film canisters?"

Guido limped over to his cluttered desk. "They were the master copies. They disappeared shortly after Margaret left Hollywood for parts unknown. There are only publicity stills left, and not many of those." He began hunting through the stacks of papers. "Where did I put that… Ah, here it is." He waved a recent copy of the L.A. *Times* at her. "Straight from the enemy camp. Don't tell Sally. You know how she is about the competition."

Sam, who knew only too well, laughed.

Uncurling her legs, she stood and dusted off. Her sleeveless purple pantsuit appeared cool, but nothing short of a bikini would have been cool enough to offset the heat wave that had moved in yesterday.

"Does the article involve Mary?" she asked hopefully.

"In a way." Guido adjusted his bifocals. "This edition is two weeks' old. The article's rich for an old news glutton like me. It says that Leo Rockland is about to wed for the ninth time. He's eighty-three. His bride is…" A broad grin tugged on Guido's lips.

"Twenty-five?" Sam guessed.

"Wrong by fifty years. She's seventy-six."

"You're kidding." Delighted, Sam took the paper and read, "'Reception to be held at the home of the former producer.'" She raised her head, her mind already hard at work. "Home," she repeated. "Beverly Hills?"

Guido gave her a sweet smile. "Would you like the address?"

"You have it?"

He patted his baggy pants' pockets. "It took some finagling, not as much as you'll have to do if you're thinking of doing what I know you're thinking of doing, but…"

"No press allowed," Sam interrupted, accepting the slip of paper he passed her. "I wonder who's catering?"

Chuckling, Guido unloaded a pile of magazines and file folders into her arms. "Go on, get out of here, little Minx. Unlike you high-and-mighty repor—sorry, journalists, I work until five, then go home to my cats, Jeopardy and an earful of grief from Vincenzo Mogli downstairs who thinks that a family curse and not old age is responsible for his failing kidneys."

"I did waitressing once in college," Sam went on abstractedly. "I bet I could pull off a role with the caterer."

Guido shook his shaggy white head and ushered her, laden, through the door. As if galvanized by the click, Sam glanced downward, then headed for the staircase. At seventy years of age, the Karl Kayne Building was equipped with clanking, wheezing elevators that seldom stopped on the floor you wanted. The stairs were faster, safer and far less strenuous in the long run.

In her cubbyhole office that overlooked the famous Hollywood hill sign, Sam dialed the number of a local television station. Connie Grant's harassed voice came on the line.

"What?"

"You sound mad."

"As a damned hornet, honey. What's up?"

"Tons, but I haven't got time to explain. I need a favor."

"Anything for my best college roommate's baby girl."

Sam pictured Connie's heavily made-up face, her trademark white-blond hair that made her look like a porcupine and the pre-fad army boots and fatigues she'd worn forever.

"There's a party list—sorry, a reception list. Leo Rockland. Do you have it?"

Connie emitted an unladylike snort. "That old coot? He's press-shy as hell these days. Our show hasn't been able to wangle an interview for donkey's ages."

"But you must have information," Sam persisted.

She heard Connie riffling through papers. As far as Sam could see, everybody she knew had a computer and not one of them used it except in an emergency.

"Okay, I've got it. Like I figured, absolutely no press allowed. Big red letters on that one, honey."

"How can I get in, Connie?"

"Are you serious?"

"Do I know anyone on the list? Do you?"

"Honey, these people are stars from a bygone era. Seventy-five's the youngest of the ones whose names I recognize."

Sam watched the heat waves that blurred the Hollywood sign beyond her window. "Who don't you recognize?"

"You want me to read 'em out or fax 'em?"

Sam sensed she was run off her feet. "Fax is fine," she said.

Connie gave a rusty laugh. "Still painfully polite. You should get out of L.A. before you develop an impenetrable iron crust like me. Okay, sweetie, I'll send it right out. Good luck."

Swiveling her chair around, Sam glanced at the wall clock. Five-twenty already. Where had the day gone? "Thanks, Connie," she said and hung up, annoyed with herself for spending the past eight hours immersed in work that had nothing to do with her column.

With a soft, "Damn!" of frustration, she brought her arm and hand down on the blotter where she'd doodled Margaret Truesdale's name half a dozen times. More disconcerting were the dozen-plus times she'd scribbled Aidan Brodie's name. She was trying to stop herself from delving into the underlying reasons when a shadow fell across her desk—a shadow that had absolutely no right to be there.

Instinctively, Sam snatched up her letter opener. Her head shot up; her body tensed. She was prepared for an aging madwoman. The implacable stare that greeted her was as far from that as it could get.

Aidan Brodie regarded her through assessing green eyes, then said pleasantly, "Who's Connie?"

Sam swallowed the nasty name that had been hovering on the tip of her tongue. Shoving back her chair, she glowered at him.

"How did you get in here?" she demanded.

He noticed that she still had a stranglehold on the letter opener. "I knocked," he told her. "Twice."

"I didn't hear you."

He held her smoldering gaze. "You were on the phone."

"I know where I was, Brodie," she snapped, then took a

deep breath and composed herself. "Okay, let's try this again. Why are you here?"

"I wanted to talk to you."

The fax machine at her elbow began to whir. She ignored it and gave him a suspicious look. "About what?"

"Leo Rockland's getting married this week. He was the producer on *The Three Fates*."

"I know." Her suspicion deepened visibly. "Where did you hear about the wedding?"

"Through friends," he said with a deliberately enigmatic smile. "You?"

"Guido Bocce. He's an old friend. He works in the archives."

The fax machine whirred on. Aidan fought a sigh. Of course she would look delicious in that purple pantsuit and matching two-inch pumps. His fingers could close easily around her slender upper arm. He'd read somewhere that Margaret Truesdale possessed the same fine bone structure. Maybe Sam was the reclusive star's granddaughter at that.

She moved a negligent shoulder. "I gather invitations are scarce—for the press, at any rate." Her gaze slid to the incoming fax, started to move away then did a double take. Her head snapped up. Irritation flared deep in her golden brown eyes. "You bastard!" she declared with feeling.

She'd managed not to call him that earlier. Aidan noted the rolling paper. "What is it? A list of my childhood misdemeanors?"

She came out from behind the desk, tearing off the sheet as she passed. "Don't you dare joke. How did you do it, Brodie? No press. No one under seventy-five, according to my friend at 'Who's News.' And yet here you are, big as life on Leo Rockland's reception list."

He took the sheet she was shaking at him and scanned the names. "Dennis Rockland's younger than me," he said, apparently with sufficient wryness to fully ignite her temper.

"You son of a... Get out!"

Since any show of amusement would undoubtedly earn him a punch in the stomach, he met her glare straight-faced. Careful to keep his tone even, he said, "Ask me again why I'm here, Sam."

"I don't give a damn if you have the story of the century tucked in your hip pocket. I hate gloaters."

Aidan's Celtic humor got the better of him. His lips twitched at the corners. "You have a suspicious mind, Sam. The Irish use sarcasm like a tonic. We never gloat."

Still fuming, she demanded, "Did your brakes really fail?"

The implication would have been clear to a three-year-old. "Meaning?" he challenged levelly.

"You don't want me on this case. You think reporters are a pain, and—"

"They are."

"I beg your pardon?"

Using his height to advantage, he moved toward her. "You heard me well enough."

"Save the scare tactics, Brodie," she scoffed. "My brother's six-five and built like a bear. Get out of my office."

A grizzly with cubs wouldn't have her angry bite. "Are you finished?" he countered, his expression steady.

"Yes. Get out. No… Wait a minute. Why *did* you come?"

Back to suspicion, but at least her temper was beginning to subside. "I had a deal in mind."

She contemplated his tone. "Go on," she said at length.

"You have direct contact with Margaret Truesdale. I have contacts in other areas."

"Like Leo Rockland's wedding camp?"

He shrugged. "A pool of knowledge is better than a few solitary drops, or so my grandmother used to insist."

"The Irish one or the Scottish one?"

"Irish. It tends to dominate."

"I've noticed. Okay, Brodie, I give you access to Margaret in exchange for what? An in at Rockland's wedding reception?"

"We work together," he said. He was crazy, he knew, to make such an offer, but God help him, there it was. It wasn't in his makeup to renege.

He expected wariness and got it in spades. She surveyed him the way a cat might a new and unfamiliar opponent. "I'd have to talk to Margaret first," she told him. "She might say no. Will you still get me in to Rockland's party?"

"I'll think about it. And to answer your unspoken question from before, no, I did not rig my brakes to fail."

A trace of delicate perfume drifted past him. He felt his body tighten in response. Self-control had been his trademark since he'd been thirteen years old and his family had moved from Dublin to Boston. Even vacations in Ireland hadn't affected him adversely. Well, they had actually, but he'd never let it show except to his grandmother Maeve. He prided himself on that hard-won control and the fact that, even when sorely tested, his temper rarely got the better of him. So why, he wondered, his gaze sweeping her discreetly from head to toe, was he having such a problem with this woman? So much so that he'd spent most of last night viewing old movies and picturing Sam in the role of heroine.

If asked prior to Monday afternoon, he'd have said he didn't care one way or the other about films like *Spellbound, The Big Sleep,* or an early Margaret Truesdale film called *Trustworthy.* But there he'd laid on the sofa with his neighbor's Siamese cat sharing his mug of Guinness, watching all three of them right down to the final credits.

The tempting wildness of her fragrance floated past again, causing him to tighten further. With a resigned smile for the self-restraint that had obviously abandoned him, he started for the door. He'd made his offer; it was up to her to react.

"I'm in the book, Sam," he said dispassionately over his shoulder. "Aidan Robert Roy Brodie."

"Rob Roy," he heard her murmur in faint amusement. "I should have known. I don't trust people named Robert Roy. It's a dangerous combination."

"Only to dukes and cattle thieves." His eyes glinted. "And people who slash brake lines. If I don't hear from you, I'll pick you up at five o'clock Friday afternoon. It's black tie."

THE STRING that bound the package was black, the paper was white—just like her first movie, Mary thought in delight. Heavenly days, what a time she'd had to get this far, so close now that she could finally smell victory.

She smiled happily at the package on the table, reached for her ankle brace, a necessity ever since that fumble-fingered excuse for a doctor had set her broken leg, and shouted for Tobias.

"Get in here," she ordered, then gave an evil little chortle and scooped up the package. She would trust the man to drive her to the post office, but not to mail the thing. Tobias didn't approve of her scheme. He stopped short of objecting outright, but she'd seen the frown on his lips too often to test his loyalty all the way.

"Hurry up, you old goat," she muttered.

A cough from the doorway announced his presence. Giving him a cranky flap of her hand, she sat—or more correctly, plopped, onto the sofa and began swathing herself like a mummy in black and brown linen.

She scowled when she reached her legs. When had her ankles gotten so thick? Bet Margaret's ankles weren't thick. Well, what the hell, Margaret wouldn't have any ankles left once Mary got hold of her. Chop, chop, Mary thought, and laughed with glee as she pictured the cleaver she would use to dismember her old rival.

"Is the car ready?" she demanded, still swathing.

Tobias gave a sober nod.

"Good, me too. Let's go."

But she fell back grunting into the cushions after three unsuccessful attempts to rise. With a grimace, Tobias relented and helped her.

"Don't know why I've kept you on so long." Mary puffed as he extricated her from the sofa. "Where's my hat?"

"Right here."

"And the package?" She swiveled around. "Where'd it go? Tobias, if you...oh, there it is. Well—" her head bobbed accusingly "—you'd better not try anything, my friend. I've waited over forty years for this moment. Not you or anyone else is going to stop me."

Tobias heaved a weary sigh. "Are you sure you want to send her this—thing?"

"Of course I'm sure." A knobby finger shook in his face. "Don't you back talk me, Tobias Lallibertie. I still control the purse strings around here. No institution's changed that state of affairs. Now go and fetch the car. You know how slow mail moves these days. I want this to get to her during my current lifetime. I don't want to have to come back from the dead to get her."

Tobias hesitated then left.

Alone, Mary emitted a hoarse gabble of laughter and clutched the precious package to her bosom. She'd waited decades to have her revenge. It was worth every minute of the wait.

Chapter Four

Leo Rockland's Beverly Hills home possessed all the lavish opulence of a movie set. The air smelled of honeysuckle and lilacs. Huge vases filled with white orchids and pale yellow roses stood at every opening, from the latticed French doors to the wide, sunlit windows. Cascading waterfalls of ferns and freesia spilled along tiled walls to the gleaming parquet floor. Rosewood siding, cherry-wood handrails, teak and pine cabinets, all shone in the waning rays of afternoon sun. Guests in tuxedos, silk gowns and jewels mingled in the hallways and living areas, though some had collected on the sprawling lawn in the backyard where a pool in the shape of a peacock's tail fanned beneath willow, palm and citrus trees.

Sam had never before seen such a display of finery gathered in a single place. It would have robbed her of breath if her nerves and the sight of Aidan, long-haired and handsome in a tux with a red and black tartan cummerbund, hadn't done so first.

"Smile and pretend you belong," he said blandly, cupping her elbow in his hand as they strolled through the champagne-and-diamond crowd.

His touch sent a jolt of awareness up her arm. In retaliation, she stepped on his toe with her three-inch heel. "I know how to act, Brodie. Who's your in? You never did tell me."

"David Garret."

She searched her memory. "That name wasn't on the list."

Aidan cast her a sly sideways glance. He shifted his hold when Sam, still far more aware of him than she wanted to be, would have extricated herself. "Stop fidgeting. I don't bite. David's a boom operator at Margaret's old studio. He knows one of the bride's granddaughter's."

"I'm not fidgeting." She was, actually. "Did this granddaughter get you on?"

"She's an amateur computer hacker. The list was sacrosanct. She took it as a challenge to break into Leo's system and add my name."

Sam stopped to stare at him, her discomfort forgotten, her expression incredulous. "In other words, we could get caught anytime."

Sliding his hand to the small of her back—an even more disconcerting act—he steered her toward the canopied patio. "Not if we play our parts well."

"I'm not an actress, Aidan." Sam's protest drowned in a spurt of mild panic. "I'm not even a good poker player."

The smile that played on his lips suggested something, though what that might be, she didn't care to find out right then. Not until she could get her emotions firmly back under control. She couldn't remember the last time a man's touch had affected her so strongly. Maybe it never had.

Well, one thing, at least she looked the part of a wedding guest. Not flashy, but striking in a slim sheath of black silk with a side slit from ankle to thigh that showed off a sliver of garnet red when she walked. The design was clever. The gown shimmered under the light of a crystal chandelier, followed every curve of her body without clinging, had no shoulders or ornamentation, revealed very little, yet managed to look quite daring.

She'd swept her black hair up for the occasion with two black and silver combs. She wore a strand of black pearls at her throat, a fine silver chain around her ankle and two solitary black pearl earrings in her lobes. Guido had gaped when he'd seen her. Even his cranky neighbor had nodded in silent approval. Only Aidan hadn't made his feelings known, and that, Sam suspected, together with his preoccupied instructions to her, was what had really caused her stomach to coil into resistant knots.

Not that the situation didn't warrant an attack of nerves, but he could have offered more than an impatient, "Come on, Sam, we're late."

A string orchestra played the theme from *Cats* on a raised white stage in what could only be termed a ballroom. More French doors opened to spacious patios. Some of the guests danced, others just stood and chatted. All drank champagne from the wrong type of flat-bottomed glass.

Connie's assessment of age had been fairly accurate. There were few people under seventy-five, only the odd grand- or great-grandchild as far as Sam could see. The youngest of them played tag and hid under the linen-draped tables.

A passing waiter offered champagne. Aidan took two glasses and handed one to Sam. His green eyes surveyed her as he sipped Moët.

"In case I haven't mentioned it, you look gorgeous."

Maybe indifference was better. His gaze seemed to strip the dress from her body, leaving her exposed and vulnerable in a way she'd never been before. Still, she could be gracious. "Thank you," she said, lifting her glass to her lips—and promptly choking on the first taste.

Aidan frowned. "Are you all right?"

"Fine." She indicated the base of the stairwell outside the ballroom. "It's Alistair Blue."

Instantly guarded, Aidan's green eyes followed her gaze. "So it is," he agreed without inflection. "I wonder what he's about?"

Despite her mistrust of Alistair, Sam took a moment to smile. Aidan's accent became more pronounced when emotion moved in. The look in his eyes became more intense, as well. He might appear quiet and affable at first glance—to say noth-

ing of handsome, virile and sensual—but he could pin and
hold his quarry with nothing more than a simple stare. She
hadn't encountered that quality very often in the past, but she
had occasionally wondered what it was that made certain people so much more dominant and daunting than others.

Whatever the answer, Aidan was definitely one of those
people. Alistair Blue, ninety percent bravado, would be
hard-pressed to measure up.

"Alicia?" a man's suave voice inquired from behind.

Sam pulled her gaze from Aidan's profile, summoned a daz-
zling smile and turned. Her smile froze at the sight of him.
Even forty years after the latest photograph in Guido's files,
the elegant features and cap of thick silver-white hair were
unmistakable. Thurman Wells bestowed his own charming
smile on her.

"I'm afraid not," she said, extending a graceful hand. "My
name is Sam Giancarlo. I'm here with Mr. Robert Brodie from
the BBC." Where the lie came from she couldn't have explained; it simply formed and with it the strong sense that the
deception could indeed be pulled off. Unless, of course, these
people spent a great deal of time in England.

If Aidan was shocked, he covered well, accepting Thurman
Wells's impressed arch of brow with equanimity. "How nice.
On which side of the camera do you work, Mr. Brodie?"

Aidan had a devastating smile when he chose to use it. "I'm
no actor," he replied honestly. "Mr. Wells, isn't it?"

He'd done precisely the right thing, bringing Thurman
Wells's frequently mentioned ego to the fore.

"You flatter me," the aging actor demurred, his modesty
false yet not unbecoming. "Until recently I hadn't made a film
for more than three years."

Sam scrambled through her memory. Guido had told her the
latest title. *"Four Candles Burn,"* she recalled in the nick of
time. "You're very talented, Mr. Wells. I particularly enjoyed
some of your earlier work."

His laugh had a pleasant ring. "The prime of my life—I was fortunate to have been a part of the studio system."

Aidan used a less tactful approach. "Fortunate also that you were able to work with Margaret Truesdale and Mary Lamont?"

"Mary!" Thurman's head came up sharply as if yanked on a string. "I'm sorry." His lashes lowered at once in apology. "I have certain, er, dealings with Mary even now."

A grunt from his left shoulder signaled the arrival of another guest. Thankfully, it wasn't Leo Rockland. Beyond that blessing, however, Sam didn't recognize the man.

He reminded her a little of Anthony Quinn at eighty. His brows were a harsh slash, his eyes hazel, his hair mostly gray. Unlike Thurman he had a tumbler of Scotch whiskey in his hand and a matter-of-fact expression on his face. Straight from the hip, Sam thought, her guard lowering a few cautious notches.

"Stan Hollister," he said with a trace of a Texas accent. "Did someone mention Mary Lamont's name?"

Sam glanced at Aidan, who replied smoothly, "We admit to a certain curiosity. Ms. Giancarlo was hired by the wife of my superior to collect background information on American personalities for a book she's comprising on intriguing people of the twentieth century. Mary Lamont, Margaret Truesdale and Anthea Pennant certainly fit into that category."

At Thurman's mildly troubled expression, Sam tacked on a reassuring, "We're not connected with the media, Mr. Wells. This book will be strictly factual, based entirely on personages. There's no witch hunt involved. I agree with Mr. Brodie, however, when he says that we are increasingly curious about these women and their final unfinished movie."

"The Three Fates." Stan took a long swallow. "I directed Margie and Thea in it."

"And Mary?" Aidan asked.

Stan gave a short laugh. "There was no directing Mary by

that time. She was fired—not from the movie, that went onto the shelf when Margaret left—but from the studio.''

"She was abnormally upset," Thurman added with an ill-disguised grimace. "She's been in a similar mental state ever since."

Sam thought of Alistair Blue and realized that, as Mary's ex-husband, Thurman must still feel responsible for her welfare. It was an admirable if somewhat misguided trait.

He seemed to settle down after that, enough so that he matched Stan's wry chuckle. "I was married to both of them, you know. Margaret first, naturally."

"I'll bet Mary loved that," Aidan murmured into his champagne.

"Transparent as glass was our resident witch," Stan said with more bitterness than Sam would have expected. Mary Lamont must have been a hellion to have left so much bad feeling in her wake.

"I heard she was confined at an institution in Cypress Canyon," she remarked in a conversational tone.

Thurman choked on his wine, recovering only when Stan patted his back. "How did you learn that?" he rasped.

Aidan cast Sam a silent look of warning.

"It's not as well kept a secret as you might think," she returned carefully.

Thurman seemed horrified. "The *Times* didn't..."

"Not the *Times*, Mr. Wells, but 'Who's News' knows and I think *Hollywood Beat* as well." What they didn't yet know was that Mary had escaped.

"Figures," Stan said in an undertone. His expression, one of tempered sympathy for Thurman, who had, according to the gossip columns of the day, borne the brunt of Mary's pre-confinement rages, was laced with cynicism. "The press had damned well better not splash this all over the front pages. She's supposed to be out of the country. That's the release on her, isn't it, Thurman?"

Thurman rubbed his lined forehead. "I believe so. I hope so."

Aidan, who'd been watching both men closely, offered a guileless, "Have either of you heard the name Helen Murdoch?"

Stan's gaze snapped to Aidan's unrevealing face. Thurman simply froze. Surprisingly, it was Stan who spoke. "Where did you hear that name, Mr. Brodie?"

The lie formed quickly on Sam's tongue. "From me. As a matter of research, I spoke to some of the patients at the hospital. Not Mary herself of course," she hastened to add. "Apparently, Mary mentions the name Helen Murdoch a lot."

Stan muttered, "This has all the earmarks of a nightmare unfolding."

Aidan saved the day by procuring a fresh glass of whiskey from a passing waiter and handing it to him. "Perhaps you'll tell us about *The Three Fates* then. That should be a safe enough subject."

Thurman's relief was tangible. He finished his champagne in a single swallow and located another.

Stan merely shrugged and patted his pockets, searching, Sam presumed, for a cigarette. "There isn't a great deal to tell, Mr.Brodie. The film died before completion. The canisters went missing soon after, leaving those of us who were involved with only our memories as souvenirs of the event."

"What about Anthea?" Sam prompted. "Do you know if she's still alive?"

Thurman tossed back a full glass of Moët. His polished actor's smile returned. "Thankfully, my dear, we haven't heard from Margaret or Anthea for more than forty years now, and it's grateful that I am—good heavens, I must be catching your Irish lilt, Mr.Brodie—not to be privy to the knowledge." Lowering his voice, he leaned toward Sam in a conspiratorial fashion. "In or out of Oakhaven, Mary Lamont would ride herd on the devil if she thought he possessed information she wanted. Best to play deaf monkey where she's concerned."

"You're slurring, Thurman," Stan admonished, pulling him firmly upright. "Hello, Leo," he said in the same stern breath.

Leo Rockland? Sam stiffened, or would have if Aidan hadn't caught her arm and spun her with him to face the man.

"Good evening, Leo," he greeted, his tone and expression pleasant. "It's good to see you again." At the man's confused frown, he tacked on, "It's Robert Brodie. We met three years ago at the studio."

The man's blank face lit up. "Ah, yes, Robert, er—"

"Brodie."

Sam would have confirmed this new lie if she hadn't been in a mild state of shock. Leo Rockland was, by all accounts, eighty-three years old. If someone had told her he was a hundred and three, she would have had an easier time believing it.

He looked ancient—frail and shrunken, all skin and gnarly bone. He had a thin, sweet face, tufts of messy white hair and baby blue eyes. He was also shaking, badly, so much so that Sam feared a too vigorous handshake might knock him off balance. He used no canes, but she saw a woman in a starched white uniform hovering close by.

More unnerving than any of those things, however, she detected a trace of a Liverpool accent when he spoke. She prayed that he was unfamiliar with both the current BBC hierarchy and the British gentry.

Recognition in the latter area was unlikely, but the BBC thing could pose a problem. Why did lies always tend to backfire? she wondered forlornly.

"Sam Gian—Gian…" Leo stumbled on the name, then gave a contrite little smile. "Yes, well, it's lovely to meet you at any rate, my dear." He clasped her hand with his cold, blue-veined ones. His eyes, bird-bright despite his aged appearance, moved from her to Aidan and back again. "Are you and Mr. Brodie engaged?"

Sam opened her mouth but it was Aidan who supplied,

"Unofficially. Maybe we'll follow your lead one day, Leo. Congratulations on your marriage."

Startled by a prospect she hadn't entertained, but which was not the shock it should have been, Sam echoed Aidan's sentiment, adding a cautious, "Where is the new Mrs. Rockland?"

"Bathgate," Leo corrected. His blue eyes twinkled. "After all these years, she preferred to keep her family name."

"You mean—" a delighted smile lit Sam's face "—that this is her first marriage?"

"First and last." Ms. Bathgate joined them. The name Olivia DeHavilland sprang to mind—lovely, plump and grandmotherly; gentle Southern accent. She took her new husband's arm and offered the group a winsome smile. "I do hope you're not wearing my husband out with shop talk."

More introductions were made. Frederika Bathgate, called Freddie, nodded in somber sympathy when the subject of Sam's research came up. "Poor dear Margaret. There she stood at the pinnacle of her career and she had to leave. To this day, none of us knows why, nor where she is right now. Anthea, either."

Leo beamed at his bride. "Freddie was an actress, too."

"A bit player," she said, blushing.

"You were on Mary's hate list even so," Stan put in.

Leo's sparrow eyes met his at once in silent remonstration. Freddie patted her ample bosom in the region of her heart. "Mary Lamont. The name gives me palpitations. She was a little, well…"

"Off?" Aidan suggested.

"I think we've exhausted the subject of Mary Lamont," Thurman interrupted. Was he swaying slightly?

Sam glanced at Aidan, who made a barely perceptible motion with his head. Time to make a graceful exit.

She mustered an apologetic smile. "You're right, Mr. Wells. If you'll excuse us…"

Their departure raised no objection, only a generally murmured, "Enjoy the party," from the group, and a more frantic, "I need something stronger than this champagne-flavored Kool-Aid," from Thurman.

"Did we learn anything?" Sam asked doubtfully as Aidan, his hand once more cupped around her elbow, steered her toward the orchestra.

"Enough to know that they know more than they're admitting."

"Thurman does, anyway," she said. Giving in to temptation, she leaned against him slightly. There wasn't an ounce of spare flesh on his body. Bet he'd look better than Leo at eighty. "He sent Alistair Blue to Oakhaven—a fact you might have mentioned earlier."

"I might have," he agreed. "But I didn't know you then. As for the others, we can only guess how much they know—with the possible exception of Freddie." He frowned. "What are you doing?"

Her head twisted from side to side. "Looking for Alistair."

"He left ten minutes ago."

"Why didn't you—?"

"Punch his lights out?"

She made an exasperated gesture. "Force a confession from him."

"Here?"

"Well, no, I suppose not. All right, so what do we do now, Sherlock?" With a feeling akin to frustration, she stepped away. It was too hard to think when she was pressed up against him.

He noted the action but made no move to stop her. A slow smile curved his sensual mouth. "We move to Plan B."

"Which is?"

His green eyes glinted. "We skulk."

TERRIFIC IDEA, Aidan chided himself three hours later. They hadn't learned a damned thing except he was convinced more strongly than ever that they all knew about Mary's escape—Thurman, Stan and Leo.

Halfway through the party, the sky over Los Angeles had grown overcast. He drove his borrowed black Jeep now through the misty night toward Sam's home.

She lived in the tower portion of a twenties' hilltop mansion that had been converted into apartments in the late sixties. Stairways ascended through palm trees, rocks and willows to her front door. A mountain goat would find the climb a challenge. Lucky then that he'd been born part Highland goat, Aidan reflected with distant amusement.

"That was quite a party," Sam observed as they drove. "Not overly informative, but it felt like we stepped back in time for a while. I don't think any of them know where she's hiding, though."

Aidan's contemplative gaze rose to the turbulent blackness above. Thunder rumbled over the Hollywood Hills to their left. The scent of her perfume washed over him, causing his muscles to tighten. "I don't trust Thurman," he said finally.

"I don't trust any of them—but I still don't believe they're giving her sanctuary. I think our best bet would be to search for Anthea Pennant. She might know something that could help us. Freddie told me that Anthea understood Mary. She was one of the few who did."

Aidan sent her a skeptical look. It was a mistake to do so with her wearing that damned black scrap of a dress, but he couldn't avoid it forever. "Do you think that's fair to Anthea? She probably guards her privacy as rigorously as Margaret does."

Sam blew out an exasperated breath. By hazy lamplight her eyes appeared almost pure gold. "I only want to talk to her, Aidan, not sic every press hound in the city on her. I'm a researcher now, remember?"

"You're a bloody good liar is what you are." Aidan tugged the tie away from his throat. "If I had any doubt before about your natural parentage, it's gone now. That performance was worthy of Margaret Truesdale at her peak.''

"And yours wasn't?'' She grunted and glanced in the side mirror. "Face it, Brodie, fear was the wellspring of our joint performance today. Turn here.''

"I know the city, Sam.''

"Turn here, Aidan.''

He said nothing, merely shot her a steady sideways look and took the next right.

She leaned forward, peering into the mirror more intently. "There's a car back there, a sedan. I think it's following us.''

His eyes flicked to the rearview mirror. A frown marred his forehead. "Hold on,'' he said, changing lanes.

She didn't at first, but soon realized he meant it and clung on. He whipped the Jeep around a corner, along a semi-deserted street, up a hill and through a small back lane to a palm-lined avenue. Their tail stuck with them like a leech.

"He's good,'' Aidan noted.

"You don't need to sound so impressed.'' She pried her fingers free of the seat and attempted to twist herself around. "I can't tell if it's Alistair or... Oh, hell, he turned his headlights off.''

It might very well be Alistair, Aidan reflected, swerving to avoid a young woman on roller blades. They had no reason to trust the man, especially in light of the slashed brake line incident. On the other hand, why would Thurman Wells's hired man want to harm them?

Unless Thurman, instead of being concerned for Mary as he professed, was in fact helping her. The other answer, no less palatable, was that Alistair was working for someone other than Thurman, possibly Mary Lamont herself.

Dammit, he should have cornered the little git at the reception and had it out with him then and there.

"It must be Alistair,'' Sam said. The faint quaver in her voice betrayed her state of nerves.

Tempted to reach over and stroke her cheek, Aidan refrained with an effort.

"Who else could it be?" She shivered. "Unless one of the others hired someone to put us off. We should have been more subtle, Aidan."

"Robert Brodie," he corrected abstractedly, his gaze shifting to the rearview mirror. "And we'd have learned even less than we did if we'd concocted a different story. Besides, it's unlikely they had time to hire anyone."

"Leo could have done it. There were lots of waiters and security guards there. Who says they all have scruples?"

Aidan's brows arched in a wry challenge. "I could pull over if you'd like. That would answer our question."

"Don't be obtuse. Just lose the creep. This car chase stuff is not my idea of a fun night in L.A."

One more glance at her in that dress and a dozen enjoyable ideas would present themselves to Aidan's mind, none of them feasible and every one of them the worst mistake he could possibly make. He'd been married once; he'd vowed he would never do it again. He had his reasons, and not even Sam Giancarlo with all her beauty, wit and intelligence was going to change his mind.

The sedan continued its relentless pursuit. Aidan cut a labyrinth path through Hollywood, past immortal Graumann's, across Vine, out of Movieland and west to the ocean.

When that tactic failed, he reached down and punched off the headlights, a dangerous move, but necessary if he was correct in his assumption of their pursuer's next move.

"Get down," he told Sam calmly.

"What are you going to—"

Rather than repeat himself, he cupped a hand around her neck and yanked her sideways, directly, he realized with an inward grimace, into the region of his lap.

She fought him like a wildcat. "Are you crazy?" she demanded, and would have taken a strip off him if they hadn't received a sudden bone-jarring jolt from behind.

"He hit us," she whispered, disengaging herself from his unrestrictive grip. "It's a Lincoln. They're fast."

Aidan squinted at the mirror. "Can you see the driver's face?"

She dug into the headrest with her fingernails. "Only an outline. He—or she—is wearing a big hat."

Aidan drove full speed for the water. He'd seen this trick in the cinema. He couldn't see pulling it off, but you never knew. Maybe the lunatic behind them didn't watch movies. "A man's or a woman's hat?" he asked, his mind racing faster than the two vehicles.

"Hedda Hopper's."

"We're being chased by a dead gossip columnist?" The question required no answer, so Sam didn't bother to fashion one.

"I think... What are you doing?"

He caught the note of alarm in her voice as she was half thrown back into her seat. "Trying something."

The water loomed before them, a great wash of black, sparkling like eerie diamonds under a storm-dark sky.

Sam gasped. "You are crazy, aren't you?" She braced herself with her feet and hands. "Aidan, you can't do this. Don't do this!"

But it was too late to change his mind. And it might just work at that.

The Lincoln was less than ten feet behind them as he sped along the residential road, a dead end that Aidan hoped to hell the driver behind them didn't know about.

Unlit houses, trees and black, cracked pavement rushed past on both sides. Raindrops began to spatter the windshield. Aidan waited until the last possible second, calculated the remaining distance, counted downward from three, then gave the wheel a hard yank to the right.

The Jeep wasn't built for high-speed maneuvers. It stuttered and shook and tipped precariously. When it finally landed on four wheels, Aidan released a pent-up breath and applied the brakes. Ignoring her elegant gown, Sam scrambled to her knees and looked back.

"He's gone," she said in disbelief. "He's really gone, Aidan. He shot off the road and into the ocean."

"STUPID, STUPID, stupid," Mary muttered crabbily. She sloshed, sodden, into the house and sank unceremoniously onto the bottom stair. "Shouldn't have done it."

"Good God!"

Tobias's exclamation of shock galvanized her anger, turning it outward from herself.

"Not a word," she snapped, hazel eyes flashing a dangerous warning. "I'm in no shape for you, and I'm in a firing mood. I lost Mr. Plimley's car."

"Mr.—who? Plimley?"

"The man who owns the Canyon Grocery Store."

"But that's miles from here."

"No kidding." She eased an aching foot out from underneath her, fingering her swollen ankle. "I got a ride to town with a kid in a truck who was higher than a kite."

"On drugs?" Tobias croaked.

"Love." Mary gave a smug smile. "He'll never remember an old broad like me."

"You're not—"

"Then," she interrupted, easing her other foot free, "I took Plimley's Lincoln and drove it to Rockland's reception."

"You went there!" Aghast, Tobias closed his eyes. "That was very foolish."

"I know. It didn't work, either. I couldn't have gotten in. But I thought the girl and her champion or partner or whatever he is could use a little shaking up, so I waited outside. Always keep the enemy guessing, Tobias."

"But—"

"Shut up, Tobias. I'm explaining. It's more than you deserve. I followed them. Not too closely, but they saw the car and knew someone was after them so they tried to ditch me."

"Obviously they succeeded." Tobias's tone was dry as dust.

Mary made a soaring motion with her hand. "I went flying off the road and into the water. Lucky the car did a nosedive into three feet of water or I'd have been trapped."

"Did they see you?"

"No, but morbid snoops that they are, they poked around the empty wreck. I hid among the rocks on the beach. When they left a coon's age later, I hobbled along the beach, pulled the hood of my rain slicker up and paid a smelly guy with a beard down to his knees and pupils the size of quarters to drive me to the fork. I walked, or I should say, limped from there."

"Good God," Tobias repeated softly.

Mary made a snarly sound. "I'm old Tobias. I'm not dead. Why do so many people when they reach a certain age plop down in their rocking chairs and wait placidly for death? If my heart goes, it goes. But I don't think it will because you know I only smoke at certain times now and I also have a damned fine reason to keep right on living."

"Margaret."

"Revenge."

"There's little difference, Mary."

Her eyes assumed a glow that warmed her body right through. "I've got all my little rooks and pawns set up, Tobias, just like Sherlock Holmes did in his giant chess game. I know all the moves."

"All of them?"

"Enough to play the game," she retorted testily. "I'll win, Tobias. This time, I'll beat Margaret Truesdale." She directed a hard look at his wrinkled face. "I'll kill anyone who gets in my way, including her snippy little granddaughter."

Chapter Five

By 10:00 p.m., Sam was so tired she could have fallen asleep in a closet, and so aware of Aidan Brodie that she wanted to scream.

He moved like a cat, sleek and lazy, a little slouchy, yet never appearing to expend a great deal of energy. His skin was sleek, too, and his musculature. She was guessing on that last thing, but she imagined him to be beautifully muscled, not bulky just toned to a lithe firmness under his clothes.

When he took her home and walked her up the long outer staircase, it took all her willpower not to invite him in for a drink. He shouldn't drink and drive, and he couldn't possibly stay. Not if she wanted to maintain her emotional stability.

There were six other tenants in the building. Three of their lights were on, including sweet, snoopy Miss Busby who played piano and made hideous human sculptures that she called surreal, but most people simply called grotesque.

"What's that?" Aidan asked doubtfully of the one drying on Miss Busby's porch.

"Ed Sullivan," Sam answered, not looking.

"Where's his head?"

"She says he lacked personality. No personality, no head. No, Aidan, don't stop here. She has a dog, a big dog with even bigger teeth."

"She lets him out?"

"Her, and she chews pant legs, mail and the odd shoe. Aidan?" Pausing halfway up the last set of stairs, she regarded him somberly. "Who do you think was in that car tonight?"

He had a sensual stare. His eyes looked at a woman rather than through her. Bedroom eyes, she thought with a small sigh of regret. If only she wasn't so skittish about relationships. If only he would make some kind of move...

He regarded her half-lidded. His voice was a lazy Irish drawl. "I don't know, Sam. Maybe Alistair, but that's the obvious answer. I think there may be a great deal about this case that isn't obvious."

"That has an ominous ring to it."

She was facing him on the narrow staircase. The rain had been stopping and starting for the past two hours. It was thinking of starting again. Sam felt a light mist settle across her shoulders and hair. Various porch lights angled shadows over both of them. And yet she could see him quite clearly in spite of that.

Before she could stop herself, she had raised her fingers to trace the strong lines of his face, a classically handsome face that had no aspect of prettiness about it. His skin was warm and smooth. He exuded sexuality like a fire radiated warmth. She faltered. Heaven help her, her desire was beginning to win out over her will.

She let her hand fall away. Like his face, his hair begged to be touched. "I'll, uh, call Margaret tomorrow and see if she'll agree to meet you."

He nodded, seemed about to say something, but changed his mind and lowered his gaze to her lips. "I had a feeling I'd regret walking you up," he murmured.

Breathing with difficulty, Sam fought the urge to slide her arms around his neck. And yet she didn't want him to go, either. She wanted... The thought had barely formed before his mouth came down on hers in a move so sudden and unexpected that she had no time to react. His kiss sent a shock of excitement through her body, along her spine and right up to her brain. An odd sort of dizziness swept over her, something to do with hidden hunger and feelings too new to fully understand.

She felt his thumb stroke her jaw and the strain of desire he strove to conceal. Her breath came in a gasp when, as if driven by a demon, he broke the contact between them.

"Damn," he said softly, and dropped his head forward. "I didn't mean for that to happen."

Sam swallowed, not sure she could speak. Too many things were leaping around in her mind, jumbled thoughts that might take days to sort out. Steadying herself, she faced him, all bravado. "It's done, Aidan. We're both old enough to deal with it."

"You'd think so," he agreed cryptically. His eyes shifted to the water. "I was married once," he told her in a low voice. "For two years and four months. When I left, she set her lawyers, her brokers and her Dobermans on me."

"Sounds a bit drastic," Sam replied carefully, not sure what else would be appropriate. She was still trying to regain her equilibrium.

His smile was ironic. "That depends on your point of view. She thought she had just cause."

Sam hesitated. He felt very dangerous all of a sudden. "What did she call 'just cause'?"

His green eyes held hers in a gaze she was powerless to break. "She claimed I tried to kill her."

"HE'S LYING," Sam declared to her parakeet, Koko. The effects of Aidan's kiss lingered, but her mind was clear enough. "He couldn't have tried to kill her. I'd know if he had violent tendencies." She kicked off her high heels as she headed for the kitchen. "He'd have gone for Alistair's throat at the party if he had a flashy temper... My God, what happened?" She stopped short, her eyes widening at the mess of tattered paper on the table.

There was a note written on pink stationery with a box of Almond Rocca beside it.

Used the spare key you gave me last summer to get in. Sorry about the mess. Angel missed her breakfast. I replaced the box of chocolates your mother sent. The bills are intact, and I don't think she damaged the video itself.

Miss Busby

Sam gazed at the sorry mess. It figured the bills would survive. She didn't know what the videotape was all about—and wouldn't until she got her broken VCR back from the shop. It looked like a blank Sony, with half the cardboard jacket torn off. At least Angel hadn't mangled her leather boots this time.

On cue, Miss Busby began to play her piano downstairs. "The Beer Barrel Polka."

Sam unpinned her already disheveled hair and, humming along, let her thoughts slide back to Aidan.

He'd said those things about his ex-wife deliberately, to unnerve her. Maybe he felt the same unwanted attraction for her that she felt for him.

A horrible thought slithered in. What if her assessment of his character was totally wrong? He'd become Robert Brodie of the BBC effortlessly enough, and actors were commonplace in Southern California.

"No," she said firmly to Koko and the night. "I won't believe that."

It wasn't until she'd poured herself a glass of orange juice in the well-lit kitchen that Sam realized she was continuing to hum a tune that Miss Busby was no longer playing. The apartment below was silent. She could hear the Freud sisters upstairs instead. They were watching Howard Keel and Kathryn Grayson in *Kiss Me Kate*.

Sam grinned at the song, raising the juice to her lips. "I Hate Men." Kate had a definite chip on her shoulder.

She started back for the living room, loving the texture of the dusty rose carpet under her bare feet. Maybe she should have asked Aidan in.

A flurry of pounding fists cut short her musings. She froze, juice glass in hand, toes curling into the deep carpet.

Miss Busby's voice, muffled by the heavy door, called frantically, "Sam! Sam! There's a man being beaten up on the street. Let me in. Let me in!"

Her paralysis broke. She ran to the door, unchained it and yanked it open.

Miss Busby stood there in curlers. She was short, thin and wiry, in her late sixties and as spry as a woman half her age. She looked like a gnome, danced like a sprite and brandished her broom like an agitated witch.

"Get your gun," she ordered. "Hurry."

Sam rushed out, peering through the trees to the misty street. "I don't have a gun, Miss Busby. My God!" Her fingers strangled the railing. "It's Aidan!" She spun. "Where's your dog?"

Miss Busby's vehement headshake dislodged several of her curlers. "If I let Angel out, she'll bite them both. The man they're beating is a friend of yours, isn't he?"

Of course, she would have seen Aidan come up.

Running back into her apartment, Sam dialed 9-1-1, explained quickly, slammed the phone down and grabbed her baseball bat from the hall closet. Hiking up her dress, she raced barefoot down the outer stairs. She knew her heart was hammering at twice its normal rate and that her palms on the bat grip were cold and clammy. But two against one was unfair, especially when those two outweighed Aidan by a good forty pounds.

Distant sirens cut through the mist. Were they coming closer? Sam didn't wait to find out. She lunged at the heavier of the pair, swinging her bat full force in the direction of his shoulder blades.

The impact jarred her arm muscles and sent him staggering

into a bush. Miss Busby followed up with a whack to his head. Her broomstick cracked sharply against his skull.

The loss of one attacker was all Aidan needed. The other one, a muscle-bound ape with greasy red curls and black Boston Strangler gloves, growled but appeared uncertain without his partner to back him up.

Miss Busby ran onto the street, prepared to flag down the police car with the straw half of her broom. Sam brought the bat back over one shoulder and watched as Aidan and his attacker struggled.

It was no Hollywood fight scene, that was for sure, but Aidan did well, ducking and dodging as one might expect a movie hero to do. The greasy-haired man was too bulky and awkward to fit the role of a slick villain. He did, however, have a wicked right cross that caught Aidan, already battered from his earlier two-on-one skirmish, across the jaw.

Sam threatened the man with the bat when he drew close, but otherwise let Aidan deal with the matter. Her aim was only so-so. She might miss her target and slam Aidan on the head instead.

The man made a desperate last dive for Aidan only to wind up facedown on the pavement, panting and agitated. He swore and rolled away, almost catching Aidan's ankles as he went.

It was an old trick, one Aidan managed to avoid despite being badly winded himself. Doubled over out of range, he endeavored to catch his breath. When the man staggered upright, Aidan, reacting like a big cat, stepped aside at the last second, caught his wrist in an iron grip and spun him so that his arm was pressed behind his back.

The man let out a stream of curses that brought Miss Busby marching over. "Don't swear!" she ordered, and hit him with her broom. "The police are here," she said to Sam. She smiled in triumph at Aidan.

Sam didn't lower the bat until the two policemen climbed from their car to survey the scene. Miss Busby leaned on her broken broomstick, which in turn rested in the small of the unconscious man's back. Sam still clutched her bat and Aidan had a chokehold on the second man who, despite Miss Busby's warning, continued to swear like a sailor.

"What's this all about?" one of the officers finally asked.

It suddenly occurred to Sam that there was nothing they could say. Not if Margaret's anonymity and the secret of Mary's escape from Oakhaven were to be maintained.

A glance at Aidan confirmed it. Thrusting his captive away, he made a weary gesture. "Just a mugging, officer," he said. "Just a simple L.A. mugging."

"YOU'LL HAVE A BLACK EYE in the morning," Sam predicted, handing him a piece of raw sirloin strip. "Try that and tell me again what happened."

"They jumped me." Aidan regarded the meat, highly skeptical. "It's an old wives' tale about raw meat and black eyes, Sam."

"You're really stubborn, aren't you?" Picking up the steak, she placed it gently against his sore eye.

It had to be the cold that felt good, rather than the meat. Aidan enjoyed steak as a rule, but well-done, not bloody and raw. His stomach gave an unpleasant twist.

"Ignore it," Sam advised, reading his mind. "I wish we could have told the police the truth. Those guys'll be out in no time."

"They would anyway, you know that."

"Yes, I do. What happened?" she asked again.

"They came at me out of the bushes," Aidan told her. He tested his canine tooth with his tongue. It felt loose. "They didn't say who hired them or why—in fact, they didn't say a word—but the logical assumption would be that Mary knows we're after her and wants to stop us before we stop her."

Sam rubbed a tender thumb across his bruised cheekbone, sending a shudder of desire through Aidan's aching body. "That makes sense. It could have been one of the people at the party, but the reason's probably the same. It would just mean that Mary had an ally.''

Aidan eased himself away from her. ''I prefer to think of Mary as working alone.''

She uncapped a bottle of antiseptic. ''What about Alistair Blue?''

''What about him?'' Aidan returned in a wary tone. He didn't trust her with that bottle and tiny scrap of cloth. He didn't trust himself within ten feet of her. The side of his mouth was bleeding. The last thing he needed was for Sam to touch him there. ''I'll do it,'' he said before she could wet the cloth.

''No, you won't.'' She tipped the bottle, then unnerved him completely by bending over to grin at him. ''Men never clean their own cuts properly, at least not the men I've known.''

''Mmm, and how many would that be?''

Damn, why had he said that? Aidan gnashed his teeth. He should get the hell out of here while his heart still had a layer of resistance around it. Because once it crumbled, he'd be at her mercy. And that, he reflected grimly, was not a state of affairs he was prepared to handle.

She didn't flinch, from the question or from him. ''I've had a date or two in my life. Now hold still.'' She trapped his chin in her slender left hand and pressed the cool cloth to the side of his mouth.

Aidan swore succinctly to himself. Half a hundred questions burned in his brain, but they paled by comparison to the insistent throbbing in his lower body. One thing was sure, the name Samantha fit her like a glove. How, though, he wondered, fighting the heat, was it possible to fall under the spell of a Hollywood witch?

Feeling oddly resigned, he leaned back in his chair, a hard-backed honey oak chair in Sam's dangerously homey apartment. The kitchen was white with light wood cabinets and floor. The living room was a blend of pale greens and antique roses with splashes of deep blue to set it off. The overall effect was one of welcoming charm, a place that was neither fussy nor frivolous. She and Domina would not have gotten along.

"Can I ask you something?" Sam paused in her ministrations to regard him.

Eyes veiled, he studied her face. "That depends on the question."

"Would you tell me about your wife?"

It must be a trick of the light that she looked so beautiful right now, fine-skinned, delicate-boned—and about as fragile as a wildcat. Her black hair smelled like roses and tumbled in silken waves around her cheeks and shoulders. All he could think about was how much he wanted to make love to her, and she was asking him about his failed marriage.

"She was a witch," he said. "With a capital *B*."

A tiny smile curved her lips then disappeared. "Did you really try to kill her?"

"It crossed my mind once or twice."

She knew just where to press on his cut to provoke a stab of pain. "I don't scare as easily as that, Brodie. What did you do that made her accuse you?"

"I poured her a glass of wine."

"That doesn't sound very deadly."

"It does if there's arsenic in the glass."

She whipped her hand away and bent low again to stare him straight in the eye. "You expect me to believe you put arsenic in your wife's wine?"

Aidan forced his gaze away from the tantalizing view of cleavage and set it calmly on her face. It was his turn to trap her chin now. He did so firmly, stroking her soft skin with his thumb as he murmured cryptically, "It might be a good idea if you did." And with that nebulous warning hanging in the air between them, he urged her lower and set his hungry mouth on hers.

IT TOOK SAM an unreasonably long time to recover from Aidan's kiss. His kisses, she corrected herself as the night wore on and sleep continued to elude her. Hot, hungry kisses that made her long for things she couldn't remember wanting before. And shouldn't want now, she reminded herself firmly. There were too many problems in her life—and apparently an equal number in his. No, a sexual involvement would not be wise for either of them at this point.

Not to mention that he was a brooder, she thought, twisting around in the sheets. His mouth had burned on hers, hot, insistent and exploratory. And she'd responded with the same intensity of desire. Then, just when she'd been about to get panicky, he'd drawn away. Eyes closed, breathing decidedly uneven, he'd murmured another vague, "Damn," and pulled away from her.

She'd known what he would do even before he did it. He'd wanted distance, and so had put a full fifteen feet between them.

Sam had stared at his lean back, feeling not so much hurt as puzzled. Most men would have said something, no matter how inane. But inanity appeared to have no part in Aidan's makeup. When he'd turned to regard her, she'd been unable to read his smoldering expression. All he'd said was, "I'll go now, Sam. Thanks for the first aid."

She slept fitfully that night, more disturbed by her own feelings than by what Aidan had told her about his wife's death—or the fact that he'd been attacked on her doorstep. It wasn't until she climbed out of bed at dawn that her mind was finally able to focus on the unlikely coincidence of the assault.

A cool shower and coffee revived her. She cut up fresh fruit and mixed it with birdseed for Koko, fixed herself some toast, jam and juice, then with the surf breaking in the distance, sat and stared at the cordless telephone for thirty minutes. She had, after all, made a deal with Aidan.

Sighing, she picked up the receiver and dialed. Theo Larkin answered on the second ring.

"Is Margaret awake yet?" Sam asked. Absently, she studied

the videocassette that Miss Busby's dog had chewed yesterday. If there was a title, Angel's teeth had torn it away with the bottom half of the jacket.

Polite but firm, Theo returned, "Madame seldom rises before eleven."

Sam frowned at the mouthpiece. Margaret hadn't struck her as the slothful type. "I have to talk to her," she told him. "About a friend of mine. He wants to help me find Mary."

Theo's tone sharpened. "What kind of friend?"

"Mary's doctor at Oakhaven asked him to look for her. And there's another man on her trail, too. At least I think he is. His name's Alistair Blue. The doctor said that Thurman Wells hired him."

A throaty voice broke in. "That makes for a jolly little group, doesn't it? Good morning, Sam. Hang up, Theo. I want to talk to my granddaughter."

"Did you hear what I said about Aidan?" Sam asked carefully, unsure of Margaret's morning mood.

The line clicked before Margaret replied, "Is that his name? Aidan? Aidan what?"

"Brodie. He's an insurance investigator."

"Doing a favor for a friend, hmm? Is he young and sexy?"

The directness of her question caught Sam off guard. "I—uh—well, he'd be in his late thirties, and I suppose you could call him sexy."

"My dear girl, I'd call any man under eighty who still has his original teeth and hair sexy."

"Can I bring him over?"

Margaret thought about it. "I suppose I could risk it. He's not a blabbermouth, is he?"

"I don't think so."

"Oh, all right, bring him over. How are things coming, by the way? How was Leo's reception?"

Sam decided not to tell her about last night's—whatever it had been—or the slashed brakes, or the car chase, not over the telephone at any rate. "Interesting," she allowed, then grinned. "The last I saw of poor Mr. Wells, he was propped up in a corner doing Hamlet's soliloquy."

Margaret's voice softened. "He always loved Shakespeare. I was married to him, you know, way back when. So was Mary. However, being a journalist, I'm sure you've discovered that by now. Did you also learn about my marriage to Frank?"

Sam searched her memory. Had Guido mentioned the name or had she dug it up herself? "Frank Durwald, wasn't it? Businessman."

"He made ice cream. Parlor Shoppe Ice Cream. Had to sell the company, of course, but that's another story, nothing to do with Mary's vendetta. Frank and I separated five years after I stopped acting. I haven't seen or heard from him for more than three decades. There was some trouble, but I never knew the details. I believe, though, that he changed his name."

Tucking that information away, Sam ventured cautiously, "What about Anthea?"

"What about her?" Margaret sounded equally cautious.

"Do you know where she is?"

"I wish," Margaret said softly. "We were cousins by marriage, you know."

"I thought she was your blood cousin. Which marriage?"

"To Frank." The old woman sighed. "It's all very complicated, and unconnected to Mary's scheme in any case. No need for you to get sidetracked by old mysteries, no matter how tantalizing they might appear on the surface."

This whole thing was getting decidedly complicated. An ex-husband named Frank Durwald, cousin to Anthea Pennant. Whereabouts of both people unknown. A slashed brake line, attackers outside her apartment, someone chasing them in a sedan; an actor, a director and a producer, all behaving suspiciously. And Margaret insisting she must retain her anonymity.

"I'll call Brodie," she said, not at all prepared to let the subject of Anthea Pennant rest. Given their past relationship, Anthea might provide valuable insight into Mary's character,

he kind that stood a chance of pointing her and Aidan in the
ight direction.

"Mary is seriously deranged," Margaret warned. "Never
orget that, Samantha. She'd murder her own mother if she
tood in her way. She'd murder Anthea, too, if she believed
Anthea could tell you anything."

"I hadn't thought of that," Sam admitted, troubled.

"That's because you're applying logic where little if any
exists. Mary was an excellent actress and an even better
marksman. She could shoot the toes off a crow at a hundred
ards. Be careful, Sam. If you value your toes, be very, very
careful of Mary Lamont's tricks."

THE SQUAWK of the telephone jarred Alistair Blue out of a
dream about Ingrid Bergman, Morocco and a piano player
called Sam. Cracking his eyes, he fumbled the receiver off the
hook and growled, "Yeah?"

"You're drunk," a familiar voice said coldly.

"Hungover. What time is it?"

"Almost nine." A pause, then, "Why did you go to Leo
Rockland's reception?"

Alistair's head spun. He grunted. "Were you hiding behind
a potted palm or something, watching the door? A buddy of
mine got me in. I went to scope out the situation. I left about
the time Anthea Pennant's name came up."

"That was discreet of you. What did you do when you
eft?"

Alistair swore, partly at the painful pounding in his head,
ut mostly at the caller's accusing tone. "I went home and
ut away a case of Bud."

"I see. Nothing more helpful than that?"

Alistair reached for a beer bottle on the bedstand. When he
ealized it was empty, he heaved it across the room. It knocked
is one and only copy of *The Invisible Man* to the floor.
wearing again, he snapped, "I called my ex, okay? Or do I

have to clear everything with you first? This is a favor I'r
doing, remember?''

''A favor to yourself,'' the caller reminded him coolly
''and you've a tendency to be lazy. That's a dangerous thing
Alistair Blue. Now you listen to me, and listen good. You
ridiculous burbling has reminded me of a loose end. I'll hel
you, of course, but I want you to locate someone for me.''

Transparent as glass, Alistair thought sullenly. ''Would he
initials be A.P. by any chance?''

''Don't trifle with me, young man,'' the caller warned i
such a frigid tone that the hair on Alistair's neck momentaril
stood up. ''You find Anthea Pennant for me, and you do wit
her exactly what I tell you to do. I wouldn't argue, Alistair,'
the person added before he could form a suitably flippant re
ply. ''My mood's not the best these days. If your mother wa
here, she'd attest to the fact that I'm hell to deal with in a ba
mood. But she isn't here, is she? So unless you want to joi
her, you'd do well to follow my instructions, and follow ther
to the letter....''

Chapter Six

"Morning, Gui...do." Sam halted on the threshold, her smile vanishing. "What are you doing here?" she demanded of the man perched on a corner of Guido's overflowing desk.

Aidan gave her a bland look. "Waiting for you."

"Wouldn't my office be a more appropriate place to wait?" She took a breath to steady her nerves. "Where's Guido?"

"Behind you, Minx." Laden with a tray of coffee and Danish, he kissed her cheek. "Is there a problem?"

Sam masked a sigh. "I take it you two have met."

"Ten minutes ago," Guido confirmed. "It was my idea that Mr. Brodie should wait for you here." He set the tray on a stack of precariously piled magazines, handed a steaming cup to Aidan, then one to her. "Now, where's this mysterious videotape you called me about?"

Aidan's brows arched. He looked too good for 9:00 a.m. on a hazy California morning, too rumpled and touchable despite the wary look in his deep green eyes. The area above his right cheekbone was bruised but not as black as she would have expected given the punch he'd taken.

"What tape?" He wanted to know.

Relenting, Sam shrugged. "I have no idea. My VCR's in the shop being cleaned. I think it came in the mail. At least, it was chewed with the rest of the mail."

Aidan's lips twitched. "Miss Busby's dog?"

She bit back a reluctant smile. "She's still crowing about last night's victory."

Guido's head swiveled with the conversation. "Do I want to know what you're talking about?"

Sam couldn't help laughing. "No, but I'll explain anyway. It really isn't funny."

Guido's thin face sobered as her story unfolded. Aidan's remained placid from start to finish.

"You're right, it isn't funny," he agreed. He picked up a raspberry Danish. "What do you think about all of this, Mr. Brodie?"

"Aidan. And it's simple enough. Mary—or someone—wants us off the case." He regarded Sam, who was trying to shove the videotape into Guido's antiquated machine. "Did you say Margaret was married to Frank Durwald?"

"Yes." She poked three buttons to no avail. "Do you know him?"

"Maybe."

"I do," Guido said. Holding the bun in his mouth, he began pawing through a stack of old movie magazines. "Where is that thing? I saw it yester— Ah, here it is. *Movie Mirror.* January, 1953."

Sam felt Aidan behind her. Reaching over her shoulder, he pressed a button on the left. The video carriage immediately popped up.

"Show-off," she grumbled, glaring at the panel. "Can I play this, Guido?"

He held up a forestalling hand. "Listen first. This is an interview with Evelyn Mesmyr. She was one of the studio makeup artists who worked on *The Three Fates.* She says here that Margaret was getting, quote, 'heavily involved with the distinguished Franklin P. Durwald, of Parlor Shoppe Ice Cream fame. Trust our lucky star to land herself such a sumptuous fish. Most of us would bait our hooks with diamonds to catch the eye of such a man as Mr. Durwald. But, of course, he would want Margaret over anyone else. The irony is that

Mary saw him first. Story of Mary's life. What's that old expression? Always the bridesmaid, never the bride...?'"

"Evelyn sounds jealous," Aidan noted, sipping his coffee. "Is she still alive, Guido?"

"I can find out."

"Whatever else she is, she likes fish," Sam remarked. "Can I play this now?"

"Curious cat is my Minx," Guido remarked with an affectionate tug of Sam's long hair. "Go on, then. It's probably just a promotional..." His sentence trailed off as the screen began to flicker. The image that formed didn't look promotional to Sam. It looked like the opening scene of *Arsenic and Old Lace*.

The thought of that old movie title had her glancing covertly at Aidan, but his hooded gaze was fixed on the television, and he likely wouldn't make the connection anyway. Or if he did he wouldn't let on. She shuddered and turned back to the screen.

The black and white silhouetted house looked old and vaguely haunted. The blend of date palms, evergreens and oak trees placed the setting in Southern California, probably in a suburb of L.A.

The scene changed without warning to an interior shot. Crackling music, suitably suspenseful, accompanied the shift.

"My God, that's Margaret!" Guido exclaimed. "And Anthea's behind her. And there's Mary. This is a clip from *The Three Fates*. I'd bet my reputation on it!"

"Really?" Sam inched closer, fascinated. "They don't look like traditional witches."

"No warts and broomsticks," Aidan murmured. He was standing directly behind her, disconcertingly close, Sam realized with a shiver she chose not to analyze.

"Did you take him food and water?" Mary's character inquired. The sound recording was as scratchy as the video was snowy.

Margaret gave her a cutting look. "He's been taken care of, sister. You needn't concern yourself with details."

"Cold as ice," Guido murmured of Margaret. "But the audience would have warmed up to her in the end. I wonder who they're taking food and water to?"

"Must be a Gothic suspense," Sam declared. "Updated to the early fifties. Like *Whatever Happened To Baby Jane?*"

The videotape crackled, then faded and settled. In the next clip, Mary was talking to Anthea Pennant.

"When did she last meet our lawyer?" Mary was demanding.

Anthea continued to pour hot wax into candle molds. "Ten years ago. Maybe more. Why?"

The camera zoomed in on Mary, heavily made up to appear as devious and sinister as her character was doubtless intended to be. "No reason," she said. The gleam in her eyes suggested differently. "You'd better hurry with that, sister. Our guests will be arriving shortly."

The tape ended there, abruptly, as if it had been cut at the end of a frame. No fade, no forewarning, only a blank video screen and three puzzled faces staring at it.

Guido was the first to react. "There are no prints of that movie anywhere," he said surely. "They went missing right after the film was shelved."

"Well, they're not missing now," Sam stated. "I think we can take a good guess who sent this, too. What I don't understand is why Mary Lamont would want me to have a clip of *The Three Fates*. And how did she find out about Aidan and me in the first place? Did someone at Oakhaven tell her? Someone from the studio?"

Guido poked at his bifocals. "I can't answer those questions, Minx, but with regard to Mary's motive, maybe this tape is in the nature of another warning."

"How so?" Aidan inquired, his tone cautious. "Possession of stolen film canisters is no threat to us."

"I was referring to the nature of the movie, Aidan. Of

course the ending was never officially revealed, in the hopes that someday Margaret would return and shooting could be completed. However, it was rumored that for the first time on-screen, Margaret's character would be killed—by the Fate played by Mary Lamont.''

MARGARET'S HOLLOW CHEEKS paled visibly as Sam related the events of the past few days. She left nothing out and ended with the watching of the videotape together with Guido's gloomy prediction that it was some kind of macabre warning from Mary.

"I don't understand," Margaret said, her knuckles white around the arms of her chair. "I didn't... Theo!" she called suddenly, her tone imperative. The sprayed waves on her cheeks trembled with the force of her emotion. "Theo!"

He materialized in the parlor doorway. "Madame?"

Her gaze flicked to Aidan's watchful face. "Bring Mr. Brodie some tea."

Aidan, who'd been studying both Margaret and his surroundings while Sam poured out her story, gave his head a negative shake. "Coffee's fine, thanks."

"I thought you English preferred tea?" Margaret said.

"He's Irish, Madame," Theo told her.

Aidan knew better than to smile. Helpless this old woman definitely was not, but it must be jarring to learn to what lengths an adversary would go in order to achieve her goal.

Margaret recovered her composure swiftly—Aidan could almost see her mental defenses shoring up. Her thin shoulders beneath the black sack of her dress squared, and she lifted her once heart-shaped face as if in defiance. She regarded Sam, wickedly appealing in a pair of black pants and a deep coral designer T-shirt that hugged her slender curves to perfection and made his hands long to touch. "The woman is a viper," she stated clearly and with only a faintly discernable quaver. "But if she thinks I'll buckle, she's got rocks in her head.

Why on earth would she send you a clip from *The Three Fates?*"

Aidan leaned forward in his seat, his forearms resting with deceptive ease on his knees. "At this point I'm more curious to know who tried to run us off the road."

"And cut your brake line," Sam added. "And told Mary about us in the first place."

"An accomplice?" Margaret suggested.

"With an in at Oakhaven," Aidan said grimly.

"And no scruples," Sam said. At Aidan's steady look, she explained, "Those guys last night were huge. And mean. Maybe they were just muggers, but I don't think so. It's too convenient."

"It happens all the time, Sam."

"Well, it shouldn't."

The exchange was being carried out at right angles, with Margaret an intrigued spectator in her high-backed chair next to the fireplace.

She hadn't risen from that chair the whole time they'd been there and didn't now. She merely slapped the arms with her palms and offered a decisive, "Time. We'll call that little parlay even, shall we? Now, back to more unpleasant matters. You received your videotape in the mail, Sam, though for what purpose I'm still unclear."

"Guido said—"

"Yes, I know, a threat." Margaret's fists balled then thumped the padded chair arms. "I'm sorry if I seem on edge, but what you don't know is that I received a package in the mail, as well."

"What?" Sam's gaze flicked to Aidan's. "When?"

"Late yesterday afternoon—apparently." Her lipsticked mouth turned down at the corners. "Theo didn't see fit to deliver it to me until this morning at breakfast. It was another music box."

She reminded Aidan of a cross between Bette Davis and Joan Crawford in their dotage. The ever-so-slight tremor in her voice could be a result of age and too much alcohol, but he doubted it. She seemed genuinely unnerved, as any sane person would be when faced with their own mortality.

"It was another of Mary's favorites," Margaret went on, lighting a cigarette with bony, trembling hands. "A little marble thing that plays Strauss's 'Tales of the Vienna Woods.' Quite pretty really, but infinitely more disconcerting in its implications."

Sam frowned, uncomprehending. "What do you mean?"

"She wouldn't part with those boxes on pain of her own death," Margaret stated flatly. "Whatever her scheme, she intends to get them back. Unless, of course, she's dying."

"The doctor would have told us..." Again Sam glanced at Aidan, but he merely shrugged. He knew John Christian, yes, but not well enough to vouch for his actions in this.

"We can ask him," he said, "but he probably would have mentioned a fatal disease. Do you know where the package was mailed from, Margaret?"

"It was postmarked here in the canyon, I assume from that little outlet about ten miles farther in."

"We'll check it out," Sam promised. "And the hospital, too, in case John—Mary's doctor—neglected to tell us anything important."

Aidan didn't hold out much hope in that area, but anything was preferable to sitting around waiting for the next attack.

His gaze slid sideways to Sam's delicate face framed by masses of long, beautiful hair. God help him, there were other things than traipsing out to Oakhaven that he would rather do with Sam. However, for both their sakes, sticking to business was the wise choice. She didn't believe he'd poisoned his ex-wife. That didn't necessarily mean she trusted him.

Did he trust her? he wondered as Margaret instructed Theo to bring both music boxes. His eyes, impassive enough on the surface, surveyed her on the floral sofa. Yes, he did, but only on a mental level. When it came to emotions, he didn't trust either of them for a minute.

Sam was beautiful, bright and determined, more so than Domina had ever been. He sensed no malice in her nature and a generosity of spirit he hadn't encountered since he'd been a kid in Ireland and Mr. McBean at the local greengrocer had taken him on and proceeded to teach him the value of both money and keeping his word. Aidan had never forgotten Mr. McBean or their talks. He couldn't see forgetting Sam, either. And that, he reflected bleakly, was a state of affairs unlikely to alter with prolonged exposure.

"Put them here," Margaret bade Theo, who had returned with the delicately carved boxes.

Sam picked up the marble one. Aidan glanced at its companion, then watched as her deft hand unclasped and lifted the lid.

Tinkling strains of Strauss reached his ears. Exquisite and bewitching—like Sam.

"Mary has good taste," she admitted, inspecting the box. "How do you wind…" She stopped and touched something on the underside. "There's a piece of paper taped here."

Margaret gave a startled jerk. Her sagging neck stretched out like a camel's. "What does it say?"

Carefully, Sam removed the tape and unfolded the note. Aidan rose, bending over her shoulder as she read.

"Well?" Margaret tapped her chair arm in agitation. "Come on, you two, spit it out."

Sam handed the paper to Aidan.

Margaret grunted. "Out loud, for heaven's sake. I read scripts, not minds."

Sam shook her head, so Aidan did the dubious honors.

"Your Fate's in my hands now, Margaret. I control the twists and turns. I control you. Read the script. Here she is, the great Margaret Truesdale. In the role of her life.

In the role of her death."

JOHN CHRISTIAN looked more harried than Aidan had ever seen him. His dark, gray-streaked hair stood up at odd angles, his glasses were askew and he'd pulled his tie sloppily away from his throat.

"One of the newspapers got wind of Mary's escape," he moaned as they accompanied him on his rounds. "I put the guy off for now, but he'll be back. He's one of those bulldog types, and ten to one he's got connections at a local television station." He appealed to them. "Have you turned up anything at all?"

"Plenty," Aidan said. "But nothing that leads us to Mary."

"Can you tell us more about her?" Sam asked from his other side. "Was she sick? Physically, I mean? Could she have spies here at Oakhaven? Did any of her old cronies ever visit her?"

"No, possibly, and yes. Thurman Wells came, as you know… No, thank you, Morris, Ms. Giancarlo doesn't need any baseball cards."

The man, a bent, bald creature somewhere between forty and sixty, ambled off, clearly disappointed. Aidan hoped to hell he never wound up in a place like this.

"That's the lounge, down there." John nodded in the direction his patient had taken. "Mary spent a lot of time watching old movies there. Several of her Oakhaven friends were in awe of her past credits."

"So they could have told her about Aidan and me," Sam theorized.

John sighed. "It's certainly possible. Phone use is limited but not rigorously patrolled. There's not much harm anyone can inflict on the phone."

"Wanna bet?" Aidan murmured dryly.

John gave him a wan smile. "As I was saying, Thurman Wells visited Mary, but only once. Others called."

"Leo Rockland?" Sam speculated. "Stan Hollister?"

"Yes to Mr. Rockland. No to Hollister."

"Was there anyone else?" Aidan asked.

"I'm not sure. I might have a list. We try to keep track of

thinks like that. Ah," he interrupted himself. "Here comes Mrs. Payne. A perfect name for her, but she might be of some help to you."

The woman was short, squat and heavy. She waddled like a duck and had a voice like a foghorn. She had also, according to John, spent a great deal of time playing card games with Mary.

"She cheated," Mrs. Payne revealed flatly when asked about her former partner.

They'd adjourned to the plant-filled lounge where John chatted with the other patients while Sam and Aidan talked to Mrs. Payne.

"Mary liked the name Helen Murdoch, you're right about that," she said, peering myopically at Sam. "You're sharp, missy. Pretty, too. You an actress?"

"I'd like to be," Sam lied.

"You should talk to Mary," the woman said with an emphatic nod that dislodged two of her pin curls. "She was the best. Better'n that old Margaret Truesdale." She leaned forward conspiratorially. "I heard the reason Margaret got so much from the studio was because she acted real hoity-toity with all the bosses. Mary got given seconds every time, you know. On screen, in wardrobe, at dinners, in the hospital, with men—you name it, Mary always crossed the finish line behind Margaret Truesdale."

Something on her list clicked in Aidan's head. "What hospital did Mary get seconds in, Mrs. Payne? Not this one, surely."

Mrs. Payne emitted a raw hoot of laughter. Her hands slapped the oak table. "Lordy, no." She jerked suddenly, then ducked. "Where's that plane?" she demanded, and would have dived from her chair if John hadn't intercepted her.

"It's one of ours," he assured her. "No need to worry."

Aidan listened as the jet engines overhead faded. "Germans?" he mouthed to his friend who nodded grimly and patted Mrs. Payne's plump arm until she relaxed.

"Those were dismal days in London during the war. Carry on, you three."

It took the woman several minutes to calm down sufficiently to continue. Even then, she seemed confused about the current time period.

"My mom took me to London to see my dad during the war," she said in a small voice. "He was English, my dad." She paused then added, "She came from New Jersey, you know."

"Your mother?" Sam asked kindly.

Mrs. Payne gave her head a vigorous shake. "No, no, Mary. My mom came from Boston. She never acted. That was Mary's job when she wasn't doing some dirty deal behind someone's back. She got Morris over there to stack the cards, I know she did. She's a schemer, that one, but I like her anyway. Only talent I have is for playing the oboe. Mary, she could act. I saw her movies. She was better than Margaret Truesdale. My mom even said she was good once. That was before my dad died in the big crash and I got so scared and had to run—" She broke off, sinking lower in her chair.

Sam moved swiftly to kneel beside her. Aidan watched but made no attempt to interfere.

"You shouldn't think about the war," Sam said gently. Like John, she patted the woman's arm. It seemed to help. Her eyes blinked and began to clear.

"I hate war movies," she said in a more strident voice. "Mary made me watch one with her and Margaret in it. They did another one after the war was over. They were both still in uniform at the start." She let out a raucous squawk of laughter. "Had to change their clothes later in the film. Mary's still mad about it. She said her face got fat and Margaret's didn't."

Mrs. Payne's gaze sharpened unexpectedly. Twisting her head around, she shot Aidan a dagger of a stare. "That's the hospital Mary got seconds in, Mr. Brodie."

Aidan had no idea what she was talking about. Neither, apparently, did Sam.

"Did this hospital have a name?" she tried hopefully.

"West Something. Mountain, I think. It was private. All the big stars went here. Mary called it the Butcher Shop."

"I'M NOT SURE I want to do this," Sam said as they made their way through the maze of narrow canyon roads. "Hospitals that can be likened to butcher shops scare me as much as planes scare Mrs. Payne. Are you sure John's right about the name?"

Aidan had the borrowed Jeep geared down to avoid mishap. He didn't seem remotely fazed by Mary's hospital nickname. In fact, he looked damnably handsome and at ease as they made their way through the remote labyrinth of roads.

He was wearing a moss green shirt with the sleeves rolled back, faded jeans and a pair of old work boots. His long brown hair blew in the breeze; his expression was one of distant calm; his attitude was as offhanded as his present manner of driving.

"West Valley Hospital isn't a butcher shop, no matter what Mary says, and yes, John's right about the name. There is no West Mountain."

"Not now. What about then?"

"Not now or then, Sam." He sent her a sideways look that bordered on impatient. "You know we have to check this out, so sit back, relax, and remind yourself that as an actress Mary probably tended to blow a lot of things out of proportion."

Sam held her temper with difficulty. "I just don't see how our going to West Valley Hospital is going to lead us to Mary. So what if she and Margaret both went there for some reason? And maybe Margaret did get treated better. Mary's not likely to be prowling around the hospital grounds. So, I repeat, Aidan, what's the real point of this little jaunt?"

He tolerated her restrained tirade with nothing more than a quirk of his sensual lips. "A good investigator never dismisses any clue, Sam. If it'll help us to understand Mary's resentment, then this trip will have been worthwhile.''

Sam made a face but offered no further argument. ''Turn left,'' was all she said, then held her tongue for the remainder of the journey.

The hospital turned out to be a lavish affair, similar to Oakhaven on the outside, and not a great deal different once they passed through the doors. And yet...

''It lacks the antiseptic touch,'' Aidan observed as they walked across the carpeted...''lobby'' was the only word that fit the wide entryway brimming with large plants and antique armchairs.

Sam nudged him, aware of an odd sensation sweeping through her. ''Are you charmed, Aidan?''

He frowned. ''Should I be?''

''I think we're supposed to be, but it isn't working on me. I keep thinking about the institute where Ingrid Bergman worked in that movie she did with Gregory Peck.''

''*Spellbound*,'' Aidan supplied, glancing at a bored-looking orderly who was en route to the elevator.

Sam stared at him in profile. ''You know *Spellbound?*''

''I like Ingrid Bergman.''

''Most men do.'' She plastered a smile on her face as they neared the front desk and the stone-faced woman seated behind it. ''Hello. We were wondering if you could give us some information?''

The woman cut her off with a chilly, ''Do you have a booking?''

''I beg your pardon?''

As if talking to a five-year-old child, the woman repeated each word with deliberation. ''Do you have a booking?''

Sam, who despised superior attitudes, matched the woman's cold tone. ''As I think I explained, we want some information, not a room for the night.''

The woman bristled. ''This isn't the Waldorf. We don't have rooms as such.''

She didn't have manners as such, either. "Look—" Sam tried again, but she was neatly cut off by Aidan who seemed to realize that while this woman had no courtesy to spare for another female, she likely had plenty in reserve for a man.

"The information we're after regards an actress by the name of Mary Lamont. Do you know her?"

The woman's stone-hard countenance melted at his smile. Sam was tempted to punch her, kick Aidan and forget this whole stupid idea.

"I've heard the name, of course," she said.

"Has she ever stayed here?"

The woman's smile faltered. "That information's classified. I'm awfully sorry."

Sure she was, Sam thought nastily. Why was Aidan wasting his time with this iceberg?

"Do you know if anyone on staff was also here after World War Two?"

"Dr. Coates was an intern back then. He's not in today, but as I said—" a dimple appeared in her cheek "—all of our patients' files are classified."

Restless, and more irritated than she had a right to be, Sam left the desk. This place disturbed her on a fundamental level. It was too—something. Forbidding? Solemn? Spooky...

The last adjective seemed a bit extreme, but it did feel spooky, she decided. There were too many long shadows and dark patches behind the plants, too much black and white amid the greenery, too much artificial lavender in the air. For all its contrivances, this private hospital was no less sterile than L.A. General. Maybe, she thought in open distaste, that was precisely why she found it so repulsive. That, plus the fact that the woman behind the front desk had, in her opinion, all the personality of a corpse.

"I'm sorry I couldn't be more helpful," the woman was apologizing loudly in Aidan's wake. Sam felt his hand cup her elbow and presumed they were leaving. "I work weekdays till four if you're out this way again."

"I'd rather die on the side of the road," Sam muttered uncharitably, endeavoring to pry her arm free of Aidan's grasp. "What's your hurry? Running to the car will save us about fifteen seconds. You can't speed on canyon roads."

Shoving open the door, Aidan cast a smiling glance over his shoulder. The woman waggled her fingers in response. "Goodbye," she called after him.

"Good riddance," Sam retorted out of earshot. His hand pressed with arousing persistence into the small of her back. "Aidan, stop pushing me."

"Keep your voice down and move." He nodded to the Jeep. "We'll drive out and park about a mile back."

"What? Why?" Sam sidestepped his disturbing touch. She turned her head to glare at him, then suddenly realized what he had in mind and halted. "No way, Aidan. I'm not breaking in. There's a million better things we could be doing—like searching for Anthea Pennant or harassing Rockland, Hollister and Wells. We could even try talking to that jealous makeup artist, Evelyn What's-her-name."

"Mesmyr," Aidan told her. Opening the passenger door, he bulldozed her inside. "We'll get to all of those people in time. First I want to see Mary's hospital records."

Exasperated, Sam stared at him. "Why? What is it you're hoping to find?"

"Think, Sam," he said patiently. "What did Mrs. Payne say about that last movie she mentioned? The post-war one."

"I don't know. Something about Mary's face looking fatter than Margaret's."

"No, she said that Mary's face *got* fatter than Margaret's. She also said they had to change their clothes later in the film, that they'd been in uniforms at the start."

Uncomprehending, Sam fastened her seat belt. "What's so special about being in uniform in a movie?"

Aidan arched a meaningful brow. "Movie uniforms are tight-fitting. And Mary thought her face was getting too fat."

"I still don't..." As if pulled by an invisible hand, Sam's head snapped around. "You think she was pregnant?"

"I think it's possible they both were." He leaned closer, until his hair and breath brushed tantalizingly across her cheek. "Mary might have a child, Sam. And that child might just know where Mary is."

Chapter Seven

"This is dangerous," Sam declared in a hiss. "And incredibly stupid. We're going to get caught."

"Don't think about it," Aidan suggested, his breath warm on her cheek.

He'd jimmied the lock on one of the basement windows at the West Valley Hospital and crawled in ahead of her. Straight into the morgue, she'd bet. But she sat down on the high ledge regardless, stole a final apprehensive glance through the shrubbery and jumped into his upstretched arms.

The mistake was obvious. It was also irrevocable. She held her breath to avoid inhaling the heady male scent of soap, shaving cream and warm skin. She couldn't hope to avoid the arms that circled her waist or the fact that he would have to slide her body along the harder length of his own to set her down.

For a long, heart-stirring moment, he held her there, pressed tightly against him. She felt every part of him, right down to the bulge that burned into her stomach.

It required a visible effort, but he put her firmly away from him before either of them could get any foolish ideas.

Bad timing, Sam thought, shivering at the force of her desire. Eyes averted, voice tight, she managed to ask, "Are we in the morgue?"

"Storeroom," Aidan said from the door. How had he gotten

across the room so fast? And how dare he sound so unaffected when her insides had turned to liquid?

Eyes scanning the hall beyond the cracked open door, he held a hand backward for her. "It's clear."

It was also cold, damp and unpleasant. As she took Aidan's hand, Sam wondered if this place had been nicer in the mid to late forties. Most things in Hollywood probably had.

"Why don't we just find a computer and go through the files that way?" she whispered as they crept along a poorly lit basement corridor.

Aidan's eyes continued to dart around. "The files we want might not be on computer." Pausing, he rattled one of the doorknobs. "Start checking doors. And keep your eyes open."

She could have argued wisdom and logic again, but what would be the point? On top of which, she was curious. If Mary really had been pregnant—no hint of which had been printed in any of the articles she and Guido had dug up—then it was reasonable to assume that her child might know her whereabouts. At least it was worth a shot.

Machines whirred in noisy profusion as they moved from door to door. Central humidifiers, central air-conditioning, air filters, water purification systems—every mechanical device in the hospital appeared to have its roots down here.

Sam spied a sign that read Morgue, and avoided it studiously, so much so that she almost blundered straight into a roomful of technicians. Whether medical or mechanical, she wasn't sure. She heard a puzzled voice ask, "What was that?" as the door clicked quietly closed, then a growled, "Nothing. Give me a smoke and deal."

Must be an early lunch break, she decided, pressing her ear to the next door as a precaution. "Any luck?" she whispered to Aidan.

"No... Yes." His tall, rangy frame disappeared across the threshold. "There are cabinets and boxes in here."

"Body-size?" Sam asked.

"Could be," he replied blandly.

She pushed past him for a look. "You have a morbid sense of humor, do you know that?"

"It's the Irish. We drink, dance and sing like birds at funerals."

The door marked Morgue evidently hadn't escaped his notice. Sexy he might be, but his wicked Irish humor was entirely too well-developed. She wondered how one would go about buying arsenic, then felt Aidan move past her and shoved the unwarranted speculation from her mind.

"Those look like filing cabinets," she noted, working her way discreetly out of range of the door. She blew a layer of dust from one of the wooden tops. "Old, too. They're made of metal now." She started to kneel then caught a glimpse of a battered photo album and picked it up. "Here's Lana Turner. And Jimmy Durante. And the Marx Brothers." She glanced doubtfully at the flaking cover. "Someone must have been a fan. I wonder if celebrities still come to this hospital for— whatever it was they used to come to places like this for... God, this is a great shot of Errol Flynn."

"Drawers, Sam," Aidan reminded.

"You have no romance in your soul, do you?"

His enigmatic eyes caught hers. "I like candlelight," he said. "And wine."

Sam masked a shudder and clapped the scrapbook closed.

They rummaged in silence for a time. Once Sam detected voices, but it was only a pair of orderlies wheeling a gurney toward the elevator.

"Charming," she murmured, and returned to her task.

It seemed they must be in the right place. Some of the files dated back as far as nineteen twenty-seven. Unfortunately, discarded information required little organization, and none of it had been stored alphabetically.

"Here's Margaret's file," Aidan remarked finally, drawing out a slender folder.

Sam turned a file sideways to mark her spot and went to

peer over his shoulder. "She looked a little like Gene Tierney, didn't she?"

Aidan glanced back at her. His mouth was disturbingly close to hers when he said, "There's no picture here, Sam. What made you think of Gene Tierney?"

"*The Ghost and Mrs. Muir, Laura.* Her picture was in the scrapbook. I just think they had similar features, that's all, but then that was the 'in' look at the time. What does Margaret's file say?"

"That she had her daughter—" he flipped to the front page "—in nineteen forty-eight."

"Five years before she left Hollywood," Sam recalled.

It crossed her mind as she skimmed the contents of the medical file that she should probably be experiencing a poignant pang or two. After all, her natural grandmother had appeared out of nowhere. Search as she might, however, the pangs refused to strike. Blood notwithstanding, Grandma Lena in Baltimore was and always would be her maternal grandmother.

"Margaret showed me copies of these records," she said at length and calmly closed the folder. "It's Mary's records we need to find."

Aidan's guarded gaze told her nothing. "None of this upsets you then?" he asked in a shrewd tone.

"Honestly? No. I have a family, Aidan. They've been there for me my whole life. Someone who pops out of the woodwork at this stage interests me, but I don't consider myself a different person because of it."

"That's a very practical attitude."

"Really? I'm not usually a practical person. It's funny how you react to different things, isn't it?"

Smiling vaguely, he stroked her cheek with his knuckles. "Not really. You're practical when it counts, that's all. Like when it comes to birth families and infiltrating hospital files."

He leaned closer, and anticipation rippled through her. Was he going to kiss her? Did she want him to? Silly question. She held her breath and refused to **ac**knowledge the disappointment that washed through her when his lips merely grazed her cheekbone.

She returned to her digging, irritable and oddly unenthusiastic. Damn Aidan Brodie for making her want him. Damn herself for responding to whatever it was about him that she was responding to. Damn everyone and everything, including Mary Lamont and Margaret Truesdale, for tossing old skeletons out of their closets and into hers.

Another group of passersby forced Aidan to douse the lights. Sam heard creaking wheels coming from the morgue again but wisely chose not to look. She was hot and tired and growing hungry when she spotted Mary Lamont's name inside the third from the last box on her side of the room.

"Got it," she said, wedging the file out. "It's a lot fatter than Margaret's."

It was Aidan's turn to peer over her shoulder. She felt the warmth that emanated from him even when he didn't touch her.

"What year?" he asked.

"Nineteen forty-eight. Same year and month as Margaret. Odd coincidence."

A frown marred Aidan's forehead as he skimmed ahead. "Mary probably would have preferred the term 'curse.' Read on."

Sam followed his gaze lower. "Mary did have a baby!" she exclaimed. "A girl called…" She searched for a name but found none.

Aidan swore softly. "She didn't give it a name, Sam. Mary's child was stillborn." He tapped the bottom line. "She was detained at West Valley for psychiatric evaluation after the birth," he continued. "Margaret was packing to leave the hospital when Thurman Wells brought Mary in in labor."

Sam fanned herself with an empty file folder. "Were Thurman and Mary together then?"

"Looks like it." Still crouched next to the cabinet, Aidan

indicated the admission form. "His signature's here under 'Next of Kin' and as the person to notify in case of emergency."

Sam bit her lower lip. "Mary had to deal with the loss of the child at birth. Do you think that's why they kept her on here?"

"Partly, but as far as I can tell, Mary had been having severe emotional problems long before she gave birth."

"On top of which, Margaret's baby lived. Chalk up another grudge." Sighing, Sam started to close the file; however, a name on the birth form caught her eye. "Stan Hollister!" She stared unblinking, prompting Aidan to frown.

"What about him?"

"Mary put his name down as the father." Brow knit, she lifted her head. "Who did Margaret list as the father of her child?

"She didn't," Aidan told her. "She left that space blank. I was surprised you weren't more curious earlier."

A blush rose in Sam's cheeks. "I explained that, Aidan. Until a few days ago, Margaret Truesdale had no part in my life. I'm sorry if that offends you, but I can't think of her as anything other than a reclusive old movie star who's being stalked by a crazy woman with a music box fetish."

More gently than she would have expected, Aidan removed Mary's file from her fingers and tucked it into his waistband. "It doesn't offend me, Sam. I'd probably feel the same way in your position."

She accepted the hand he offered to pull her up. Dusting off, she murmured, "I wonder how Stan Hollister felt? Or Thurman Wells, for that matter, since he was married to her at the time. It must be hell knowing your wife's carrying another man's baby."

"Assuming he knew before the fact," Aidan said, aggravatingly logical. "It might have come as a complete shock to him."

"Whatever. They divorced in nineteen forty-nine, four years

before Margaret went into hiding." Easing the door open, Sam checked the corridor in both directions, then hastily pulled her head back into the room. "Damn," she gasped. "It's Alistair!" She leaned on the door to close it, flinching as the latch clicked loudly. "He's coming down the hall, and ten to one he's not heading for the morgue."

Aidan muttered an oath and grasped her wrist. "We'll have to duck behind one of the cabinets."

Maybe he wouldn't come in here, Sam thought, trying not to bang into any of the precariously stacked boxes. But of course he would, because he was undoubtedly after the same information as they were.

"Stay down," Aidan ordered, pulling her to her knees in front of him. It was not a position she cared to be in.

He tucked her against him, so securely that when he spoke, his lips grazed her temple. "He's coming in."

Sam held her breath and watched as the doorknob turned. The shadow that was Alistair Blue slipped soundlessly across the threshold, closed the door and began groping for the light switch. When he located it, Sam had to swallow another gasp, this one a blend of surprise and panic.

Shoved roughly into the belt of his ragged jeans was a very large, very lethal-looking gun.

AIDAN CONSIDERED lunging but retracted the thought as Sam shifted closer. Teeth grinding more from her proximity than Alistair's presence, he considered his options. The cabinet was not a good hiding place. Alistair could spot them anytime. And that .45 he carried was no toy store trophy.

"Hell," he swore under his breath, then tensed as Sam leaned into him.

Ahead of them, Alistair, who'd been shoving boxes around with his sneakered foot, suddenly spun to face the door. Aidan saw his hand go to the gun. He started to pull it free, hesitated, then changed his mind and bolted like a jackrabbit for cover.

He was crawling through a gap in the cabinets when he came nose to nose with Aidan.

Either he'd expected them to be there, or he was too agitated to care. Jerking his head backward, he rasped, "Someone's out there," and scrambled past to the shelter of the next shadow.

Less than five seconds later, the door was thrust open. "Just put him here for ten minutes," a nasally voice ordered. The speaker tugged fretfully on the foot of a gurney. "Is it my fault they're dropping like flies, today? I'll clear a slab as soon as I can."

Even half obscured, Alistair looked decidedly green. Sam hadn't moved a muscle since she'd spotted the gurney being wheeled in, and even Aidan's stomach tightened at the thought of a corpse languishing less than ten feet away. Not that he hadn't seen dead bodies before, but he'd seldom done so at close range and he'd never viewed them tidily arranged on a stretcher. There was something particularly gruesome about the blank—some people called it peaceful—expression that settled on the human face in death.

The doctor and attendants left, still bickering. Aidan waited until the door clicked shut, then, setting Sam aside, made straight for their companion. His movement was so swift and agile that the younger man had no chance to dodge him.

On his knees, Aidan took a handful of rumpled cotton sweatshirt and shoved Alistair into the wall hard enough to rattle the taut muscles in his neck.

"Talk," he ordered, and although at first he seemed reluctant, Alistair finally nodded. One thing Aidan had never done was bluff when roused to anger. Alistair would either confess or lose a number of teeth. Aidan was in no mood at this point to be kind.

"I heard Mary'd been confined here once," the younger man said in a petulant voice. His fingers worked futilely to pry Aidan's hand away. "I wanted to see her records."

"Bull," Aidan said, and shook him. "The truth, Blue. Who sent you here? Who do you work for?"

"Thurman Wells..."

"Has never heard of you. I called him from Oakhaven earlier."

"You did?" Sam had crawled over to watch. Now she turned resentful eyes on Aidan. "Why didn't you tell me?"

Aidan kept his level gaze focused on Alistair's unmoving face. "I didn't want to worry you." Another shake. Alistair grimaced but wouldn't relent.

"I can't tell you," he said, his tone that of a child being scolded.

Aidan refused to slacken his grip. "Is it Mary?"

"No!"

The denial was vehement and oddly startled.

"Who then?" Sam wanted to know.

"I promised not to tell."

"So it could be Mary, and you're just lying to us," she retorted.

Alistair's head came up in defiance. Chin jutting, he challenged, "I could ask you the same question, you know—what you're doing here."

"You know why we're here," Aidan said coldly. "And who sent us."

"Sent you, yes." He nodded awkwardly at Sam. "We don't know sh—anything about *her* reasons."

Aidan half expected Sam to slug him. But only half. She was far too refined for such a vulgar display.

"Creep," he heard her mutter. Eyes darkening, she demanded, "Did you cut Aidan's brake line?"

"No."

Aidan's instincts, not his ears, caught the lie.

"Did you hire two men to attack him?"

"No."

"Was that you chasing us after Leo Rockland's reception?"

"No."

"You're lying, Alistair Blue," she declared, disgusted. "And you're a coward to boot. All this time Aidan's been holding you, and you haven't reached for your gun once."

Alistair's already blotchy cheeks burned deep red, though whether with rage or embarrassment Aidan couldn't tell. His fingers began to fumble for his belt.

"Don't bother." Sam produced the .45. "I've got it now."

Outrage brought a surge of energy to Alistair's muscles. He strained against Aidan's hold. "You give it to me!" he shouted.

Aidan shook him for a third time. "Shut up or we'll have the whole hospital on us. We're getting out of here, now. If you want information on Mary, Blue, you'll have to sneak in again some other time."

Alistair called him a crude name, certain, apparently, that Sam was not volatile enough to use the gun. He smoldered for the few seconds that Aidan allowed him, then finally nodded and said, "Yeah, all right, let's blow this joint."

The worst part lay in getting past the corpse without touching it. Once that task had been accomplished it was a simple matter of locating the nearest exit and the comparatively fresh canyon air beyond.

Not surprisingly, Alistair bolted the instant he saw the threshold. He took a desperate moment to try to snatch the gun from Sam's hand, but she was faster and sidestepped him.

Giving the wall a frustrated thump, he took off, plunging through the tall shrubbery like a fleeing deer.

Aidan stared after him, running a hand through his long hair. He automatically reached for and found Sam to his right. "Weird guy" was all he said.

Whether she would have added to that or not, he wasn't sure for a man's ingenuous, "What's that?" at close range had both their heads swiveling in surprise.

"Morris," Sam breathed, then did a double take and demanded, "how did you get here from Oakhaven?"

He grinned toothily. "Came with Little Boy Blue."

"Alistair," Aidan grunted.

"He came looking for you. Dr. John told him where you went."

Aidan's eyes glinted. "I'll have to have a chat with Dr. John."

"He has a nice car," Morris went on in his childlike way. "Better'n my grandpa's Model T." He blinked at the object in Sam's hand. Before either of them could stop him, he reached out and grabbed it from her.

"Pretty," he said, stroking the metal. His formerly soft eyes shone with malicious glee. "Makes a good bang." Lifting the barrel, he took aim—and squeezed the trigger.

MARY LIKENED HERSELF to the crone her character in *The Three Fates* would have become if she'd been alive. Her name was Esme and she'd have wanted her turncoat sister, played by Margaret, dead just as surely as Mary wanted her old rival gone forever.

She hobbled around her rented house and told herself all was fine with her plan, splendid in fact. No need to concern herself with minor problems, like—well, no, best not to start that again. She'd already worked herself into one frenzy today. Two, and her sorely strained ticker might give out.

She scuttled like a naughty child from bedroom to kitchen to living room, checking each one thoroughly before moving on. No sign of Tobias anywhere. Good. She could get back to work.

Clearing her throat, she reached for the phone and dialed. Nurses at Oakhaven were easily circumvented. Mary knew the procedures upside down and backward. "Mrs. Hilda Payne," she repeated in one of her best stage voices. "This is Mrs. Crocker." The nurse sounded rushed. All the better, thought Mary smugly as she tapped the lid of her cigarette box with knobby fingers.

Mrs. Payne's exuberant, "Yes, what is it, Betty?" greeted her.

"Mabel," Mary corrected, taut-lipped.

"Sorry. Don't worry, no one's listening. There's big trouble here. I think someone else got out. No bombers though, thank heaven."

Mary endured her comments then drove straight to the point. "Has she—have they been to see you yet?"

"Came and went donkey's ages ago," Mrs. Payne informed her.

Stupid lout, Mary thought contemptuously. "How long is that in hours?" she demanded.

"Three, maybe. I don't remember. We can't find Morris, you see, and Dr. John's going crazy."

Her loud guffaw made Mary's stomach tighten. Between that and her annoyance at having missed her quarry's helpers, she felt testy enough to snap, "Did you see them?"

"See? Hell, I talked to them. That's okay, isn't it? You told me if they ever came by—"

"It's fine," Mary interrupted. "Now listen to me, Hilda, I need you to do me a favor. The next time you see them, and there will be a next time, I promise you, I want you to mention the name Frank Durwald. Say it back to me—Frank Durwald. Tell them I said that name all the time when we played cards."

"You said it while you cheated at cards," Mrs. Payne retorted.

Mary snorted. "Don't be ridiculous. I never cheat. I just don't always let everyone see what I'm doing."

"You cheat," Mrs. Payne maintained.

Although it galled her to give in, Mary needed a strong ally, and as mental patients went, Mrs. Payne's allegiance was unswerving.

"All right, I cheat," she said in a clipped voice. "Just tell them the name Frank Durwald for me. Did the girl—Sam—leave you her card?"

"Yeah. She's a knockout, Mary."

Mary's frayed temper snapped. She heard the front door open and close. Dammit, Tobias was back. "She's a knockout, all right, just like her snooty grandmother.'' She lowered her voice, cupping the mouthpiece with a gnarly hand. "Remember what I said, Hilda. Frank Durwald. It's important. Phone her if you have to."

She hung up abruptly, shoved the phone away and flopped back in time to see Tobias pass by the entrance. He didn't say a word, simply went about his servant's duties. But he had one ear open all the same. One ear and both eyes. Oh, well, at least he'd never turn her in.

Her eyes began to glitter with vicious anticipation. She'd have to make sure he was miles away when she went for Margaret's jugular. She wanted everyone to be miles away when that happened. The moment would be hers to savor and Margaret's to despair. And any and all who dared to interfere would die right alongside her nemesis—just as surely and every bit as painfully.

Chapter Eight

It was one of those long, hideous days that Sam wanted to end, but circumstances refused to cooperate.

"If Mary doesn't get us, I swear my heart'll give out," she mumbled to Aidan as people in pink, white and blue uniforms rushed out of the hospital to see what the gunfire was all about. Thank heaven and his conscience that at the last second Morris had shot the grass instead of them. And thank God he'd dropped the gun afterward, shaken by the kickback of exploding bullets.

He'd looked lost and bewildered as the hospital staff led him away. He couldn't even recall how he'd gotten to West Valley from Oakhaven. Naturally Sam was obliged to explain that situation since Aidan seemed more fascinated by the vegetation than by their near-death experience moments before.

Forty minutes later, she discovered him seated beneath a sprawling oak tree, contemplating the hazy afternoon sky.

He didn't notice her approach at first, muffled as it was by the thick carpet of lawn. If only he'd had a big white rabbit for a friend the way Jimmy Stewart had in *Harvey,* then she could dismiss him as a nut and be done with it. But there he sat like—she didn't know what. His namesake perhaps, minus the kilt but every bit as sexy as the movie version of Rob Roy MacGregor.

The afternoon breeze stirred his long hair, lifting several

strands and blowing them across the angled plane of his cheek.
He looked contemplative, unmoving, with his head averted,
his forearms resting on his raised knees and his hands dangling
loosely between them. Sam felt a pang of suppressed desire
and had to take a deep breath before she could shove it back
into the shadowy recesses of her mind.

"Find any four-leaf clovers?" she asked with only a trace
of a sigh.

He moved just enough to look up at her. His expression was
inscrutable, but she sensed something troublesome lurking beneath the surface.

"What?" she said cautiously when he didn't answer. "Morris is being taken care of, if that's what you're wondering.
Alistair Blue drives a souped-up Chevy with a big trunk and
a faulty lock. Morris had no trouble climbing in. Apparently
he hasn't set foot outside Oakhaven for seven years. I guess
he got curious. Anyway, John's been contacted, and lucky for
us no real harm's been done."

The compelling weight of his stare caused her to ramble on
longer than necessary. She would have continued to ramble if
he hadn't interrupted her, saying solemnly, "They were
blanks, Sam."

She halted a full six feet away. The wind ruffling her hair
from behind carried with it the threat of a storm. "What are
you talking about?" She had a feeling she knew, but the answer made no sense and therefore couldn't be correct.

"Alistair's gun. I looked at the grass all around where Morris was shooting. There was nothing. Alistair's gun was loaded
with blank bullets."

SAM TOPPLED into bed that night, exhausted, confused and
unutterably sick of the whole mess. If she'd become an ac-
countant as her father had suggested, maybe none of this
would have happened. But then what child ever did what their
parents suggested?

The phone gave a purring ring in the living room. She ignored it and thumped her pillow with her fist. It wouldn't be Aidan at 1:00 a.m., and anyone else could leave a message.

Damn you, Margaret, she thought in rising vexation. You've handed me a problem I don't need, and now I'm mixed up with a man I don't want to care about. I'll be the one in an institution before this is over.

The answering machine picked up on the fourth ring. Even through the bedroom wall, there was no mistaking the squawk that passed for a woman's voice.

"You there, Sam? It's me, Hilda Payne. You came to see me today. There's something I forgot—"

"Hello? Mrs. Payne?" Sam rubbed the bare toe she'd stubbed en route and pressed her lips tightly together. "Isn't it a little late for you to be calling?"

A hoarse cackle reached her. "First chance I've had all night. They're all running around like chickens with their heads cut off around here. Morris jumped the fence today, you know."

"Yes, I do. You, uh, said there was something you forgot?"

"Right. She—I mean, I—that is, you were asking about Mary when you were here, and I forgot to tell you about this person. I don't know who he was, just that she used to say his name a lot. Frank Dur... Something"

"...Wald," Sam finished. "Frank Durwald."

"Yeah, that's right." She sounded relieved. Sam considered that for a moment then set her doubts firmly aside.

"Did she say anything in particular about him?"

"Nope, only the name. Don't know if it'll help at all, but I figured you'd want to know."

"Yes, I do. Thanks, Mrs. Payne." Sam gnawed on her lip. "Er, Mrs. Payne, did you say that you and Mary were close friends?"

"Close as sisters," Mrs. Payne said proudly, then quickly back-pedalled. "Well, maybe not that close, but friendly. Chit-chat friendly if you know what I mean."

"I might," Sam said slowly. "Thanks again, Mrs. Payne. Good night."

She hung up with thoughtful deliberation. Something about that telephone call struck a nerve. It hadn't felt right. It seemed in keeping with the woman's character, and she really hadn't said much except a name Sam already knew. Still...

"Oh, hell," she muttered. Standing, she crossed barefoot in her red football jersey nightshirt to the computer. This was definitely not her favorite tool; however, if it would help...

She sat with a thump and a sigh, switched on, dialed and typed in the name she strongly suspected Mary Lamont wanted her to pursue, that of onetime Parlor Shoppe Ice Cream owner, Frank Durwald.

AIDAN SAT in slouchy comfort in a deck chair on the roof of Guido's apartment and listened as the older man prattled on about the good old days in Hollywood. Guido had invited him over for coffee and conversation before they headed to the *Break.*

"Over there used to be the Brown Derby," he said, his dark eyes soulful. "And Graumann's Chinese, what a showplace that was in its heyday. Do you know, my uncle Ricky saw John Wayne sign his block? It was quite the glamorous time."

Ricky and John Wayne? Aidan checked a smile at the picture his mind flashed of Lucy and Ethel prying up John Wayne's footprints—the ultimate Hollywood souvenir.

If there'd been a storm in the offing, it had veered away, leaving sunshine and a pale blue sky in its wake. Sometimes Aidan missed the vivid blues and greens of Ireland, but less now than he had five years ago and not once since he'd laid eyes on Sam.

Guido turned, his fond smile fading. "I did more digging with regard to Anthea Pennant. Can't find a blessed thing on her after nineteen fifty-three. Alive, dead, in California or the Casbah—I have no idea and no thought at this moment where to look next. What about you and Minx? I hear you had a little trouble at West Valley Hospital yesterday. Found Mary's medical file, too, I gather. It's hard to imagine her with a child.''

Aidan rubbed his forehead, willing away the headache that lurked behind it. He'd drunk too much Irish whiskey last night in the company of too many Irish sots whose solution to everything was to tip back another one.

"Drown the bad," Paddy McGillvrey had advised. "Bed the woman. And tell old friends you don't do favors that involve getting your head blown off."

Sage advice, Aidan reflected, except for the part about bedding Sam. One, it wouldn't be that simple on any level or from any perspective, and two, he wasn't now nor was he ever likely to be prepared to deal with the consequences of such an action.

Guido sent him an odd look but said only, "I think this case is getting to you. Am I right?"

"Dead-on," Aidan agreed. "It's a mess from top to bottom."

Guido drew a philosophical breath and settled on a stack of bricks next to an antiquated aerial. "Do you see the fine sort of mist that hangs over the city most days? I see that mist and liken it to ghosts from another time, lingering in the city that was the birthplace of movie magic. Celluloid glamour got many of us through the Depression and the war that followed. We were even more hungry for glamour in the fifties, and Hollywood obliged willingly."

"You don't see stars like Margaret Truesdale these days," Aidan noted.

Guido smiled sadly. "No more Lana Turners discovered at drugstore soda counters. The days of classy pinup girls like Betty Grable are long gone. But the memories live on in film, and maybe, as I said, in more than film. There's a feeling that comes over me sometimes at night when I look out on the city. I'm transported and yet I'm still here. Maybe, then, it's the old stars coming to visit me, reminding me of a lost age and a more civilized code of behavior."

"People like to remember the old."

"Exactly. We need to preserve the facade. Of course there were drugs and sex and dirty deals done in those days, too, but never in such a blatant fashion as today. Corruption lived behind the walls of the studio and the 'in' star's home. We knew that, and yet it didn't dampen our enthusiasm one bit."

It had taken Aidan a few minutes to understand Guido's point. Now at last he thought he grasped it. "You're saying that this matter involving Margaret and Mary should be handled with discretion in order not to shatter anyone's illusions, is that right?"

"In a sense. The secrecy surrounding Margaret Truesdale's life is a mystery that many of us enjoy pondering. It gives us pleasure, takes us away from our everyday lives. I'd hate to see that mystery reduced to gritty reality on the front page of some trashy tabloid—which by the way the L.A. *Break* is not. Also, there is Sam to consider, as I'm sure you've already done several times.

"As Margaret's natural granddaughter and very likely only surviving descendant, the media attention she would receive would be untenable. She doesn't want it and we shouldn't want it for her." He paused, nodded decisively, and continued, "This case requires a delicate hand, Aidan. Three delicate hands, in fact. Yours, mine and Sam's. We must keep searching and slogging and digging, because as competent as they are, the police operate in a manner that is decidedly less than delicate. Mostly for Sam's sake, Aidan, and partly for the sake of sentimental old fools like myself, please have patience with this case. The answers are there, all of them. We simply have to unearth them."

"And if we can't?"

The old man's expression grew grave. "We must, Aidan, because the phrase 'murder of necessity' seems to have a very broad meaning for Mary. We could all of us wind up dead.

And the monstrous thing is, we don't know how many of 'us' that might entail.''

"FRANK DURWALD no longer exists," Sam stated. "He disappeared the same time as Margaret and Anthea and hasn't resurfaced since."

She'd finally located Aidan in Guido's office at the *Break*. That they seemed to be becoming good friends played no part, she vowed, in the scowl that settled upon her lips. However, the guarded look they exchanged caused her to wonder if she might not have been the subject of their conversation.

Was that a vain thought or a jealous one? Probably both. She dismissed all of it with an effort and focused on Guido's apparent consternation.

"Have you spoken to Margaret?" he asked.

"First thing this morning. She says she'll explain as best she can later today."

"Which leaves us with many hours to fill. Sit, Minx, and have some coffee. You look as though you could use it."

Not quite sure she felt up to meeting Aidan's penetrating gaze, she cast him only a quick glance while she poured. He was half perched on Guido's low filing cabinet, sipping coffee and looking incredibly sexy and rumpled in a pair of worn jeans, work boots and a white jersey shirt. His black eye was healing; his hair was messy—and she wanted very badly to kiss him. She swallowed a mouthful of scalding coffee instead.

"I called Margaret's old studio this morning," she said. Turning, she leaned against the stuffed bookshelves. "I was surprised to learn that a good one-quarter of the people who worked with Margaret, Mary and Anthea on *The Three Fates* are still active in the industry. In fact, Stan Hollister's currently directing Thurman Wells in a midbudget thriller. Mr. Wells plays a psychotic killer, disguised as a conductor for the Los Angeles Philharmonic Orchestra."

"An old plot but interesting," Aidan noted.

Sam shrugged. "Stan Hollister's good at twisting old plots.

The Three Fates would have been a subtle thriller if it had been completed. Anyway, neither of them was available. I said we had some questions about Anthea Pennant and left messages for them to call you on your cell or home phone. I was glad to see you're unlisted.''

Aidan's forehead wrinkled. "Unlisted? Ah, the BBC exec."

"Remember your role, Robert Brodie. Can't have them finding you in the phone book."

"If one of those studio people is involved with Mary, my cover's already been blown."

Sam had no response for that and so regarded Guido, a silent spectator slumped behind his desk. "What about other people who worked with them? Did Mary have any friends then who might be helping her now?"

"Few that are alive. Fewer still who would be in a position to offer assistance either physically or financially."

Aidan left his perch and strolled to the window. "Mary has plenty of money," he said, surveying the sultry hills beyond the city. "And access to it, if John's guess is accurate. He told me the first day I spoke to him that Mary was a secretive creature. He never knew what surprise she might pull out of her hat next."

"So she's a rich, crazy, homicidal woman," Sam said with a sigh. She dropped into the nearest chair, tired suddenly down to her bones. "Why doesn't that surprise me?"

"Because," Guido said briskly, "your subconscious recognizes the truth of the situation even if your conscious mind prefers to ignore it."

"Psychology 103," Sam remarked to Aidan. "He wanted to be the next Carl Jung." Sweeping the dark hair she wished she'd braided from her face, she asked of no one in particular, "What's next, then? I managed to get hold of Leo Rockland, but he had no comment. He said he was honeymooning blissfully with Freddie and had no desire to discuss either Anthea or an old thorn in his side at this time."

From the window, Aidan said, "You read us an article,

Guido, an interview given by a woman who seemed to feel sorry for Mary.''

Sam brightened. ''That's right. She sounded jealous of Margaret.''

Guido searched for the magazine. ''She was talking about Margaret's marriage to the vanishing ice-cream magnate. Melman, wasn't it? No, here it is. Mesmyr, Evelyn Mesmyr. She was a studio makeup artist.''

''Is she alive?'' Sam asked.

''I remember, I checked into that. Unless she's died within the last six months, yes. She was in charge of makeup on a made-for-television production that aired two weeks ago. 'Dark— Something.'''

Sam looked with renewed hope at Aidan who made an obscure go-ahead motion. ''Can you get an address on her, Guido?''

He could and did. Five minutes later, Sam and Aidan were heading toward Brentwood and Evelyn Mesmyr's fashionably situated home.

It was a typical posh neighborhood with wrought-iron gates, shrubbery-lined stone fences and swimming pools in every backyard. Kidney-shaped in Evelyn's case, and a preferable setting, in Sam's opinion, to the woman's den, which was filled with an array of mounted animal head trophies so disgustingly popular in the Hollywood of the fifties.

''I'd rather see big game hunters' heads up there,'' she muttered, her anger ill-disguised despite the maid who hovered uncertainly in the doorway.

Aidan, naturally, revealed nothing of his feelings. He did, however, shoot the old woman who swept in with the panache of a famous movie queen a level look from under his lashes.

She wore something that Sam likened to a quilted silk lounging robe. It was floor-length, pale green and had wide-legged tea pants beneath it. Both sash and pants were royal blue as was the thick satin band she'd wound around her upswept blond hair. Her makeup was bold and applied with a liberal hand. She'd had at least four face-lifts, possibly more, the result being that her mouth appeared to have been stretched to twice its normal size. Her face as a whole shone like plastic. What sags remained had been meticulously powdered down.

Despite that, Sam's attention was riveted to her eyes. Hadn't peacock blue shadow died with the sixties? And those false lashes must take an hour apiece to apply.

She had a cigarette smoldering in an ivory holder—another blot against her, Sam thought, her doubts growing steadily—and enough perfume on to choke the elephant who'd undoubtedly been killed to give her an implement into which she could shove the filtered tip. Sam disliked her on sight.

"You must be Robert Brodie," Evelyn said in a practiced voice that oozed false charm and condescension like honey. She acknowledged Sam with a measuring stare and a slight sucking in of her cheeks. "Sit, please," she bade them, and proceeded to arrange herself artfully on the antique settee.

"Ms. Mesmyr—" Aidan began, but she cut him off with a contrived laugh.

"Evelyn, please, or Miss Mesmyr if you must. I've never been married, and I'm proud of it. I always thought Kate had the right idea."

"Katharine Hepburn." Aidan's demin-covered knee brushed Sam's as he shifted on the low sofa. She fought a tremor and got right to the point. "We were wondering, Miss Mesmyr, if you've had contact recently with Mary Lamont."

This time Evelyn's laugh sounded a trifle stiff. "Good Lord, no. Mary? She's locked up, isn't she?" Her black-rimmed eyes narrowed. "What's your interest in Mary Lamont? I thought you were researching a book for someone's wife."

"She is," Aidan said blandly. "We're intrigued by the feud between Mary Lamont and Margaret Truesdale. Do you recall the time when it reached its peak?"

"Recall it? Heavens, I was in the thick of it. Margaret outshone Mary, Mary fought back tooth and nail, and Anthea, poor little mouse that she was, stood meekly on the sidelines and watched. Well, she rooted for Margaret, but I think deep down her feelings weren't all that different from mine.''

"And those were?" Aidan prompted.

Evelyn gave a small shrug. "That it could just as easily have been one of us in Margaret's shoes under different circumstances. I considered acting once, you know, but decided it was too vicious and went to work backstage instead.''

In other words, she had no performing talent. Sam summoned a polite smile. "No one could blame you for that decision, Miss Mesmyr. How did you feel about Margaret, Mary and Anthea?"

The woman had lipstick on her teeth when she laughed. "Cool," she replied. "Except to Anthea. Although I understood Mary, that's not to say I liked her. No, I don't think I'd have minded one bit if Mary had followed through on one of her screaming threats to kill Margaret. Then Margaret would have been gone, Mary'd have been in jail for murder and I—I mean, Anthea would have had the spotlight all to herself.''

One of Aidan's brows rose in a vague challenge. "And you'd have had Frank Durwald?"

Eveyln jerked back as if slapped. Hand clasped to her throat, she managed an incredulous, "What on earth makes you think I had designs on Frank Durwald?"

Sam reminded her about the old magazine article.

Evelyn blinked, then offered a shaky chuckle. "I may have wanted him once, it's true, but whether I did or not, he chose Margaret. Truth to tell—" a bitter edge crept into her voice "—I doubt if he even knew I existed. He was besotted with Margaret, so much so that he actually stopped gambling for a time. Perhaps not for good, but certainly at the outset of their courtship."

Gambling? Sam straightened, her interest renewed. "What form of gambling? Poker? Blackjack?"

"Horses." She drew heavily on her cigarette. "He owned one once. Sold it before he married Margaret."

"To whom?" Aidan inquired.

It puzzled Sam that Evelyn should start at such a simple question, but she did. Her answer, after a few noticeable stutters, contained all the warmth of a poked rattlesnake.

"I have no idea," she said, her tone flat and final. "Ask Frank, if you can find him. He took to the shadows with his wife and hasn't been seen or heard from since. Yes, what is it, Elizabeth?"

"I'm sorry, ma'am," the maid who was eighteen at best apologized from the doorway. "There's a man on the telephone. Says he's from a collection—"

Evelyn cut in. "Tell him I'll return his call within the hour." A smile, phoney from top to bottom, curved her mouth. "Collection for charity," she said breezily. "Once the requests take hold, they never stop."

Sam and Aidan exchanged skeptical glances. Opulence, it seemed, was more facade than fact in Evelyn's case. She might, Sam reflected with a renewed surge of resentment, be forced to sell some of her prized animal heads.

The woman puffed several times on her cigarette, then shocked Sam by demanding, "Have we met before?"

Sam controlled a spurt of panic. "I—don't think so."

"I think she looks like Gene Tierney," Aidan drawled, broadening his Irish accent for effect.

Evelyn tipped her head to one side. "You know, she does a little at that. Gene had a lovely bone structure. Exquisitely delicate."

"Maybe we should go," Sam murmured, but Aidan restrained her with a discreet hand around her wrist.

"One or two more things," he said, and gave his full, charming attention to Evelyn. "*The Three Fates*, you worked on that movie, didn't you?"

"For months in open production," she agreed. The bitter edge returned full force. "It was a good script, and a wonderful challenge for any makeup artist. None of the effects could be obvious. I had to soften Margaret progressively and at the same time create a more evil look for Mary. Anthea stayed about the same—which was, in a way, reflective of her life. Theirs, too, I suppose. Margaret went from a nothing in the chorus to a superstar on the silver screen. Mary went from exuberant chorus girl to impatient starlet to bitter hag.''

"In other words," Sam translated, "Mary's hatred grew in direct proportion to Margaret's fame. And Anthea played referee from the sidelines.''

"Not a bad assessment... Are you sure we've never met?"

"Yes. I'm sure." She buttered her tone deliberately. "I'd remember you if we had, Miss Mesmyr. You were the Edith Head of the makeup department in the nineteen fifties.''

Her ego stroked, Evelyn beamed. "Why, thank you. I was rather good, wasn't I? Oh, I still do the odd bit of work here and there, but only when sorely pressed. I'm mostly retired these days. By choice, of course.''

Sam smiled. She would have tried leaving again if Aidan hadn't inserted Thurman Wells's name into the conversation.

"A talented actor," he observed shrewdly. "I hear he was married to both Margaret and Mary.''

"Yes, though not so happily to Mary as it turns out. Shrews make poor wives. Not that Margaret was any better in that sense. Granted, she didn't rant and rave like Mary, but she was terribly career oriented at the time.''

This woman loved to gossip, Sam realized. She also enjoyed finding fault. So far, the only mildly interesting thing she'd told them was that Frank Durwald had been a gambler—which probably wouldn't be overly useful in their endeavor to track Mary down.

"Thurman was another of Margaret's castoffs by the time Mary snared him," Evelyn disclosed. "She only wanted him to prove that she was as good as Margaret at getting what she wanted. It was during that time that the sh—I mean, the dirt really hit the fan. Margaret told the studio execs that she was pregnant. Unmarried and pregnant, I might add. That was taboo in those days for reigning movie queens.''

"Did she ever name the father?" Aidan asked when Sam didn't.

"Nope." Evelyn stuck a fresh cigarette into her holder and lit it. "Which says to me that it was no one who mattered."

"Everyone matters, Miss Mesmyr," Sam said firmly.

"Not in those days. Only fame mattered, and hushing up secrets best not disclosed to a gossip-hungry public."

Speaking of gossips... Sam folded her hands demurely in her lap, avoided Aidan's eyes and said clearly, "Is it possible that Stan Hollister was the father of Margaret's child?"

Instead of appearing shocked, Evelyn pursed her lips and considered the notion. "That's a thought, isn't it?" she agreed at length.

"An unexpected one," Aidan murmured, studying Sam through veiled eyes.

Sam moved a slender shoulder. "Not so unexpected if you think about it. We know—we heard—that Mary was having an affair with Hollister. We also know that Mary usually ran second to Margaret. It's possible, even probable, that any relationship between Mary and Stan Hollister came on the heels of a breakup between him and Margaret."

Aidan's expression remained dubious. Evelyn's transformed into one of calculating speculation.

"That does make sense." She warmed rapidly to the idea. "I'm sure Stan had no intention of marrying Mary. He told her to go home to Thurman and dumped her like a hot potato. To be honest, I don't think there was much to the relationship. It was more like a fast fling. A few nights in the sack, possibly to compensate for losing Margaret, and that was it."

Sam wondered distantly if Mary's baby had gone to term. It seemed unlikely in the face of Evelyn's remarks. Not that any of this was going to help them locate Mary.

A feeling of impatience pushed its way into her head. She tugged circumspectly on Aidan's sleeve. "I think we've taken up enough of Miss Mesmyr's time, don't you, Robert?"

"Yes, I'm sure Mrs. Higgenbothom will be delighted." He

took the hand that Evelyn condescended to extend and bent over it in a gesture of Old World charm. "Thank you for your time, Evelyn. You needn't call your maid. We'll show ourselves out."

Sam held her tongue until they reached the covered porch. "Mrs. Higgenbothom?" she repeated, tempted to laugh in spite of her annoyance with Evelyn Mesmyr's habits and affectations.

Aidan propelled her forward with a hand pressed to the small of her back. "*The Luck of the Irish.* Tyrone Power and Anne Baxter, nineteen forty-eight. I know one or two old movies, Sam." He slanted her a questioning look. "Are you calm now?"

She refused the bait. "I was never not calm, Brodie. Except that I wouldn't mind seeing Miss Mesmyr stuffed and mounted on her own den wall."

"She's broke, you know," Aidan said.

"I gathered as much."

"She also has an expensive house to maintain."

At the Jeep, Sam sighed. "Make your point, Aidan."

He leaned his forearms on the roof, regarding her over the vinyl top. "Think about it, Sam. Evelyn needs money. Mary has money."

Sam glanced at the shuttered white house with its cotton candy trim, its pretty flower beds and its sculpted shrubbery. "You think she's harboring Mary?"

"I think she knows more than she's telling."

"That's all well and good, but we can hardly break in and demand to search the rooms, can we?" She frowned. "Or can we?"

A faint smile curved Aidan's sensual lips. "I can't see demands getting us anywhere with her, but a break-in might not go amiss. Let's wait and see what happens."

"You mean wait for the next attempt on our lives, don't you? You're braver than I am, Brodie. I vote we break in tonight."

An Important Message from the Editors of Harlequin®

Dear Reader,

Because you've chosen to read one of our fine romance novels, we'd like to say "thank you!" And, as a __special__ way to thank you, we've selected __four more__ of the books you love so well, __plus__ a beautiful cherub magnet, to send you absolutely **FREE!**

Please enjoy them with our compliments...

Candy Lee

Editor

P.S. And because we __value__ our customers, we've attached something extra inside...

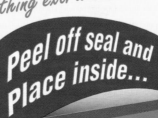

Peel off seal and Place inside...

EDITOR'S FREE GIFT SEAL THANK YOU

How to validate your
Editor's FREE GIFT "Thank You"

1. Peel off gift seal from front cover. Place it in space provided at right. This automatically entitles you to receive four free books and a beautiful cherub refrigerator magnet.

2. Send back this card and you'll get brand-new Harlequin Intrigue® novels. These books have a cover price of $3.75 each, but they are yours to keep absolutely free.

3. There's no catch. You're under no obligation to buy anything. We charge nothing—ZERO—for your first shipment. And you don't have to make any minimum number of purchases—not even one!

4. The fact is thousands of readers enjoy receiving books by mail from the Harlequin Reader Service®. They like the convenience of home delivery...they like getting the best new novels BEFORE they're available in stores... and they love our discount prices!

5. We hope that after receiving your free books you'll want to remain a subscriber. But the choice is yours— to continue or cancel, any time at all! So why not take us up on our invitation, with no risk of any kind. You'll be glad you did!

6. Don't forget to detach your FREE BOOKMARK. And remember...just for validating your Editor's Free Gift Offer, we'll send you FIVE MORE gifts, *ABSOLUTELY FREE!*

GET A FREE CHERUB MAGNET...

This charming refrigerator magnet looks like a little cherub, and it's a perfect size for holding notes and recipes. Best of all it's yours ABSOLUTELY FREE when you accept our NO-RISK offer!

The Editor's "Thank You" Free Gifts Include:

- **Four BRAND-NEW romance novels!**
- **A beautiful cherub magnet!**

PLACE
FREE GIFT
SEAL
HERE

YES! I have placed my Editor's "Thank You" seal in the space provided above. Please send me 4 free books and a beautiful cherub magnet. I understand I am under no obligation to purchase any books, as explained on the back and on the opposite page.

181 CIH CCRE (U-H-I-01/98)

Name

Address   Apt.

City

State   Zip

Thank You!

Harlequin Reader Service® — Here's How It Works:

Accepting free books places you under no obligation to buy anything. You may keep the books and gift an... return the shipping statement marked "cancel." If you do not cancel, about a month later we will send yo... 4 additional novels, and bill you just $3.12 each plus 25¢ delivery per book and applicable sales tax, if a... That's the complete price, and—compared to cover prices of $3.75 each—quite a bargain! You may canc... at any time, but if you choose to continue, every month we'll send you 4 more books, which you may eith... purchase at the discount price...or return to us and cancel your subscription.

*Terms and prices subject to change without notice. Sales tax applicable in N.Y.

He opened the driver's side door, his expression wry. "In that case you're the one who's brave, Sam. Because not only does Evelyn Mesmyr keep dead animal heads on her walls, she also keeps live ones outside. They strolled past the window while we were talking to her."

"What did?"

"Two black Dobermans, an Irish Wolfhound and a pit bull."

EVELYN'S PLUMP FINGERS tapped the telephone for five long minutes after her visitors left. Should she? Shouldn't she? She'd better.

She pressed the numbers carefully. A private number, recently given to her—she'd never thought she would have occasion to use it. It was answered on the third ring.

"A man and a woman were here," she said, worrying the cord with her right hand. "They were curious about *The Three Fates*, the real ones, if you know what I mean. Their names? Sam—yes, that's right, Samantha—Giancarlo and an Irishman named Brodie. That's what he said. Oh, yes, I'm sure you have ways. I understand. Of course, you'll handle it… A check? Well, that would certainly help… I'll watch for it. Yes, thank you. Goodbye."

Her hands were shaking as she hung up. This Mata Hari stuff was definitely not for her. Someone might very well wind up dead before this was over. She hoped to hell it wouldn't be her.

Chapter Nine

Margaret expelled a long-suffering sigh and rubbed her forehead in a gesture of infinite weariness.

"I was hoping I wouldn't have to go into details," she said from the corner of her shadowy parlor. "Frank's and my problems were private. However, your questions are reasonable and deserve proper answers."

Thunder beyond her canyon home walls made the crystal fronds of the chandelier quiver. The delicate tinkle sent a chill of unnamed terror down Sam's spine. Somehow that one small sound seemed worse than the noise of the storm that underscored it. Rain pelted the walls, roof and windows as Margaret lit a cigarette and explained.

"Frank and I were in love. It was a wonderful time. Most of Hollywood was in love back then."

Her voice shook with the force of her emotions. A veil of smoke encircled her carefully coiffed head, clouding her features. Sam couldn't see her brown eyes clearly, but she thought she glimpsed raw pain in their depths.

Margaret's gaze flicked to Mary's music boxes, still prominently displayed on the coffee table. "Unfortunately," she sighed, "Frank loved the ponies, too. I'd hoped his feelings for me might be stronger than his addiction to gambling, but to my disappointment, that proved not to be the case. He got in over his head and had to borrow money."

"From you?" Sam asked.

"Lord, no. He was far too proud a man to beg a loan from his wife. It simply wasn't done in those days. No, he went to a loan shark."

Aidan, who'd been pacing behind Sam, murmured, "I think I see where this is heading. It was your husband and not you who thought it prudent to go into hiding."

Margaret toyed with her cigarette holder. "Call it a mutual decision. I was getting tired of all the back-stabbing necessary to move up in the film industry. At any rate, who ever knows how long one's flicker of fame will ultimately last. Best sometimes to get out while you're ahead. So we faded into oblivion together."

"Did your husband ever pay back the loan shark?" Sam inquired.

"Not during our marriage, though he might have done later. I hope for his sake he did. Dorian Hart was not known for his patience, and a racehorse was small compensation for the sum owed. I'd have paid the man off myself, but he lives and works by a very strict set of rules. Old-fashioned to be sure, but rigid to a fault. 'A man,' he insists, 'must pay his own debts.' On the other hand, a woman can certainly get a man to pay hers." Wicked brows arched in Sam's direction. "A boorish attitude, don't you think?"

"A sexist one, anyway," Sam agreed. She leaned forward in earnest. "The truth, Margaret—is Frank Durwald still alive?"

"I don't know, and that *is* the truth."

"What about Dorian Hart?" Aidan stopped pacing to inquire.

"I have even less of a guess on that one, but it shouldn't be difficult to find out. Dorian was never big on keeping a low profile. You won't get an audience with him, but you should be able to determine his present status."

Aidan resumed his to and fro circuit behind her. Sam's mind drew a picture of an edgy feline. He was obviously deep in thought, no doubt wondering what new and deadly tricks Mary might have in store for them. Perversely, Sam wished that clinical mind of his would stray, even for a moment, in her direction.

"I'll see what I can turn up on Mr. Hart," she said, placing Aidan firmly at the back of her mind. Although he continued to remind her of a caged tiger, and his hair and face tempted her to touch, that was simply one more battle she'd have to wage in bed that night. For now they both had more imperative problems to deal with.

Holding her cigarette in her mouth, Margaret rang a small crystal bell for the butler. Theo materialized, gaunt and ramrod straight.

"The movie, Madame?" he inquired with his usual butler's aplomb.

"Er, yes," she said gruffly. "Go ahead and show it to them." She addressed Sam and a distracted Aidan. "I received a clip from *The Three Fates*. It appeared with the afternoon mail. No postmarks," she added, anticipating Aidan's question. Her mouth tightened. "It must have been hand delivered."

"Did you see anyone?" Aidan directed the query at Theo, who shook his head.

"Not a soul." He produced the unmarked video. "Shall I play the tape, Madame?"

A wave of her hand supplied the answer.

Margaret's extensive entertainment system was housed behind the bookshelves. The videotape copy, although snowy and old, was much clearer than the one Sam had viewed on Guido's office TV.

Margaret—no, Mary, appeared, creeping up a darkened stairwell, a covered tray in hand. She cast several surreptitious glances behind her before mounting the final few steps to the door and tugging aside a heavy bolt.

Eerie lighting coupled with Evelyn Mesmyr's makeup gave her features a sinister look. An evil little smile played on her lips as she entered the attic. The camera panned her rather than the room's occupant.

"Nothing to say?" Mary challenged.

Now the camera shifted. Sam spied a shadowy movement in the corner.

"Maybe you're too weak to answer," Mary taunted the indistinguishable figure. "Maybe a little food would help, hmm?"

She rocked the tray in a tantalizing fashion. "Just say the magic words, and you can eat till you explode."

Silence broken only by the sinister rumble of thunder in Laurel Canyon supplied the response.

"I see," Mary said. "In that case..." She held the tray higher, and would have dropped it on the floor if a voice hadn't emerged clear and strong from the shadows.

"Your cruelty will be your downfall, sister. That and your predictable nature. He isn't here."

Sam recognized Margaret's on-screen voice. So did Mary's character. A closeup of her face showed her cheeks mottled with rage, her eyes blazing with unbridled fury.

"Where is he?" she demanded. "What have you done with him?"

"He's been moved," Margaret said calmly. She rose from the cot to confront her evil sister. "I don't choose to tell you where."

Mary's mouth opened and closed. Finally through bared teeth, she demanded, "How dare you? I won't allow this, sister. You're not omnipotent, not at all. Two of us together can still defeat you."

Margaret stepped into a tiny pool of light. Her features glowed with strength rather than rage. "Our sister supports me," she said. Her delicate brows rose in defiance. "And so, you see, you stand alone, alone and thirsty for the power that should not and never will be yours to command. We had no right to imprison him."

Mary's anger seemed about to choke her. "You didn't let him go? You couldn't."

"I've done nothing," Margaret informed her coldly. "Yet. But when I do, sister, remember that the choice resides with me. Now go back downstairs and rejoin the party. And don't bother to threaten our sister. She is not so easily swayed as you think. And I—" she took a menacing step closer "—am not so susceptible as you suppose."

She walked past Mary and was immediately swallowed up in the shadows of the stairwell. For a moment, Mary stood perfectly still, then her face contorted, and she spun to confront the darkness in her sister's wake.

"One day," she vowed, "you'll pay for all the hurt and humiliation you've caused me. I'll beat you, sister, and then, I swear, I'll kill you."

THE STORM WORSENED as they left Laurel Canyon. The restlessness that had driven Aidan to pacing earlier lingered despite the directives from his brain that told him to back off.

Although he didn't consider himself particularly streetwise, he'd learned enough growing up in Dublin to know when his instincts were trying to tell him something. The frustrating thing was, try as he might, he couldn't interpret the message.

That would be in large part Sam's fault, he reflected, casting her a dark sideways look from the driver's seat. Her delicate beauty, her doggedness and determination, her wicked sherry brown eyes that challenged and seduced him at every turn...

Aidan gave himself a hard mental kick and endeavored to shut down the more lascivious part of his brain. Sam slid him a canny sideways glance that had him grinding his teeth in frustration.

As if regretting the action, she sighed and fixed her gaze firmly on the slapping windshield wipers.

Wind lashed the trees on the side of the road, bending the smaller ones almost double.

He saw firmness melt into vague suspicion when she realized the direction he was taking. "Wait a minute. We're heading for Topanga Canyon. I don't live out here."

"I do," Aidan told her. He kept his voice even while his eyes swept the road ahead. He saw only darkness and the outline of wind-battered trees all along the winding strip of pavement.

Somewhat to his surprise—or perhaps not—Sam offered no objection. She merely laid her head against the vinyl seat and kept her thoughts and feelings to herself.

An old Lipton Tea-sponsored radio program called "The Inner Sanctum" accompanied them as they made their way to his home off Topanga Canyon Road. The place had been a private mansion once. It was an extensive if not lavish structure. Built of old stone and redwood, it sat well back from the road and rose like a tree-bound fortress out of the side of the hill. It had been divided two decades ago into four suites. His apartment was on the top floor. Beside him lived a semi-successful composer who dreamed of creating the next "Phantom of the Opera." Below was a woman who painted movie scenes both new and old, then sold them to a national poster company.

Sam sat up straighter as he braked by the curb. "It's fixed!" she exclaimed. "When did you get it back?"

She meant his black Cadillac which sat, good as new on the surface, directly in front of them.

"It doesn't run worth a damn," he said, reaching over her to push open the Jeep's door. "My place is up the stairs to the right. There's a porch. If you run you shouldn't get too wet."

A ridiculous statement if ever he'd made one. The rain pounded down so hard and fast that they arrived on the porch soaked to the skin, panting and laughing at the futility of the attempt.

Sam wiped sopping strands of black hair from her eyes while Aidan located the front door key. "I feel like—what's that old expression—a drowned duck?"

The slow grin that curved his lips came from self-denial as much as amusement. The white T-shirt clinging to her breasts couldn't have been more alluring if the neckline had plunged to her waist. "A rat, Sam," he corrected, dealing with the simultaneous stabs of desire and regret that shot through him.

"Whatever. I haven't been this wet since I fell into the log ride at Knotts' Berry—" She stopped suddenly and frowned at the door. "Is that your telephone?"

Aidan listened. Diverted by the rain and thunder and his lustful thoughts, he'd missed the ring. Pushing open the door, he stepped inside and reached effortlessly across the plant stand and low bookshelf to the oak sofa table.

"Brodie," he said without preface.

A woman's soft-spoken voice ventured an uncertain, "Mr. Robert Brodie of the BBC?"

Aidan hit the speaker button and gestured for Sam to close the door and listen.

"That's right," he confirmed. "Can I help you?"

"I doubt it," came the wistful reply. Her tone altered, as wistfulness gave way to efficiency. "Perhaps, though, I can help you and…well…others. My name is Anthea Pennant."

SAM'S HEART CATAPULTED into her throat and lodged there. She couldn't utter a sound, not even a disbelieving gasp as Anthea continued.

"I've kept in touch with an old friend from the studio over the years. Or rather, I gave him the means by which to contact me should the need arise."

Sam's fingers curled around Aidan's wet sleeve. Her nails bit into the warm flesh beneath. He didn't flinch and she didn't loosen her grip. Anthea went on.

"I was told you're an executive with the BBC, Mr. Brodie. Possibly you are. However, it's the girl, woman who accompanied you to Leo Rockland's reception, who really interests me. You might not know this, but Leo has an extensive video surveillance system. One of his guests that day had a funny feeling when he saw this young woman—the weird sensation you get when you meet someone you think you should know but know you don't. He asked Leo to provide a still picture of her. Leo complied and he sent it on to our contact point. Having seen it, I'm extremely curious to meet her. Is she..."

"I'm here, Ms. Pennant," Sam said, tamping down her excitement. Her nails continued to bite into Aidan's arm.

Anthea wasted no time. "Do you know who your grandmother is?"

Inexplicably, Sam's insides tightened. "My blood grandmother is Margaret Truesdale."

Anthea's voice gentled. "And how do you know that, dear?"

Sam took a deep breath, considered briefly, then blurted, "Margaret told me."

"Margaret!" She sounded appalled but covered well. "I mean, I see. Er, I take it you've spoken to her."

"Several times."

"Have you met her?"

"Yes."

"Where?"

"At her home." She stopped short of mentioning that that home was in Laurel Canyon. Margaret had asked her to tell no one. She explained about the threats Mary had made on Margaret's life instead.

Anthea remained silent for a time. Thunder rumbled portentously over the Canyon Road, causing Aidan's wineglasses to rattle in their rack. Sam heard a series of clicks and attributed them to static on the line. Finally, the woman cleared her throat.

"I think," she said carefully, "that we should meet face-to-face. You're in grave danger, my dear. Mary Lamont is not a woman to be trifled with. I of all people learned that the hard way. So did Margaret, and poor Frank. I—" She broke off. "What was that click?"

"It's the storm," Sam told her. "It's bad here."

"Here, as well," Anthea concurred. "As I was saying, we must meet. There are too many things you don't know, and the telephone is not the place to go into them. Can you come tomorrow?"

Sam glanced at Aidan who was absorbed in his view of the street below. "Yes," she said, watching as a black Jaguar slunk past his newly repaired Cadillac. "Where?"

"My home is north of Santa Barbara. You have to exit the freeway early and take back roads through a collection of woods. The town is called Cedar Valley. It's very lovely and very secluded. The house is just off Cedar Hill Cross Road. Number three. There are no other homes nearby. You can see my barn from the road. It's umber as opposed to red. Do drive carefully. The roads can be treacherous after a rain. We're often flooded out."

Aidan interrupted with a brief epithet. "They're stopping. Get a time for tomorrow," he told Sam and shot through the door before she could protest.

"Eleven in the morning," Anthea obliged. "What's going on? Is there trouble?"

"As usual," Sam muttered under her breath. Louder, she replied, "Ai...uh, Robert can handle it." She peered through the vertical blind. "Make that, he did handle it. Whoever they are, they just made a U-turn, hit the gas and fishtailed out of here."

"Good." Relief weakened Anthea's voice. "Take care, then, my dear," she said softly. "I'll explain all tomorrow."

She hung up with a muffled click. Sam's hand hovered above the Phone Off button as Aidan returned, sopping wet and breathing hard from his exertions.

"Alistair?" she guessed.

He shook his head. "These guys had short hair." The phone clicked and he motioned for her to hit the button. "Hang up."

"What? Oh, yes." She tore her gaze away from his rain

slick body only long enough to comply. "You, uh, should probably change."

His hooded eyes never left hers. His uneven breathing might have been the result of the long descent and climb, but Sam sensed it stemmed from another source entirely. And if it did...

No, absolutely not, she admonished herself. No entanglements. He'd had a wife once; she was dead now. And even if Sam didn't believe for a minute that Aidan had poisoned her, she did know he was a man with the potential for danger, not physical perhaps, but the kind that could cause her a great deal of pain.

His dark green eyes impaled her from the doorway. Her tan leather boots had glued themselves to the carpet. Heat and the unfulfilled promise of sex vibrated in the air between them. Sam wanted his mouth on hers, his sleek body molded against hers, his hands undressing her with exquisite slowness in the steamy, shadow-laden warmth of his apartment.

"Sam..." he said, and she recognized the half question, half denial in his tone.

Tension, palpable enough to cut, flowed between them. Sam felt a cramping surge of desire between her legs and a throbbing born entirely of sexual longing in her limbs. With a boldness she hadn't realized she possessed, she stepped out from behind the table and started toward him.

"Did you get the license number?" she asked, not really caring at that moment.

His eyes tracked her approach. "It was too dark. Sam..." he warned again, his chest still rising and falling unevenly. He sighed and closed his eyes. "Maybe bringing you here wasn't such a good idea after all. Maybe we'd be smarter to let things between us be."

"I've been doing that for days, Aidan. I'm not afraid of you."

He made no move to avoid her, but countered with a steady,

"I didn't poison Domina with arsenic, but you've only my word on that."

Sam halted directly in front of him. Tipping her head back, she regarded him calmly. "Were you charged?"

"I was investigated."

"It isn't the same thing. Was anyone charged?"

Aidan's tone grew vaguely bitter. "It was decided that she'd done it purposely to herself in the hopes that I'd be blamed. Her doctor assured the police that she had strong suicidal tendencies."

Something in his tone cautioned Sam against any further brash questions. Instead she ventured quietly, "And did she?"

Grim was the only way to describe his handsome features. "Not to my knowledge. But she wanted me gone, and that's a fact."

Sam refrained from brushing the damp hair from his face with her fingers. "Gone?" she repeated, her dark brows rising. "As in…"

"Dead. It was Domina who tried to poison me."

ALISTAIR'S CAR SLOWED to a crawl and finally halted on the road below Aidan Brodie's apartment. No headlights, no light-colored clothing, no conversation between himself and the person beside him who sat there with headphones on, holding a piece of machinery that was in turn hooked up to a laptop computer.

Alistair put the car in park, opened his mouth to yawn, then gave a sudden start and yanked his passenger down below the level of the windshield.

"What are you doing!" his companion demanded.

"Stay down," Alistair snapped. "He'll see us."

"Who?"

"Brodie."

The older head inched up. "I don't… Oh, yes, there he is. He's after that black car, Alistair. He doesn't see us."

"He will if you don't stay down."

The person beside him gave his arm a smack. "You're leaning on my equipment. I'm trying to trace a ca-all."

The word fragmented as Alistair yanked them both to a low crouch. "The car's making a one-eighty turn," he said through his teeth. "It's heading straight for us."

Again, the stubborn head popped up. Eyes strained for a clear view through the streaming glass. "Why, that's one of Dorian's men, I'm sure of it! His grandson and soon-to-be successor. You know Dorian Hart, Alistair. I've told you about him many times."

The gangster Dorian Hart? Alistair's stomach twisted into icy knots. A picture of Bugsy Malone planted itself in his head and refused to leave. He hauled his companion forward until their noses almost touched. "What does Dorian Hart have to do with this? What's his grandson doing at Brodie's place? You said—"

A hand swatted at him. "Shut up. I need to hear this."

"Not until you tell me what's what here."

Even by feeble streetlight dappled with patches of rain, Alistair saw his companion's eyes glow in anticipation. The name "Anthea" fell from the aging lips. "So you really are alive—and living in Southern California." The headphones were removed completely. "We've done it, Alistair. Or rather, I have."

Alistair jammed balled fists into his jacket pockets. It was either that or wrap them around his passenger's throat. "I did look," he mumbled sullenly.

"Not hard enough." A glance at the receding taillights of the black Jaguar, then, "I hate to think what Dorian's intentions are. Once on the scent he'll no doubt find a way to leap ahead of all of us. Damn Anthea for holding back her address. We'd be blundering around like a pair of idiots if we went out searching for her in the dark."

"So what then?"

"We'll have to wait." White-knuckled fingers gripped the headphones, threatening to break them. "And hope that we can get to Anthea Pennant first."

Chapter Ten

He'd done it again, Aidan thought, wincing as a shaft of sunlight broke through the overcast shrouding the hills north of the city. Did Nick Charles feel like this on mornings after? Or did movie magic extend to blowing off hangovers like so much loose dust?

The thought of Dashiell Hammett's famous Thin Man detective brought a weary smile to his lips. Another hazy ray of sunshine turned it to a grimace.

He headed for the kitchen and a cup of yesterday's coffee, reheated and strong enough to strip paint. The first sip stripped the residue of whiskey from his stomach but had no effect on the pounding in his head.

Two more cups helped. Sam's determinedly cheerful arrival on his doorstep at quarter to ten did not.

He'd made dinner for them last night, burned steaks, red wine—and conversation. He hadn't expected the last part. In fact he wasn't sure why he'd brought Sam to his home. Or if he was, his intentions had altered after Anthea's phone call.

They'd gone to a local bar after that, he recalled with a grunt, for stand-up comedy and far too much whiskey on his part. And later, alone in his bed, he'd dreamed of her....

They'd been hot, lusty dreams, of Sam and silk sheets and ''The Shadow'' playing on the radio. It must have been a period dream, he reflected now. Sometime after the war but before "I Love Lucy."

The obvious analogy sprang to mind. Aidan loved... No, he didn't. He shoved the thought away. The scent of her perfume, something exotic and knock-down potent, had lingered long after he'd put her in that cab and sent her home. Now here it was again, it and her, standing right in front of him at the door, looking beautiful and alert and sexy as hell in a slim-fitting moss green dress made of sinfully soft cashmere. Professional yet sensual, it hugged her slender curves and drove him straight to bloody distraction.

"You look like hell," she told him, and while her candor stung, at least she had the decency to keep her voice down. He saw her fight back a smile. "There are advantages to drinking only cola, Brodie. I'll drive. Jeep or car?"

He chose her recently repaired Miata. It had better shock absorbers, and coffee or no, his head still felt suspiciously like a live mind field.

He stared half-lidded at her hands as she drove north. Long-fingered, and delicate like her. God, he wished he would stop noticing things like that.

"It's almost eleven o'clock," she remarked as they bumped their way cautiously along a muddy back road. "Do you see an umber barn?"

Aidan forced his eyelids open all the way. What he saw was a California mist thick enough to have done Nick and Nora proud on New Year's Eve. He massaged his aching temples. He must be in bad shape to be stuck on "The Thin Man" series for so long.

"There," he said, squinting through the cedars. "That looks like a barn."

Sam turned into the first opening wide enough to be a drive-way. "I hope you're right, otherwise we'll be late."

Not entirely to Aidan's surprise, the overgrown drive broad-ened into a Spartan yard. Sam stuck to the traveled path, brak-ing only when a brown pickup materialized out of the mist.

"It's a '49 Ford," Aidan noted, impressed. "In good condition, too."

Sam switched off the lights and slid out. She was in the process of smoothing down her dress when she stopped abruptly. Her eyes fastened on the foggy outline of the house before them. "Aidan, the front door's open."

He brought his head around. Dammit, it was, wide open. And there was music spilling out.

The door hit the outer wall, swung inward, then banged again.

"'Bless Your Beautiful Hide,'" Sam whispered, still watching.

Aidan skirted the car to join her. "What are you talking about?"

"It's a dance, from *Seven Brides For Seven Brothers*. Howard Keel and Jane Powell, nineteen fifty-four. The barn dance is a classic...never mind. She might be watching the movie."

"With the door swinging back and forth on its hinges?"

"No, but I don't like the alternatives." She edged forward as she spoke. Aidan moved to stop her, then decided against it. She'd only shake him off and do exactly what she wanted to anyway.

"Anthea?" Sam called the woman's name at a level loud enough to be heard above the music. "Anthea, it's Sam and Robert. Are you there?"

Nothing but an eerie gust of wind swirling around the corner of the clapboard house answered her.

They mounted the four outer stairs like a pair of prowlers. The door banged twice, then almost blew closed. Only Aidan's quick reflexes allowed him to catch it.

"Anthea?" Sam tried again. "This isn't right, Aidan. She has to be here. She..." Her voice trailed off. "My God!" she exclaimed. "It's Alistair Blue. Again!"

Aidan spied the man inside the door. He was crouched on the checkerboard floor, staring openmouthed at—something.

Sam's voice seemed to rouse him from his trance. Using the wall for support, he stumbled awkwardly to his feet.

"I didn't do it," he declared, making a flat gesture of denial. "I only just got here. I had no part in—" he waved an agitated hand "—this."

Beneath her light tan, Sam's cheeks paled. But she was across the threshold before Aidan could stop her and staring at the floor where Alistair had indicated.

"You bastard!" she raged as her eyes located the unmoving body. "You slimy little bastard."

Alistair backed away, palms raised in surrender. "Wait a minute, lady, this was none of my doing. I had to follow you to find this place. I just got inside faster than you, is all. Ten seconds faster, I swear that's all it was. I didn't kill her. I don't even have a gun."

No, they had that, and it was still half loaded with blanks.

Aidan regarded the person who lay in a crumpled heap at the foot of the kitchen staircase. She looked to have been a very slim and attractive elderly woman.

On her knees, Sam bent over her body, swallowed hard and sat back on her heels. "I can't find a pulse."

"Of course you can't find a pulse," Alistair shouted, badly rattled. "She's got a bullet through her heart."

They heard it at the same time, the powerful roar of a car engine near the umber-colored barn. Aidan made it around the front porch in time to see a black Jaguar take off in a spray of mud and water.

No plates this time, he thought grimly, but he sensed it was the same Jaguar that had been skulking around his street last night.

He didn't realize Alistair was behind him until he heard a sound like a mournful moan emerge from his throat. "It's him, I know it is. They'll think I saw the murder, and I didn't. My name'll be in his computer. By tomorrow morning, I'll be toast."

Sam arrived, holding her high-heeled shoes like hammers.

"Whose computer?" she demanded of a quaking Alistair. "Do you know that Jaguar?"

Wild-eyed, he spun to face her. "Don't you? My God, didn't you bother to run those plates last night?"

"The car's registered to a Dinah Cobbett from Santa Monica," Aidan said coldly. "And what do you know about last night?"

Alistair scuttled away as Aidan advanced. "Surveillance. I was only watching. It's the people in the Jaguar you need to worry about." His Adam's apple bobbed. "Dinah Cobbett, you said? She must be his grandson's latest bed partner, because it was his grandson who was in that car last night."

"Give us a name," Sam demanded again. Her temper, Aidan noticed, sounded as frayed as his.

"Jimmy Visey."

Aidan's brain made the connection with amazing swiftness. He'd seen that name in one of Guido's magazines, as well as on Dinah Cobbett's file.

"Who is Jimmy Visey—" Sam began, but Aidan interrupted.

"He's Dorian Hart's grandson."

Her brow furrowed. "Dorian Hart? The same Dorian Hart that Mar—Guido mentioned?"

Good cover. Alistair stared at her as if she'd sprouted a second head. "How can you stand there and be so calm? Don't you know what kind of bodily damage Dorian Hart can inflict? He's done it more times than any of us can probably count. And don't expect his grandson to be a pushover even if he did go to Harvard." He took a vicious swipe at the railing, then stiffened and swung around. "What am I doing? I've got to get out of here."

Angry, Sam retorted, "You can't leave, Alistair. You're a witness to a murder."

Alistair uttered a short, explicit curse, glanced at Aidan who really didn't care if he stayed, went or jumped in the nearest lake, and darted around the side of the house.

Sam flung an exasperated arm. "That's it? You're letting him go?"

"I don't think he did it, Sam. He was too shaken."

"Maybe he saw something then."

A loud crash from inside the house had her jumping into the side of his body. She didn't scream, merely sent him a frightened look and tugged him away from the window.

A ream of possibilities shot through Aidan's bleary mind. The Jaguar and its occupants had roared out of the yard as if chased by the devil. Had they left one of their own behind? If so, why? Because he couldn't see the logic in that, he searched for an alternative. A cat, possibly. Or a small dog.

"I'll look," he told Sam, and held a hand out to keep her, if not motionless, at least behind him.

It took an eternity to circle the large house. No other sound emerged from inside. Only a squirrel chattering as it ran up a tree broke the silence in the yard. That and presumably Alistair's car as he floored the gas pedal and made for the nearest highway.

A board creaked beneath Aidan's weight before he reached the back door. Sam, who'd wrapped her fingers around his waistband, tightened her grip but didn't tug. Cautiously, because he didn't relish the idea of getting his head blown off by a trigger-happy gangster, Aidan glanced around the frame.

A low curse, similar to the one Alistair had used, came from deep in his throat. With a single, agile movement he entered and crossed to Anthea's crumpled form. "She isn't dead, Sam. She grabbed the cookie jar and broke it."

"What?" Shocked, Sam ran in after him. "I thought..." Her eyes widened in horror. "I'll call an ambulance," she whirled and raced to the phone.

"Use a handkerchief," Aidan warned, then saw she'd already grabbed a potholder and returned his attention to Anthea. Behind him, Sam turned off the movie.

Anthea's face was deathly white. Her lips made a soundless

fluttering movement. "Got part of it..." she croaked. "She tried to take it, but I tore..."

Aidan cradled her head in his hand. It surprised him how small she was—and how pretty she must have been. "What did you tear, Anthea? Who did this?"

He didn't expect an answer and so was surprised when she gasped in a spiteful tone, "Mary. She's..." A sharp pain seized her and she went rigid in his arms. "Crazy. Don't be deceived... She *was* good, damned good... Wants revenge... Always has. Just...like...Three...Fates..."

She emitted a soft sound like a groan, nothing remotely like the dreadful death rattle Aidan had been anticipating, and released a deep breath. Her head rocked sideways; her taut little body went limp.

Aidan closed her sightless blue eyes with his hand, then closed his own eyes and let his head fall forward, ordering himself not to draw comparisons. He refused to relive that godawful moment in his life when Domina had died. An unsuccessful actress, she'd forced him to witness a death scene of her own creation. She'd drawn it out, of course, exaggerating the process in order to punish him. But in the end, death was death, and it was a sight he'd prayed like hell he would never see again.

Sam sounded very far away when she asked, "Is she—gone?"

Aidan managed to nod.

He heard her at closer range, caught the scent of her perfume and braced for the sensual kick that was bound to follow. This time he met it halfway and blotted it out with an image of Domina's contorted face.

"What's that in her hand?"

God, she was bending over him. And, dammit, he was reacting. A woman lay dead in front of him, and all he could think of was Sam and her luscious, living body. His nephew in Dublin would call him "one buggered up dude."

He dropped his gaze with an effort to Anthea's hand. In

typical murder mystery fashion, her left palm was partially open. Between it and her cuff, Aidan spied a small piece of paper.

"She must have hidden it up her sleeve," Sam said as he removed the thing. "Is it a note?"

"We already know who did it, Sam." He smoothed the wrinkles and held it up. "It's part of a photograph. Must be a picture of Mary. It isn't Anthea or Margaret."

"I guess." Taking it from him, Sam studied the plump features and dyed honey-blond hair.

No face-lifts; a modicum of makeup. Aidan got no sense that the woman was clinging to the last days of her youth. Large brown eyes, shrewd, discerning and perhaps a trifle secretive, stared back at them. Laugh lines crinkled the corners; strength of purpose glimmered within.

"She doesn't look crazy," Sam remarked.

"Neither did Lizzie Borden, but she was. Appearances..."

"Can be deceiving, I know." Going to her knees, she cast a guilty glance at Anthea. "I feel terrible. She might have lived if I'd called 9-1-1 when we got here."

Aidan shook his head. "Alistair's right. The bullet passed very close to her heart. Not a chance she would have lived." He stood, bringing her gently with him. While feelings of tenderness weren't foreign to him, the depth of his emotions at this moment had the power to terrify—more so when she rested her forehead against his shoulder and fitted her trembling body to his.

He released an inward sigh of relief as a distant wail of sirens filled the air. Cops and paramedics to the rescue. Wonder what Humphrey Bogart would have done in this situation?

He was losing it, badly and fast. He needed air and time alone to think. A car crunching along the driveway, red and blue lights flashing, told him he wasn't likely to get either of those things for several hours.

The first police officer to arrive, Sergeant Lionel Dempsey, was well into his fifties. He regarded the body doubtfully, asked the usual plethora of questions and made notes in a dog-eared book. "What's her name?" he inquired of Sam.

Her composure semirestored, she replied dully, "Anthea Pennant."

The sergeant's pen halted in midair. His eyes snapped to her face. "*The* Anthea Pennant?"

Sam nodded.

"Well, who on earth would want to murder her?"

Sam looked angry and resentful. "Mary Lamont," she stated without hesitation. She met Aidan's steady gaze. "We weren't supposed to say anything at the request of her doctor, but Mary escaped from Oakhaven a couple of weeks ago. She killed Anthea Pennant, Sergeant. And I don't believe for a minute that she intends to stop there."

SAM SAT, swamped with guilt, in Guido's cluttered, comfortable office. *The Sins of Elizabeth,* a vintage Margaret Truesdale film, played on his television. She had a pile of magazines on the desk and three more stacks on the floor beside it. She'd been through half the collection, a full pot of coffee and two jelly doughnuts. She wanted to phone Aidan and apologize for snapping at him earlier. She wanted to forget this entire day had ever happened.

"I had to tell Sergeant Dempsey the truth," she'd insisted at the restaurant where they'd stopped after the nightmare at Anthea's. It had a *Bishop's Wife* theme, charming as Michel's had been, elegant yet trendy and strongly reminiscent of the late forties. A collection of booths and tables had afforded them only marginal privacy. They'd had to keep their voices low.

Aidan had held his temper well in the face of her aggressive outburst. Maybe he'd known it had nothing to do with him. Her anger had been and still was entirely self-directed.

"You didn't mention Margaret," he reminded her. "And you're right, you had to tell the sergeant some portion of the truth. You did fine, Sam."

She sighed. "You're being kind. I'm not sure I deserve it. Fine translates to acceptable. I can't believe I didn't see her breathing. Anthea had to crawl to the counter and smash a cookie jar to get our attention. I don't think that's fine at all."

"She'd be dead now, regardless. There's no blame involved—except for the person who killed her."

He was right. Guilt was not an emotion she handled well. The only thing she hated more than feeling guilty was feeling foolish—and right now she felt both those things and angry to boot. If she accomplished nothing else, she was determined to avenge Anthea's death.

The glossies in Guido's old movie magazines blurred. Closing her eyes, Sam folded her arms on the desk and laid her forehead against them.

Thoughts of Aidan moved with the tumult in her mind. Tall, lean, sexy Aidan, the Rob Roy of insurance investigators. Would he be as good in the bedroom?

"Forget it, Sam," she murmured into her arms. "He's not for you."

On the television screen, Margaret as the title character Elizabeth slipped into the second of her four personalities. Mary hadn't been in this movie, but she'd been in the first one Sam had watched, a picture titled *The Dark Horse*. As she was trying to do in real life, she'd plotted to kill Margaret throughout the film.

"Doing penance?" drawled a voice from the doorway.

She braced but merely raised her head and shot a nasty visual dagger at him. "What are you doing here, Brodie? How did you get in? I thought you went home for soccer, pizza and a good night's sleep."

He leaned a lazy shoulder against the door frame. "You didn't turn the lock, soccer and pizza lost their luster, and sleep eluded me. It's almost 1:00 a.m., Sam."

She dragged her gaze from his sinewy body and placed it on the flickering TV. "I need to know more about Dorian Hart."

"Why?"

"Because according to Alistair, his grandson was at Anthea's today."

"Anthea said Mary shot her," Aidan reminded her, still
trapped in the shadows of the doorway. "Dorian Hart's people
arrived after the fact."

Sam brought her eyes reluctantly back to his face. She
couldn't see much of it in the murk. "After what fact, Aidan?
Why, if Margaret's husband owed him money, would a gangster or a loan shark or whatever Dorian is, want to find Anthea?"

"I can think of a reason or two."

"Exactly. Say Margaret's husband Frank never paid Dorian.
Say Frank disappeared, along with Margaret and Cousin An-
thea. Time passes, Dorian fumes, and still there's no sign of
Frank Durwald or a payback. No self-respecting gangster
would be willing to let that go, not even after forty years. So
Dorian keeps searching.

"Then one day he hears about a man and a woman who've
been asking a lot of questions about Margaret Truesdale and
Mary Lamont. He decides to have them watched. Maybe he
even taps one of their phone lines. Your phone was clicking
a lot last night, Aidan. So was mine this morning when I called
Anthea to confirm our appointment. After that it would be a
simple matter of logistics and logic. Dorian Hart wants his
money. The best way he would know to find Frank Durwald—because he wouldn't necessarily be aware of their divorce—would be through Margaret. And the best path to Margaret would very likely be through Anthea. It's probably the
first link he's ever found." She paused to look away, frown-
ing. "Can you get an address by tracing a telephone number?
I wonder if he did bug my phone. His people got to Anthea's
before us, so he must have known where she lived. But he
couldn't have known for long, or else... What are you doing,
Brodie?"

He'd come in, unzipped his jacket and dropped onto the

sofa. "Helping you," he said, and reached for a handful of newspapers.

Sam hesitated then picked up the microfiche box. Having him here would be torture for her nerves, but it was preferable to sitting alone mired in guilt.

She'd told Margaret what happened and extracted a promise from Sergeant Dempsey and his associates not to volunteer any information to the press. She'd also spoken to her editor, Sally Dice, before she left today. Sam's human interest column was down to its reserve stories, and Sally was getting understandably anxious. To her surprise, and suspicion, Sally had waved her explanations aside.

"No problem, Sam. We'll run a few of your more popular back columns." Then her eyes had gleamed, and Sam had seen Guido's hand clearly. "I'll expect an exclusive, of course. 'The Story Behind Margaret Truesdale's Disappearance.' We'll beat the rest of the industry to the punch and put our paper on the map at last."

Sam could have objected. If it had been anyone except Sally, her seventy-year-old editor and mentor, and Guido's checker-playing partner, she would have. But since she'd only told Sally a minute portion of the whole story, she couldn't see the harm in making the promise. After all, it wasn't as if she planned to splash Margaret's Laurel Canyon address over the front page.

Her pricks of conscience on that score came and rapidly departed. Which left only Mary—and Aidan—to deal with.

She glanced up, noticed he was studying a certain picture poster, and contained a heavy sigh. "Margaret wasn't in *Dr. Jekyll and Mr. Hyde,* Aidan. If you really want to help, stop ogling Ingrid Bergman and find what you can on Dorian Hart."

Aidan sent her a dark look but made no comment.

Three exhausting hours later, Sam swept the long hair from her face and switched off the microfiche. "One lousy reference," she said, deflated. "Dorian Hart attended a wine-tasting convention in San Francisco in October of nineteen forty-nine, in, quote, 'the company of several of Hollywood's finest.' Terrific, but the least they could do is mention who those 'finest' were. Maybe he met Margaret on that trip, or—"

"He didn't meet Margaret there," Aidan interrupted. "She was in *Calcutta* at the time."

Sam missed the subtle inflection. "She went to India?"

"No, she went to the backlot. *Calcutta*'s a movie, not quite as exotic or visually stunning as *Casablanca* but along the same lines. I doubt if it was one of her bigger hits. The reporter who wrote the article on it said she appeared subdued and unhappy during filming."

Sam snapped the lid on the mircofiche box. "Maybe that's because she gave her child up for adoption the year before. Some form of delayed postpartum blues, except in her case there was no baby to lift her out of her depression."

"That's a very clinical analysis, Sam."

She faced him unabashed. "I feel clinical, Aidan. Margaret's…" She wasn't sure how to put it. "Fine," she said at last.

Aidan saw entirely too much. He stood. His hands hung loose at his sides, his brown leather jacket was open, his long hair was rumpled, damp and windblown. She couldn't read his bland expression, and didn't think she wanted to when he started slowly toward her. "'Fine,' Sam?" he challenged in a mockery of her earlier charge. "Just 'fine'? That's the best you can say about your maternal grandmother?"

Her defenses surged. "I don't have anything to say about her, Brodie." She stood, stubborn and defiant, her heart racing, her palms damp. "I'm doing the job I promised to do. It has nothing to do with blood—you know what I mean." She made an impatient gesture when he would have offered a comment. "I don't have to explain my motives or my feelings, not to you or anyone else."

The defensiveness of her tone made her shudder. Or was that Aidan's effect on her? He continued to close in, smoothly, soundlessly, his eyes steady on her face. The predator preparing to pounce on its prey, she thought, then firmed up her resolve. She was nobody's prey, male or female. However, since she also wasn't invincible, she made a point of putting Guido's swivel chair between them.

"Don't," she warned when he would have shoved it aside. "You're too complicated for me, Brodie. You have angst and ghosts and danger swirling around you like a miasma. I have goals and a strong desire for simplicity in my personal life. We don't go together."

"Neither do oil and vinegar."

"Don't be obtuse. We've got people chasing us all over L.A. Mary's one of them, and there must be others. I don't like crazy, murderous people, old-style gangsters or the unknown. Not when any of those things might leave me dead. Our getting involved beyond a professional level would be stupid. It could even prove fatal." When she stopped for breath, she noticed that he looked bored rather than annoyed and infinitely more sexy than seductive. Had she misread the intent behind his approach? Had she been wrong about him from the start?

He made no further attempt to push aside the chair. Sam ran a tired hand over her eyes and let the tension drain from her body. She was being ridiculous, overreacting to the events of the past week. Overreacting to Aidan's powerful brand of sensuality.

"Are you done?" he asked when she didn't add anything more.

She hesitated, not trusting him or herself. "I don't know. Maybe. It depends what you have in mind."

"What makes you think I have anything in mind?" Same dispassionate tone as before. Her suspicion mounted.

"Because you're too agreeable, that's why."

"Yeah?" He moved and she jumped, her backside colliding with the wooden windowsill. His eyes narrowed on hers. "You're not afraid of me, are you?"

He'd told her once that she should be. And yet... "No," she said, swallowing the knot of sudden panic that had inched up into her throat. "Of myself."

That stopped him. Only for a moment, but he stopped, dead in his tracks. Then he swore softly and started to turn away.

"Aidan, wait." Her action was purely involuntary. She grabbed a handful of jacket and held on. "What is your problem?" Frustration bubbled to the surface. "You come here, make me as defensive as hell, break it all down and finally get me to admit that I'm more afraid of my own feelings than yours—and then you walk? Do you also pull the wings off flies in your spare time?"

He stared at her, his expression grim and unyielding. "Only when they come into my parlor. I came looking for you, Sam. I don't know why. I don't want to know. I let my guard slip and so did you. Fortunately, we did it at different times, otherwise..."

"Otherwise what?" Her chin came up. "I'm not a push-over, Aidan. Andy could tell...well, no, he couldn't, but trust me, I don't fall to pieces at the sight of a handsome male. I like my life the way it is. Besides which, what I don't know about you could fill half the city library. So forget 'otherwise', Brodie. We're working toward a common goal. Let's leave it at that and figure out our next move, okay?"

He thought about it, though what he thought was anyone's guess. Sam had never met a man who could shut down his facial expressions so completely. He must be half Irish actor, half Scottish chameleon.

Finally, a single wicked brow rose. "Would dinner be an acceptable next move?" he asked.

She staved off a smile but couldn't hide the amusement that danced in her eyes. "At one-fifteen in the morning?"

"The last food I remember eating was at Lulu's this afternoon."

She wrinkled her nose. "That pretty place was called Lulu's?" Yet even as she asked, she was reaching for the red knit jacket that matched her dress. "Our poor world needs a good stiff shot of fifties-style romance."

Aidan stared at *The Sins of Elizabeth* for a moment, saw Margaret wrestling with her antagonistic, soon-to-be lover, and pushed the Stop button. "Fifties romance was an illusion, Sam," he told her. Reaching out, he pulled several trapped strands of dark hair from her collar. "Hollywood hype dished it out by the plateful to a war-weary America. The illusion's just gotten tarnished over the years. It'll be back. We need it back. Computers may be a fact of life, but they have no heart, no soul. People have basic urges. They also love sensual pleasures."

"Do you love sensual pleasures?" Sam asked softly.

A glint appeared deep in Aidan's green eyes. "Right now I'll settle for satisfying a basic urge."

Her mood had lightened considerably, although a trace of wariness lingered. You could never really trust a hungry cat. Smiling succinctly, she picked up her shoulder bag. "I assume you're referring to food."

"Food, dancing. And maybe," he added as she passed him at a dangerously close range, "a glass of homemade elderberry wine."

Chapter Eleven

Two in the morning.

Mary rubbed her sore feet, her excruciatingly painful feet. She wasn't up to a shoot-and-dash-and-drive-and-walk. But she'd seen Dorian Hart's eyes and nose on his grandson's slender face and wisely hightailed it out of there before he'd slithered inside the house.

She'd seen the Jaguar, too. Hell, she'd almost stumbled headfirst into it. She'd had to walk half a mile around it to reach her own little Legacy and its nearly empty gas tank. Now her corns hurt, her bunions stung and her arthritic ankles throbbed. Trust Anthea to live in the back of beyond. Trust Tobias not to fill her stupid tank.

Crankily triumphant, she shouted, "Tobias! Bring me hot water in a basin. And plenty of Epsom salts. Then park your presumptive backside in here. I have a bone to pick with you."

Five minutes later she'd picked it clean and the poker-faced Tobias Lallibertie with it. "I'm warning you, Tobias," she finished ominously. "My deeds go no further than the walls of this house. It's been you and me for a long, long time now, partners in crime as well as employment."

He looked displeased. "I'm not a criminal."

"An accessory then, willing or un. I'm on top of everything here, Tobias. This is my game, and we're going to play by my rules. Now fetch me a Magic Marker. A fat red one. And no more of your clever tricks. I'm onto you, old friend. I'm also better than you at subterfuge.''

She knew he rolled his eyes, but like the professional he was, he didn't argue. Mary chuckled nastily and removed the torn photograph from her pocket.

The missing portion had bothered her at first, but when she'd realized it couldn't possibly hurt her, she'd simply chalked up another victory and carried on with her plan.

She removed a picture of her own from the desk drawer. She was chortling merrily when Tobias brought her the red felt marker.

"Poor old Anthea," she said without a scrap of remorse. "She never made it to the conclusion of any film. Story of her life—she always missed the climax."

Anthea Pennant's face smiled up at her as she uncapped the marker. "One down—who cares—and one to go. And one and one—'' her eyes slid sideways to the door "—and then one more." She held the picture up in front of her, blowing on the wet ink. "Now you tell me, Margaret Truesdale, who controls the Fates in the end?" Her tone altered until it matched that of her movie character. "I'll get you, sister. And I'll do it with the most fitting weapon in the world—the weapon you gave me way back in nineteen forty-eight."

CANDLELIGHT AND ROSES it definitely was not. But Aidan offered—against logic and his own good judgment—to knock together a batch of Irish stew. Visibly amused, Sam snapped the offer up.

The stew was mediocre and Sam was a glutton for punishment. She ate two helpings, sipped an Irish Cream and spared only one uneasy look at the elderberry wine sitting in plain view on his pantry shelf.

Obviously she'd seen *Arsenic and Old Lace,* the old Cary Grant comedy about two elderly women whose nephew had been appalled to discover that they not only poisoned lonely old men, but also buried them in their cellar. She actually had the guts to refer to it after dinner.

Raising her liqueur glass to eye level, she studied the creamy gold contents. "Teddy used to take his aunts' victims to Panama," she told him. "What do you do with yours, Brodie?"

"Loch Ness," he replied, not missing a beat.

The question had surprised him slightly. She couldn't possibly be drunk. But she could be bold in spades.

Sheer perversity had him pouring himself a tall glass of elderberry wine; truthfully, he despised the noxious brew. "Nessie has to be fed, and she's a fair hand at keeping secrets."

Sam grinned. "Morbid, Brodie. Your Scottish ancestors must turn in their graves when they hear you talk." She took another sip, then ventured a determinedly casual, "Why did your wife want to poison you?"

His blood turned to ice. If it showed on his face, however, the effect didn't daunt her.

"You might as well tell me," she said without a hint of apology. "You have to tell somebody sometime. It's cathartic to talk. Besides, I already know the worst of it. Was she paranoid?"

Aidan swallowed a mouthful of wine. It tasted sour and weedy. "Something like that," he answered less irritably than he would have thought possible. "She had a persecution complex. That's what the doctors called it. She thought the world was against her, and me most of all."

Sam's expression grew puzzled. "Why?"

"I don't know. I doubt if anyone did. She had a lot of hatred inside her and a lot more jealousy."

"Toward whom?"

"Anyone who could do anything better than she could."

"Did that include you?"

"Probably."

"Do you blame yourself for her death?"

That hit home, a swift, accurate gut-punch that Aidan absorbed like a boxer's blow. "I don't believe in blame, Sam. She wanted me dead. She wound up killing herself instead. Who knows, maybe she would have taken her own life afterward anyway. Murder-suicides aren't all that uncommon. There are any number of theories about them. In Domina's case, killing me would have eliminated the object of her deepest hatred. Remove that and what's left? Once you've killed the thing you dislike most, your hatred needs a new direction. I'm not sure Domina would have bothered to look for one. Better, possibly, to end it in her moment of triumph."

He suspected it was impulse that made Sam cover his free hand with both of hers. "I think you do blame yourself just a little, Aidan," she said. "But you shouldn't. Domina sounds like Mary in some ways. Jealous, spiteful, angry at the world. Only they narrow their world down to one person. For Domina it was you. For Mary it's Margaret."

He stared at her slender hands. "And Anthea."

"I don't think so. I think Anthea was incidental. Maybe killing her soothed Mary's frazzled nerves, but I'd guess that her main goal was to keep Anthea from telling us anything. What I can't figure out is how Mary was able to find her. She had to have gotten there at least five minutes before we did."

"You said it before," Aidan reminded her, glancing toward the living room. "Phone taps. Yours and mine. It isn't hard to do."

Her fingers curled around his hand, digging in to his flesh. "Should we, uh, check that out or something?"

It had crossed his mind. But then so had a few other things, the kind of things he preferred not to dwell on.

Shoving back his chair with his foot, he rose and headed for the phone. He felt Sam behind him all the way. With a shudder that was only half desire he snatched up the phone and examined it.

"Nothing," Sam said finally, disappointed. "I don't get it—unless it's my phone that's tapped. I don't think so, though. I had a funny feeling about all the clicking on the line this morning so I unscrewed the removable parts and looked.'' She peered closer, then pointed at the underside of the base. ''What's that?''

Aidan spotted the device. It was the smallest he'd ever seen, not the most sophisticated but adequate if the installer had a computer backup.

Sam sat with a despondent thump, cupping her chin in her hands. ''Anthea gave good general directions on this phone,'' she mused out loud. ''Still, if Mary's responsible for the tap, she'd have to have done a little searching to find the place—which, I suppose, might explain why she was only a few minutes ahead of us. On the other hand, it doesn't explain how Dorian Hart found her home.''

She blew out an exasperated breath and started ticking items off on her fingers. ''This is getting painfully complicated. All we have are questions, three names and no faces. Dorian Hart, Frank Durwald and Helen Murdoch—which might or might not be Mary's alias, and a lot of old studio people who won't talk.'' Flopping back in the leather chair, she folded her arms across her chest. ''So what's the answer, Brodie? Host a dinner party and hope all concerned not only show but that one or more of them also coughs up a confession?''

''No.'' Using a shamrock paperweight, Aidan destroyed the little device with a satisfying crunch. His deceptively placid gaze slid to the streaming window, then returned to Sam's mutinous face. ''We go up to my roof,'' he said, battling back a smile at the ridge that formed between her delicate brows.

''What's up there?'' She wanted to know.

''You'll see.'' He held out his hand to her. ''Coming?''

She remained seated and unmoving for two seconds, no more, then pushed herself from the chair. When she placed her hand in his, he wasn't sure whether to be pleased by her show of trust or terrified to the center of his bones....

HE ACTUALLY OWNED a compact disk of Bing, Perry and Frank. Crosby, Como and Sinatra all crooned out mellow, nostalgic lyrics that brought to mind a simpler day, before micro-waves, Virtual Reality and surfing the Net. Sam loved it. She had a very strong feeling she also loved Aidan, but that was not a thought to be dissected at the moment.

Warm rain trickled down her back. Her hair and dress were soaked; her shoes, too. It didn't matter. Like Eliza Doolittle, she could have danced all night and right into the next day.

A clock chimed in one of the apartments below: 4:00 a.m. She should be dead on her feet. Why did she feel so alive and tingly?

Aidan's hand caressed her spine. His touch brought goose bumps to her skin and a hot, scratchy feeling to her throat. She pressed herself closer, swaying against the lean, hard length of him, savoring the feel of his arousal where it dug into her abdomen.

He must have heard the sound she made in her throat because he moved away to look at her. His features by misty lamplight were somber and unrevealing. Nothing new in that, she decided with a sigh.

He pulled her close again, until her head rested against his broad shoulder. His hand continued to stroke her back, bringing all manner of delicious sensations to her heated skin. "You're too trusting, Sam," he said softly.

She roused herself to stare up at him, torn more about whether she should take the initiative and kiss him than about how to respond. "In that case," she said cheerfully, "we're even. You're not trusting enough. Call it a good balance."

"We're not divvying up a bag of Hershey's bars. It isn't that simple for us."

She ran an experimental finger across his cheekbone then along the line of his jaw. "It is as far as I'm concerned. You're healthy, aren't you?"

"That isn't exactly—"

"It's important," she insisted.

The corners of his mouth twitched as if he found her attitude humorous as well as vaguely annoying. "You remind me of a cat I had once. I called her Gracie. I should have called her Francis."

"As in the talking mule, female version?"

"She had a mind of her own."

"That has the earmarks of a compliment, Brodie." Deciding it was worth the risk, Sam went up on tiptoe and touched her lips to the side of his mouth. He tasted of salt, rain and sex. "Maybe we're being a little too analytical here. Maybe you're afraid I'll be another Domina, but…well, no," she amended at his spearing look. "I guess that doesn't really come into it. I'm sorry. I know better than to make comparisons, especially unpleasant ones. It's just that you give me next to nothing to go on. You can't be that relationship-shy."

"Gun-shy's the phrase you're looking for, Sam. And I doubt that you'd feel a whole lot bolder if you'd watched your husband choke out his dying last breath at your feet."

"An accusing breath, too, I'll bet."

"You'd win," he said dourly.

Aware of his continued state of arousal, Sam wriggled closer, running her fingers through the silk of his brown hair. "Let it go, Aidan," she suggested. "For tonight, let the past slip away and yourself relax."

"This from the woman who, a few hours ago, wanted to keep things between us on a professional level?"

She lowered her eyes. "I was wrong about that. I didn't mean it. Well, I did, but only because it seemed like a smart thing to say at the time." Her head came up in a challenge. "Now, I'm not so sure that thinking every choice through to its theoretical conclusion is the right way to live. Loosen up, Brodie. Go with your feelings. They can't be that far wrong."

She arched herself toward him, but didn't kiss him again. He was the stubborn one now. She wanted him to kiss her.

With his thumb, he grazed her full lower lip. His gaze skimmed her face, coming to rest on her eyes. "You're like a drug in my veins, Sam,'' he said at length. "Potent as hell and ten times more frightening.''

Frank Sinatra sang "New York, New York'' in the background. Rain fell from the night sky like a heavy mist. Grainy pools of light spread out around them. They were alone and, for the moment, suspended in time. Sam thought briefly of Margaret's passionate film embraces and long lost glamour. Then she felt Aidan's breath on her cheek and swayed into him as seductively as she knew how.

She heard the groan that emerged from his throat and knew it only covered her own. Then his mouth came down on hers, and every conscious thought fled into the warm, wet shadows of the night....

AIDAN HAD NO IDEA how they arrived in his bedroom. He remembered picking her up like some kind of errant knight and carrying her through the living room, but he couldn't recall navigating the stairway from the roof.

Her kiss had been more than a drug to his senses. She'd tasted like cognac, sweet, with a hint of mystery and delicate danger mixed in. He'd longed to strip off her clothes, piece by tantalizing piece, on the roof, ease her onto the tiles and make love to her in the pouring rain.

He'd checked that urge, but couldn't, if he'd lived to be a hundred, have hoped to stop himself from wanting her. Damn the woman, namesake of a sixties' witch. She should have listened to his earlier arguments. He should have made her listen—or left.

In the bedroom, he let her slide, standing, to the floor. Eyes opening, she cupped his face in her palms and regarded him seriously. "Second thoughts, Brodie?''

"No.'' Twelfth or thirteenth, but not second. He forced himself to take a deep breath. "But now that you mention it…''

"Pretend I didn't.'' Her lips found his again in a kiss that would have caused a dedicated monk to abandon his vows.

Aidan was no monk. Nor was he a masochist. Both his hormones and his heart wanted her badly. And right now he couldn't drum up a single reason to deny them.

Their clothing was soaked through. Sam's dress had literally molded itself to her slender body. Aidan took his time unfastening it, allowing his eyes to linger on the swell of her breasts and the gentle curve of her hips. Her legs went on forever, and they were as silky and shapely as the rest of her.

A shiver started deep inside him. His self-possession had blown away during their dance. Only his hunger for her remained—and perhaps another feeling that he refused to acknowledge right then.

"We'll get the sheets wet," Sam protested as he guided her toward the queen-size mattress.

"They'll dry," he said into her mouth.

She had a fascinating mouth, all sweetness and witchy fire inside. He didn't sense a tremendous amount of experience, but her lack of inhibition was more than sufficient to send his mind into a tailspin.

His palms, calloused but not rough, traced the outline of her luscious body. The damp red dress fell in a sodden heap around her ankles. Beneath it, she wore a black lace camisole and bikini briefs. Her lightly tanned legs required no panty hose.

She moved against him even as he pulled her hips closer. Panic spiked momentarily in his chest and stomach, radiating swiftly outward as her curious hands ran down his spine to the waistband of his jeans. Then it died and a purely primitive reaction shuddered through him.

With a gentleness he'd forgotten he possessed, he lowered her onto the bed. Sweat replaced rain on his overheated skin. The pulsing in his loins threatened to explode. Closing his eyes, he permitted a groan to climb into his throat. His tongue slid into her tempting mouth, delving deeply, testing, tasting. If fire could be heady, then he was intoxicated, more so than he'd ever been on whiskey.

Her fingers clawed lightly at his back. Her breathing was as rapid and uneven as his own. Raising his head for a moment, he splayed her long, dark hair over the ivory pillowcase, then paused a few seconds longer to drink in her beauty.

She smelled of roses and a walk in the woods. A fine Irish day; a fine Irish lass… Good God, since when had he become a poet? A rueful smile played on his lips. Maybe there was a glimmer of hope for him at that.

His eyes strayed to the creamy flesh of her breast visible above the lace cup of her bra. Bending his head, he touched the hidden nipple, first with his tongue then with his whole mouth. Damp, the lacy fabric only heightened the friction. Her nipple hardened as he suckled. He felt her fingers in his hair, holding him in place as her body moved beneath him.

She made a series of soft, hungry sounds in her throat. Then her fingers left his hair and slid once again to his waistband. She unzipped his fly and pushed on the wet denim. When it refused to slide over his hips, he reached down and yanked the jeans lower, kicking them unconcernedly onto the floor.

Even aroused, she could tease. "You half-Scots are so efficient."

He ran a suggestive finger along the inside of her bikini briefs. "A little Irish impatience helps." He sobered, then, his eyes taking in her flushed cheeks and wild hair. "Are you sure about this, Sam?"

For an answer she wrapped her arms around his neck and pulled. "Positive," she said. And using her bewitching mouth, proceeded to show him just how much.

NO STREAKS OF DAWN light graced the sky outside. Sam saw only darkness, heard only Bing's dulcet tones and the thunder of her own heart as Aidan entered her. She pushed on his shoulders with the heels of her hands, not in an attempt to push him away, but in an effort to bring him deeper inside her. If it had been possible, she'd have crawled through his pores and under his skin.

Right now, that skin felt like hot silk over bone. The muscles beneath were stretched taut like piano wire. Sam glimpsed a blend of pain and pleasure on his face as his head fell back, then heard herself gasp as a sudden burst of heat and energy filled her. Her head moved from side to side; her hands gripped his shoulders. The sob that rose in her throat stemmed from desire. She wanted more, so very much more.

She savored the intoxicating male scent of him, something to do with cool Irish nights, hot Irish whiskey and his body rubbing insistently against hers.

Blood throbbed in her ears and at the base of her throat. His mouth skimmed over her cheeks and eyelids, her collarbone and both of her breasts. She emitted something akin to a whimper but knew it was really a cry for him to continue, to hold back nothing physically, even if he couldn't give his emotional all.

She sensed something in his touch, perhaps a hint of panic. Or did that come from her? Then the tempo increased, and her shaky logic dissolved. Nothing mattered except that she was here with Aidan, making love in his apartment. It felt like the early fifties even if it was the nineties—and she wanted this moment to go on forever.

Now a stronger cry begged for release. He stroked her with his hands, ran his tongue lovingly around the diamond-hard tip of her nipple. The rhythm altered, growing faster, deeper, more fiery. Sam responded, digging her fingers into his buttocks and raising her needful body to meet his thrusts.

She knew what to expect, yet even knowing was robbed of breath when the first fierce shudder tore through her. The second left her gasping out loud. The rest was little more than a blur.

She remembered feeling wonderfully light and giddy, floaty—until Aidan collapsed on top of her. Even then, her mind wasn't eager to return. So she wrapped her arms around him and held him close, absorbing the feel of his warm, hard body and the sound of his ragged breathing, knowing full well that her own heart pounded at a similar, erratic rate.

"Stubborn namesake of a witch," she heard him mutter into her shoulder. "I should have known better."

Sam swallowed hard around the pain that burned at the back of her throat. He didn't mean that. He couldn't. She wouldn't believe it. If a house had to fall on her, so be it. Until then, she would believe he could love her. Anything was possible. Anything and everything. Even the morbid Irish believed in miracles.

That left only his Scottish side to deal with—and the memory of a woman who'd wanted him dead. Perhaps a difficult memory to offset when they dogged the footsteps of a much older woman who appeared to desire another person's death.

With a shiver for the unknown danger lurking beyond the apartment walls, Sam snuggled closer to Aidan and prayed for a miracle.

Chapter Twelve

"Wait here."

It wasn't a request but an order barked at her by a bent old woman wearing a maid's uniform. She had steel wool for hair, a pointed chin with visible whiskers, a gravelly voice and an air of absolute authority. Sam waited as instructed.

The maid had led her to Stan Hollister's study, a spacious room with a mushroom leather sofa, matching chairs, a large walnut desk and stuffed fish instead of animal heads mounted on the walls. Floor-to-ceiling windows overlooked a yard dotted with orange and grapefruit trees, a gazebo, a rectangular pool and, far in the distance, a dog kennel and runs. As Sam watched, a tall, thin scarecrow of a man, possibly the handyman, with a billed cap, long blond hair and a protruding Adam's apple shuffled past.

Sighing, she turned. Photographs of old movie stars and vintage cars adorned the space above the sofa. She'd also glimpsed a long row of garages outside, in front of which were parked no less than a dozen collector automobiles.

All of those things registered, yet none really held her interest. Curiosity had been eating her up since eight-thirty this morning. That's when Stan Hollister's call had come via Aidan's phone—his untapped phone, she was relieved to recall.

Aidan had been dead to the world. Sam had heard the ring, untangled herself reluctantly from the bedsheets and Aidan's slumbering body and stumbled to answer it. Stan seemed both surprised and grimly pleased to find her there.

"I need to talk to you," he'd said by way of a greeting.

She'd stifled a yawn and propped her eyelids open. "What about Aid—uh, Mr. Brodie?"

"I think it would be best if we kept this meeting down to two. I live in Bel Air. Can you be here by ten?"

"I—well, yes, I suppose so."

"Please be prompt," he'd said brusquely before she could question him further. "I'm on a tight schedule these days." He'd rattled off the address so abruptly that Sam had barely been able to locate a pad and pen in time. She'd had to scrabble through Aidan's desk drawer, and at that she'd had to use a three-year-old check stub and a dull pencil.

But those weren't the only items in the drawer. In the process of closing it, she'd glimpsed a wrinkled photograph partially hidden under a stack of road maps.

The older woman must have been his grandmother, the Scottish one since she'd been wearing a tartan scarf. But it was the younger woman who'd really caught her eye. Domina? she'd wondered, and held the photo up to the morning light. She was very pretty, beautiful in fact. She had bright red hair, a dusting of golden freckles—and a glint in her pale green eyes that could have been rooted in either mischief or malice. Sam had suspected the latter, shivered at the prospect and shoved the picture back under the maps. God help Aidan if he'd misread those gorgeous green eyes.

He'd continued to sleep soundly while she dressed in a borrowed pair of jeans that were miles too big for her and a white cotton shirt, the tails of which she tied around her waist. Barefoot, she'd collected her still-damp clothing from the night before, kissed the nape of his neck and crept out to her car. She hadn't been relishing the awkward morning after and couldn't deny the faint sense of relief that washed through her that the moment would be indefinitely postponed. Maybe later she'd be equipped to handle her spinning emotions. A portion of that ability would undoubtedly depend on what Stan had to say.

In the director's study now, she paced, arms folded, tapping her elbows with her palms in agitation. She'd worn a black wraparound dress for the occasion, short, simple and businesslike. She'd snapped on her gold Gucci watch, added a pair of black and gold earrings, swept her hair up on the sides with combs and now here she was, ready to do battle—assuming a battle was necessary, and that Hollister bothered to put in an appearance.

At the opposite end of the room a door opened and a middle-aged woman with short blond hair and layers of makeup emerged. Sam stopped pacing to exclaim, "Connie! What are you doing here?"

Connie Grant pulled on her spiky hair. She was clearly as surprised to see Sam as Sam was to see her. "'Who's News' wanted an interview. Harvey was out with the flu so I volunteered to cover. I think Hollister forgot, though. Some crusty old maid demanded to know who I was, then marched off in a huff. When she came back she said her boss was on a long distance call, and she shoved me in here." Stabbing a painted thumb over her shoulder, she added, "There's a ladies' room if you need it. Three cups of coffee and thirty minutes later, I needed it badly." Adjusting her oversize green sweater, she pulled Sam toward the sofa. "So do tell. What brings you out here?"

"It's a very long story," Sam replied honestly, too keyed up to sit. She circled instead. "Stan Hollister called me at eight thirty this morning. I have no idea why."

"Did you infiltrate Rockland's reception?" Connie asked with a canny grin. At Sam's raised brows, she sat back, legs crossed. "Ha! Thought you might have." She waved a manicured hand. "Don't sweat it, kid. Hollister probably has the hots for you. He sure did for every starlet he met in his youth."

"Including Margaret Truesdale?" Sam wondered out loud.

"Probably. Just watch your step and his hands and you'll be fine. Besides, Mama Bear's here to make sure he doesn't overstep the mark. You feel like sharing any secrets as long as we're alone and cozy?"

Sam thought about it, but knew she couldn't, not without divulging the whole sordid story. What bothered her most was Stan Hollister's reason for asking her here today. Not Aidan, or as he knew him, Robert Brodie, just her. What was it that Stan wanted to keep between them? Did it concern Anthea's death, or was he in cahoots with Mary?

She offered Connie a preoccupied denial and continued to circle. Now she knew how a caged tiger must feel. The study seemed to be shrinking by the minute.

Connie lit a cigarette and blew out a long stream of smoke. "I guess you heard about Anthea Pennant, huh?"

"I heard she was discovered dead in her home." That information and little else had appeared in all the city newspapers, including the *Break*. Restless, Sam allowed her fingers to sift idly through some of the papers on Stan Hollister's desk.

"Shot dead," Connie specified, and stretched her arms over her head. "I'm betting it was a fluke, you know, a robbery gone bad. Happens all the time in La-la Land."

"Cynic." Sam would have added more to the gibe if she hadn't glanced down and caught sight of a name on Stan's blotter. With an unintelligible gasp, she ran behind the desk and started shoving papers aside at random.

Connie hopped up, clearly appalled. "Have you gone mad?" Scurrying over, she grabbed Sam's right wrist. "That's private stuff. You could get sued."

Shaking free, Sam kept pawing. "I saw a name, Connie. If he has it written down he must be working with her."

"Name? What name? What are you talking about? Sam, stop this." Connie rounded the desk to grasp her shoulders. "You're going to get us both in hot water. I mean it. I'm as gung ho and game to play spy as any reporter who's worth her salt, but plowing through personal papers in someone's home is going a bit too far, don't you think?''

Sam jabbed at the name on the blotter. ''Helen Murdoch, Connie. He wrote it down. Here, go through this file folder. There's got to be more than just her name.''

Too baffled to object further, Connie riffled through the file. ''Who the hell is Helen Murdoch?''

''Mary Lamont.''

''Get out,'' she scoffed. ''Lamont's in the loony bin.''

''Oakhaven,'' Sam corrected. ''And she isn't there now. She escaped.''

''Really?''

Sam recognized the avid tone. Looking up, she leveled her friend with a glare. ''Off the record, Connie. I'm sworn to secrecy. Anyway, there's more to it than even your inventive mind could imagine. Keep quiet and I'll talk Sally into letting me share my exclusive with 'Who's News.'''

Connie, thankfully the best of friends, shook a warning finger. ''Swear it?''

Sam held up her right hand; her left kept shuffling papers. ''I swear... Damn!'' Her head shot up. ''Footsteps!''

Connie had already dropped her file. Red-tipped fingers hooked Sam's arm and yanked. ''Sit.'' She thrust her into the leather chair, perched on the arm and emitted an indignant snort. ''Sounds like you'll have your hands full with that one, honey. I'd tell Sally to put on—ah, here he is.'' She catapulted from the arm, hand extended, eyes casting a pained glance at her cigarette, which smoldered in an ashtray across the room. ''What a pleasure to see you again, Stan.'' She bussed him, kissing the air on either side of his ruddy cheeks, and giving Sam the opportunity to slip over and pick up the cigarette. She took one distasteful puff, exhaled quickly and crushed it out.

''Good morning, Mr. Hollister.''

''Stan,'' he said automatically. The frown on his lips grew more pronounced. ''Nellie!'' he bellowed. When the old maid clumped in, he demanded harshly, "Why did you put my guests in here?"

Uncowed, she planted blue-veined hands on her hips and scowled back. "I put 'em where you told me to."

"Where I told you *not* to," he said through his teeth. "This is my private study. You should have showed them to the salon."

Nellie's lips curled in contempt. "Mr. Lush is in the salon. I thought you wouldn't want anyone to see him and that's why you told me to bring them in here."

"I didn't tell... Oh, what's the use. Go and ask Mr. Wells to amuse himself for a while. If you don't mind," he spoke to Sam, "I'll give Ms. Grant her interview—"

"Forgotten interview," Connie corrected cheerfully.

"Yes." His smile was thin. "Then you and I will have our talk. Nellie, show Ms. Giancarlo to the drawing room."

Nellie jerked her head sideways. "This way," she ordered, her hands still on her hips. Sam followed without a word and no reaction to Connie's conspiratorial wink.

"Make it snappy," Nellie barked as they walked along the broad corridor. Snatching a feather duster from her apron, she passed it over a few of the larger plaster busts. "Grecian white. Old fool. More work for me, that's what it is." She made an irritable arm gesture. "Listen to that unholy racket, will you? Mr. Lush tinkling the ivories. Only gets one note in five right. The drawing room's here." She shoved open a pair of double doors. "Stay put while I stop that hoo-ha in the other room. You want tea?"

"Yes, please."

"Humph. Thought you looked the tea type. I got muffins, too. Baked 'em fresh last night."

Sam spied a telephone on a stand near the window. She waited until the grumbling maid had departed and hastened over to it.

"Pick it up," she said softly. "Pick it—Aidan? Is that you?"

"I was in the shower." He sounded vexed and maybe just a little relieved. "Where are you?"

"At Stan Hollister's. Didn't you get my note?"

"Yeah, I got it. You little idiot, why didn't you wake me? He could be working with Mary."

"I think he is—and I'm not an idiot."

"You are if you went out there alone."

"Do you sweet-talk all your lovers like this?"

"Only when they go off half-cocked. Where is he?"

"With Connie Grant from 'Who's News.' Don't worry, I'm safe enough for the moment. Thurman Wells is around somewhere and so's his cranky old maid. Can you get over here right away?"

Suspicion thundered in. "I thought you said you were safe."

"I am, but I doubt if I'll be able to get back into his study."

"What…" He forced patience. "Go on."

"He wrote the name Helen Murdoch on his desk blotter. There was a ton of papers on top, but he showed up before I could go through them. I thought you could sneak in and look while I kept him busy."

Aidan sighed, and her mind drew a vivid picture of him, naked and dripping wet, raking his fingers through his long hair and shooting a dagger at the receiver. As hot and cramped as that made her feel, the image also made her grin. She must still be high from their lovemaking.

"Well?" she repeated when he didn't answer.

"All right. Give me forty minutes. Where is it?"

"Bel Air." She gave him the address. "The French doors were open when I was in there but not the front gate. You'll have to…" The rattle of a door handle brought her head around and had her inserting a hasty, "Yes, thanks, Sally. No, I'm sure I'll be finished by lunchtime. Yes, I will, goodbye." She replaced the receiver and turned to smile at a glowering Nellie. "My editor doesn't like delays," she explained simply.

Nellie made an undignified sound. "Neither do movie directors. I should know. I've been slave to one for more 'n forty-five years. Sugar? Milk? Lemon?''

"Milk, please, and one sugar. You've worked for Mr. Hollister all that time?"

"Yup."

"Have you met anyone other than Thurman Wells?"

Nellie regarded her as if she needed a brain transplant. "I guess I've met 'em all over the years. Liked Tyrone and Grace. Pretty thing, she was. Married a prince, you know."

"Yes, it made the news." Sam accepted the teacup and saucer, glanced at the surprisingly appetizing muffins and smiled again. "They look delicious. Tell me, did you ever meet Margaret Truesdale or Mary Lamont?"

"Yes and yes. Liked Margaret, hated Mary. Bran or oatmeal?"

"Oatmeal." Sam paused. "Why did you like Margaret?"

Nellie shrugged. "Just did, is all. She treated everyone the same. Her maid Jenny and me were friends. Jenny used to figure she had the nicest boss in L.A. Maybe she did, though Bob Hope's a real gentleman if you ever have occasion to meet him. Margaret never caterwauled constantly about this, that and the other. Lots of 'em did that, you know."

"Did Mary do that?"

"Mary was a snippy so-and-so, as I told her that more 'n once, straight to her snooty face. Aw, hell, he's at it again. Sit and eat. Mr. H. won't be long."

"Wait a minute," Sam called to the woman's departing back. "Do you know someone named Helen Murdoch?"

Nellie didn't break stride. "Never heard of her," she said over her shoulder. Yanking open the door, she shot Sam a stony look. "If you know what's good for you, missy, you've never heard of her, either."

AIDAN WAS IRKED and crotchety, and he knew he'd have to deal with both feelings if he intended to get out of here in one piece. The gate had been a nightmare of barbed wire, spikes and a pressure alarm he'd noticed at the last second. His jeans and olive drab army jacket had matching tears in them; his hair had snagged on a spike and he'd caught his hand on the sharp edge of a wrought-iron spike. This had better be worth the effort.

Someone was singing down the hall as he let himself into the only ground-floor room that boasted a set of French doors.

"Sing a song of sixpence," a man's voice caroled happily. "Thurman wants more rye…"

"Lush ass," a growly voice responded. Aidan had to duck behind the floor-length curtain as a woman in an apron and cap thrust open the door, grabbed a bottle of liquor from a rosewood trolley and stomped out. "Keep your pants on," she shouted. "I'm coming. Only got two legs, you know."

Amusement at the grouchy attitude of a person who could only be Stan Hollister's maid brought a grin to Aidan's lips and wiped away his less charitable thoughts. Blotter, he reminded himself when he was sure she'd gone.

The name had been scrawled in the lower right-hand corner, recently, too, by the look of the ink. He started going through the paperwork, methodically as he'd been trained by his investigative mentor, but faster than he would have liked.

It didn't take long to ascertain that the desktop held nothing of interest. Neither did the mail baskets. Maybe the teak filing cabinet would prove more lucrative.

Sliding open the top drawer, he flipped through the files one by one. Adams, Hallmark, Alcott, Sessoni, Bruhner, Yalta… No order to the names. This was going to take longer than he'd anticipated.

Because he seemed to have lost complete control of it, his mind wandered to Sam. He'd expected to find her beside him when he'd woken up this morning. It had disturbed and annoyed him that she'd been gone.

Her note pinned to the fridge had outlined Hollister's phone call, but had done nothing to ease his mind—about her safety or the unacceptable hold she seemed to be gaining over his heart. He'd needed that ice-cold shower she'd interrupted to clear his head. Unfortunately, all it had done was remove a few cobwebs. Domina's malice no longer haunted his every waking thought; Sam did that now, and in a fashion that simultaneously annoyed and terrified him. God help them both if he'd fallen in love with her.

The top drawer contained no file on Helen Murdoch. He moved onto the second and finally the third. Sunshine streamed through the windows, flooding the room with golden light and causing perspiration to form on Aidan's forehead and neck. Once, a painfully thin man wearing overalls and a billed cap walked past outside the window, but he kept his hands stuffed in his pockets and didn't glance in the direction of the study.

Damn Sam and her impulsive dead-end clue. If Stan had any knowledge of Mary's whereabouts, he'd hidden it too cleverly for Aidan to unearth.

He persevered through a series of initialled files: D.V., L.R., T.W., S.F., A.P., N.J.

A light of recognition flickered in Aidan's head. A.P.? As in Anthea Pennant perhaps?

He extracted the file and opened it. The first thing to topple out was a picture of Anthea from *The Three Fates*. It was followed by other pictures from different movies. Margaret and Mary appeared in only one of them. A clump of newspaper clippings dropped onto the carpet. Among those, Aidan's sharp eyes picked out the name Dorian Hart.

He studied the yellowed photo. Anthea was there; so was Margaret, far in the background. They each held the arm of a distinguished-looking man who must have been Margaret's husband, Frank Durwald. The year on the clipping was nineteen fifty-three. The caption read, "In Questionable Company. Dorian Hart Dines with a Gathering of Hollywood Stars. See page two for details."

Naturally, there was no page two. But there was a woman on the gangster's arm. Aidan studied her more closely. In her prime, and smiling upward, that woman looked suspiciously like Mary Lamont.

SHE KNEW SOMETHING, damn her. Nellie knew something about Helen Murdoch, and she refused to tell Sam what it was.

"Stay out of it, missy" was all she had to say on the subject. "Mr. H. won't appreciate you or anyone opening that can of worms. Got a temper, that man. Not like the lush in there."

The lush. Yes, of course, Thurman Wells. Sam's mind opened itself to a dozen possibilities. People who drank too much frequently said too much, as well. If she could corner Thurman and start him talking, who knew what incriminating tidbits might slip out.

Nellie tromped ahead of her through a tricky maze of corridors. None of them wound past the study. Sam could only hope that Aidan had arrived and snuck in undetected. It didn't cross her mind that he would fail to show. Maybe, she reflected, her faith was a positive sign.

"Where are we going?" she asked Nellie five minutes and several turns later.

"To the sunroom, I thought," the old woman grumbled. "But now that I think again, I remember he mentioned the garages."

A man lurched unexpectedly into her path, startling Sam. However, Nellie merely poked a warning finger at his chest. "I'll bring you more to drink later. Mr. H. is waiting for his guest at the garages."

"Ms. Giancarlo. How delightful." Inebriated or not, Thurman Wells knew how to charm. Straightening, he adjusted his Armani sweater, fiddled briefly with his ascot and gave his cap of silver-white hair a pat. Except for his bloodshot eyes, lopsided grin and slight stagger, he looked almost sober.

Flapping a dismissing hand, he shooed Nellie aside. "Buzz off, and bring me a bottle of Scotch this time. I'll escort Mr. Hollister's guest to the garages. Buzz," he repeated when Nellie didn't budge.

"I'll buzz you, you old coot. Can you walk?"

"Certainly, my good woman. I've done a thousand stage shows more tanked than this."

"Recognizes his flaws anyway," the maid said with a disdainful sniff. "You go straight to the garages, you hear, Mr. Lush? And no Scotch till after lunch."

"Snarly old biddy," Thurman muttered in her wake. "I'd have sacked her years ago. Stan's too soft, always has been."

He offered his arm, and Sam took it. "I left a message for you from Mr. Brodie," she remarked conversationally. "We were hoping to talk to you and everyone else we met at Leo Rockland's reception."

"Everyone except Anthea," he replied mournfully.

"Yes, I was sorry to hear about…" She brought her head around. "Was Anthea at the reception?"

He patted her hand. "In spirit, my dear, not in the flesh. Sadly now, the spirit is all that remains of my lovely lady friend. As you can imagine, we're all of us quite devastated by her death."

All of them? Sam wondered, but held her tongue.

Connie must have left, interview in hand. Sam hadn't seen a camera crew so it had probably been for one of "Who's News'" thirty-second gossip spots.

Stan's tall, broad figure was easy to separate from the rare autos. He closed the hood of a vintage '22 Mercedes and wiped his hands on a rag.

"Why are you here, Thurman?" he asked, scowling. "I came out here specifically to get away from you. This was to be a private conversation."

Thurman made an airy gesture. "Surely you can talk in front of me. I was married to the woman, you know."

"Which woman?"

"Take your pick. Ah!" His keen eyes located a silver flask on the trunk of a Model T inside the garage. He made a beeline for it. "Come along, Stan, fess up to dear Sam. Tell her we think her interest in Margaret Truesdale and Mary Lamont extends beyond the boundaries of research. What we don't know is how far beyond or for what reason. Isn't that right, Stanley?''

Stan glared openly now. "Go away, Thurman."

Thurman regarded the flask. "At a guess," he stated, enunciating each word carefully, "I would say that my good friend Stan has his own agenda. Whatever that may be, the fact remains that you, Samantha, and your British friend popped up out of nowhere asking questions about our three beautiful Fates mere days before one of them was blown away. I for one do not believe in coincidences. You also look damnably familiar to me. You know something, or you're up to something. Which is it, my dear? And please be honest. I may be a pushover, but Stanley here can spot a bogus story a mile away."

Throughout Thurman's spiel, Sam kept her eyes on Stan Hollister's granite-hard face. He'd had a purpose for inviting her to his home, a specific purpose. She also sensed that he had little time for games.

"Were you the father of Margaret Truesdale's child?" she asked so softly that Thurman, busy draining the silver flask, didn't hear.

Stan's formidable dark brows lowered. "And if I were?"

"Then we might have grounds for an in-depth conversation. On the other hand, Mr. Hollister, in our research, Robert and I learned that you were named by Mary Lamont as the father of her child."

To her surprise, he chuckled. "That's never been proven, Ms. Giancarlo, but I must admit I was rather flattered that she did it. I'm also rather surprised by your tenacity. For a researcher, you're quite the little spy. West Valley Hospital records are not easy to obtain."

Sam saw no advantage in lying. "Yes, well, it might interest you to know that Robert and I weren't the only people who wanted them. Do you know a man by the name of Alistair Blue?"

She could almost see the Rolodex in his brain flipping over. "No, I don't." He frowned. "Are you sure about the name?"

"It's the one we were given."

"By whom?"

Deciding it was time to take the proverbial bull by the horns, Sam squared her shoulders and said, "By Mary Lamont's doctor at Oakhaven."

Chapter Thirteen

Whatever reaction she'd expected, it was not the one she received. Stan grasped her roughly by the arm and hauled her into the garage. Thrusting a blearily oblivious Thurman out onto the macadam, he punched the switch to bring down the doors.

"Thurman's right, you do look damnably familiar," he growled. "Who's Brodie, really? More to the point, who are you?"

She wrenched free and stepped away. "I'm who I said I was."

"But not *what* you said you were."

It was a three-car garage. On the shadowy far side, an engine sputtered to life, but Sam was too frightened to investigate, and Stan apparently too angry to notice. She'd done a foolishly impulsive thing. What on earth had prompted her to mention Mary's name?

He stood there breathing like an enraged grizzly. "You're involved in this up to your eyeballs, aren't you? How are you involved? By God, if Mary's doctor—"

"It has nothing to do with her doctor," she lied. "He didn't contact me, I contacted him. She's out, and you know it. You and Thurman Wells and probably Leo Rockland, as well."

If a human could resemble a thundercloud, Stan Hollister

did so at that moment. "Dammit, you're either a reporter as Leo insists, or you're—something else."

She worked her way around the Model T, her eyes glued to his face. "I am a reporter, actually. What kind of something else do you mean?"

He faltered visibly, gave a short cough and seemed to rein in the worst of his anger. "I'm not prepared..." he began, then coughed again and twisted his head to the side. "Who started my Rolls-Royce? Who's there?" When no one answered, he forged a path to the Rolls and yanked on the door handle.

"What's wrong?" Sam asked when he stooped to peer in the driver's window.

"Someone's locked the keys inside."

Belatedly, Sam realized that her vision was beginning to blur. And her lungs hurt. Waving at the bluish exhaust, her fear temporarily set aside, she joined him, tugging on the back door.

Years of smoking took a swift toll on the director's lungs. He rubbed his chest, coughing hard. "The main door," he gasped, but Sam was way ahead of him.

"No good," she called, wiping her tearing eyes with the heel of her hand. She fought hard to combat the panic that poured through her. Her limbs felt rubbery. That was either extreme fear or the carbon monoxide affecting her.

Had Thurman done this? Possibly, but she didn't really believe that.

"Ax," Stan choked, pointing. "It's... Damn!" His fist hit the polished hood.

"Gone?" Sam assumed. She slapped the large door one last frustrated time.

Behind her, Stan sank to the floor. Sam saw him go, and stumbled over. She managed to prevent his head from hitting the hubcap, but had a horrible feeling it might not make a difference in the end. Nevertheless, she was determined to try.

Breathing into her sleeve, she made her way back to the big

door. Not one, but all three were locked tight. "Thurman!" she shouted, coughing. "Thurman, please, open the door!"

"No use..." Stan roused himself to rasp. "Doors are three inches thick...solid oak... Spared no expense..."

Sam spared a great deal of mental expense willing Aidan to hear her. Forget Thurman, concentrate on Aidan, she told herself.

Head bowed, forehead pressed to the thick center door, she murmured his name like a mantra—and prayed one last time for that elusive miracle.

"WHAT THE HELL are you doing here, Blue?"

Furious, Aidan grabbed Alistair's arm and swung him around. He'd spotted Thurman tottering drunkenly through the backyard and had gone out to see what information he could pump from the man. That's when he'd caught sight of Alistair hovering around the garages. He'd also seen the blond man in the cap but he was sauntering toward the rear gate, not skulking as Alistair was.

Aidan had the newspaper photo of Dorian Hart in his jeans' pocket and an unpredictable gleam in his eyes. Alistair shuffled his feet ineffectually on the gritty pavement.

"Talk, Blue," Aidan ordered, shoving him.

Alistair took a staggering step, caught his balance and turned his head from side to side. "I followed your lady friend out here. She...she went into the garage with Hollister. He dragged her in, actually. I—I thought I should see if she was okay."

"Why, Mr. Brodie, as I live and breathe." Thurman Wells gave Aidan a resounding thump across his shoulders. "Not looking so dapper today, are we? Who's this—" he examined Alistair as if he were a bug "—person? A friend of yours?"

"Yes," Alistair said quickly.

"No," Aidan countered. "Where's Sam, Thurman?"

"Haven't got a clue. With Stan, I suppose."

"I'm telling you, they're in the garage," Alistair insisted. "I think we should, uh, look."

The hair on the back of Aidan's neck had been prickling for several minutes now. Unwilling to acknowledge the sensation, yet unable to ignore it any longer, he snarled, "If she's hurt, Blue, you're a dead man."

Thurman tut-tutted and wagged a reproving finger. "Never make threats in public, dear boy. A friend of mine taught me that once. They locked her up for it."

Possibly because Hollister's neighbor had been mowing his lawn, Aidan missed the sound at first. He heard it now when the mower cut out. He probably wouldn't have thought twice about it even so, except for the worried glances Alistair kept sending over his shoulder.

He focused on the distant engine rattle and attempted to identify it. An air conditioner? Pool filter? Those noises wouldn't be coming from the garage. What then? A car?

His blood froze. Alistair had gone decidedly pale. Thurman tossed back a double Scotch and held the glass out to an invisible bartender. "One more hit, Nellie," he slurred. "I can still see her face in my mind. Bet she did it, the old crock. Mean streak in her as long as fifty cobras tied nose to tail. Smart, though, and you'd better believe she knows how to use that mean old mind. Crazy smart people'll drive you around the bend every time, make you crazier than them in the end." He blinked at his empty glass. "I need another shot."

His babble barely registered. Shoving Alistair aside, Aidan followed his instincts and the engine sound to the row of garages. "Sam!" he shouted. "Are you in there?"

Did he hear a tiny cry? He could definitely smell car exhaust. Tendrils of it seeped out from under the doors. Alistair had run over with him. The other man pulled and twisted and finally kicked the stubborn release handles.

"They're stuck," he yelled, his voice half an octave higher than normal. Another kick. "How can all three of them be stuck?"

Aidan's eyes scanned the ground. There was a window on the side but what could he use to break it?

Thurman supplied the answer by bumping into an exposed spare tire. "Stupid protrusions," he muttered. "Idiotic design made by idiotic designers. Now see here, Mr. Brodie," he sputtered as Aidan brushed past. "It's rude to shove your elders."

Aidan ignored him and yanked open the trunk. "Jack," he said, grabbed it and ran back. Holding it like a bat, he smashed the garage window, diamond panes and all.

Exhaust fumes poured out, fogging his vision and making him cough. "Sam?" he called inward. "Sam? Blue, get over here."

Alistair and Thurman appeared together. "Are they there?" the younger man demanded.

"I can't tell. The opening's too small for me to climb through. You'll have to do it."

"But—oh, hell." Saving Aidan the trouble of tossing him inside, Alistair clambered onto a flower box and hoisted himself over the narrow pane.

"Use the tire iron to smash the windshield," Aidan shouted to him.

Ten endless seconds later, the engine stopped. Aidan heard Alistair coughing and banging on the large center door with the iron rod. "Stupid, stupid, stupid," he yelled in time to each bang. "I think I've got it, Brodie. Give the handle a pull."

Aidan did, almost tearing the door and his shoulders from their sockets.

He saw Alistair sidle out and break into a run, but his only concern right then was for Sam. He caught sight of her behind the fender of a Model T, not quite unconscious but well on the way. Hollister was passed out next to the rear tire.

Gathering Sam up in his arms, he carried her outside, past Thurman who was grinning like a bloody idiot. The actor fell with a plop underneath a tall palm tree.

"Put her next to me," he instructed Aidan. "Air's good and clean over here."

"Hold still," Aidan advised when Sam would have sat up. Groggy but as obstinate as ever, she used his hand to lever herself onto her elbows. "You came," she croaked, her tone a blend of smugness and amazement. "I knew you would." Fighting to keep her eyes open, she asked, "Did you find Helen Murdoch?"

Thurman gave a rich hiccup. "Helen Murdoch, you say?" The idiot grin broadened, caricaturizing his distinguished face. "Won't find anyone by that name lurking 'round these parts, my dear. Alas, and to my infinite relief, Helen Murdoch is no more."

"THREE, FOUR, FIVE hundred dollars." Mary counted the bills into the blond man's outstretched hand. He wore no expression on his narrow face. Only his Adam's apple moved and then only when he swallowed. He came and went without a word. She knew he'd done his job. Whether it would have the desired effect or not, it would have rattled their nerves, of that she had no doubt. As for the other matter, she'd hear about that soon enough.

Had she forgotten anything, overlooked anything, neglected to cover any base? Heaven knew, she might have done all those things, but the end result should still be the same. It only required that things proceed to that end, that shining, glorious goal she had established so many years ago.

"You're going to get caught." Tobias's droll remark from the garden doorway surprised her. He stood there in his vest and striped gardener's gloves, holding a spray of yellow and pink gladiolus. She hated yellow and pink. She tolerated Tobias.

"Maybe," she agreed, hobbling over to him at a good clip. "But it'll be after the fact, you can be sure of that."

"I saw that—flunkie—drive away. How much did you pay him, and to do what?"

"Enough, and you'll find out." Her shrewd eyes gleamed wickedly. "I shouldn't think anyone was hurt, if that's worrying you."

"So it had the potential for harm, then, did it? Why?"

"Same reason as before, old friend. To keep you in line and them guessing."

"I think you just enjoy torment."

"That, too. Wouldn't you if you were me? That wretched Margaret Truesdale has tormented me for fifty years now. I deserve to get a little of my own back."

"I'd be careful if I were you—and I've never been out of line."

"Ha!" She hooted with laughter, then immediately sobered. "Why would you be careful?"

"No reason."

Yes there was, but he hadn't meant to mention it. Did he think Mr. Adam's Apple might run to Stan with his story? For five hundred big ones, he'd better not. Dammit all, she would not be double-crossed by a brainless dolt.

Scuttling into the hall, she took a gray raincoat from the brass rack. Tobias sounded highly mistrustful and vaguely horrified when he said, "Where are you going?"

She gave him a complacent smile. "Out."

"Out where?"

"To send a package. Special delivery this time." She tapped a box wrapped in brown paper on the entry table. "Don't worry," she said, chuckling throatily at his anxious look. "It won't explode. I want a local postmark on the thing this time, that's all. I want them to know just how close I am. It'll make them sweat."

"I'm sure they're doing plenty of that already. Why don't you…"

"Let it go?" she finished wickedly. With her cane, she reached out and knocked the heads off the flowers. "How often in our very long association have you known me to let anything go?" The question required no answer, so she went on. "Oh, no, Tobias. I've been waiting for this, plotting and planning for this, for more than fifty years. I'll see that woman dead, and not you or anyone else is going to stop me. All I have to do is keep everyone off balance and my ass covered till the scene is as I want it. Then, bam, I'll close in for the kill and the curtain will come down for the last time on Margaret Truesdale's life."

Going slowly to one knee, Tobias began gathering up the bruised petals. Point made, Mary decided. Scooping up the package, she opened the door, checked left, then right, and scurried to the garage and her fully gassed Legacy. She had two errands to run. The first was to set up delivery of the package. The second was to see a man about a car.

Grinning at the irony of that thought, she gunned the engine and took off in a most fitting roar of exhaust.

"I SAW A MAN," Thurman trilled thirty minutes later inside the house. "He had dirty blond hair and a face like a weasel."

"Did his Adam's apple stick out?" Sam accepted the tea Nellie thrust at her and handed it to Aidan.

"I really couldn't say, my dear. Possibly. Nellie, I said Scotch. What is this godawful green slime?"

"Shut up and drink," Stan ordered querulously. "The man Thurman saw is Randy Paliss. He comes around twice a week to weed the garden. He's not the brightest person in the world but he's no killer."

"Does he like money?" Aidan asked. His discreet fingers around Sam's wrist took her pulse. He'd wanted to call an ambulance, but everyone, and Sam most of all, had negated the idea.

"We're fine," she'd insisted. "Aren't we fine, Mr. Hollister?"

"Stan. And yes, we are—no thanks to whoever started that damned car and locked us in."

"It was Alistair," Sam declared staunchly.

Aidan didn't think so, though he couldn't have said why.

God knew, the man's track record was poor, and he'd been hanging around, which gave him plenty of opportunity. But he'd also been adamant about looking for them in the garage.

"Don't you see, though?" Sam had challenged when Aidan argued the point. "If he was so anxious for you to search the garage, it means he knew we were in some kind of danger. And how could he know that if he didn't cause the situation? Anyway, what was he doing there if he wasn't gassing us?"

"Eavesdropping?" Aidan suggested.

"To what end?" The hint of a pout in her voice enchanted him. "He can only be working for Mary, Aidan. Mary knows where Margaret is, and Mary does not want to be stopped. Mary's behind all of the things that have happened to us, and Alistair's her pawn. It's simple logic."

"Nothing's simple as far as I can see." Stan was still rubbing his chest. "Mary, Margaret—I thought that nightmare ended years ago."

Since Sam's pulse felt fine, Aidan settled for stroking the inside of her wrist with his thumb. "Are you saying that you didn't know Mary had escaped from Oakhaven?"

"Of course I knew. We all knew. Thurman found out and came running to tell us."

"I wanted someone else to know," the actor defended. He waited until Nellie marched out, then pushed himself upright and wobbled over to the teak liquor trolley. "I bore that burden alone for years. Finally I thought to myself, Why should I be the only one enduring this hell? Stan knocked her up, he should have some part in it. Not that any of them wanted to do a blessed thing to help the woman, but I figured they could at least go and visit the odd time."

"It sounds like you still love her a little," Sam observed, sliding closer to Aidan on the sofa.

Thurman smiled, a melancholy, fatalistic smile. "No, my dear, I don't love her at all. Never did. That's why I feel so guilty."

It made sense to Aidan. "So everything you've done for her, you've done out of guilt."

"It's a nasty emotion," Thurman agreed, pouring himself a tall glass of bourbon. "It'll eat you up if you let it."

"Tell me about it," Aidan murmured.

Stan thrust himself forward in the leather chair. "No, you tell us about it. Who are you, really, and what do you want with Mary?"

At Sam's subtle caution, Aidan shrugged. "Sam's a reporter and I'm an insurance investigator. Mary's doctor asked us to locate her as a favor to him. Simple as that." Before Stan could begin a lengthy cross-examination, he shifted his attention back to Thurman. "What did you mean earlier when you said that Helen Murdoch is no more?"

Thurman blinked. "Did I say that? Can't imagine why. I've never heard of the woman."

"You certainly have," Sam said to Stan. "I saw her name on your blotter."

Grim-faced, Stan stood. "I have nothing further to say on the subject. I asked you to come here today because I had—and still have—a nagging suspicion about you. Not you, Brodie." He pointed at Sam. "Her. Unfortunately, at this juncture, we seem to be exchanging only ill-concealed barbs and pointless half-truths. I want time to think this through. That's my way."

"And a ponderous one it is at that." Thurman raised a cheerful toast to him. "Sorry to interrupt, but while I'm still semicoherent, ditto for me on the information exchange thing. Excuse my bluntness, but whatever we on this side might suspect, we don't in fact know either of you from Adam. I suggest we end this little tête-à-tête and indulge in some serious solo thinking."

"One question," Sam said to Stan. "Did you ever have an affair with Margaret Truesdale?"

His eyes shot to her face, then seemed to soften slightly.

"Yes," he said, bowing his head, "I did. And to answer your next question, I loved her very much."

"Did you love Mary?"

"No, and she didn't love me, either. If she tells you we cared for each other, it's a bald-faced lie."

"We've had no contact with Mary Lamont," Aidan reminded them.

"You've also lied to us in the past." Stan stood, drew a deep cleansing breath and bellowed for Nellie. "Give me time to think this through again. There are too many forces at work for me to offer my blind trust to anyone right now."

Aidan could accept that. Sam didn't want to, but she knew better than most how to be gracious in defeat.

"I wish things weren't so complicated. It's hard to straighten out so many tangles," she sighed to him as they walked across the driveway. "At least Stan agreed to keep my car for me overnight." A weary smile touched her lips. "Mind if I hitch a ride, Brodie? I still feel the tiniest bit woozy."

Aidan resisted a fiercer urge to take her in his arms. If they went back to his place and made love as his mind and body longed to do, who knew what clues might slip through their fingers. Mary was entirely too dangerous at this stage. She wanted to kill Margaret and apparently no roadblocks, human or non, were going to stand in her way.

In the Jeep, Sam turned to regard him. "It was Alistair who locked us in and started the car, you know. It had to have been him. Who else was there?"

"Randy Paliss." Aidan removed a square of folded paper from his jacket pocket. "Hollister gave me his address."

Sam closed her eyes. "Oh, no, Aidan, tell me we're not. What could Stan's handyman know that we already don't?"

"Any number of things—including who masterminded today's debacle. Who did it," he repeated with absolutely no emotion in his voice, "and where she is right now."

"Is that you, Linnie?" Randy Paliss stuck a six-pack in his stained white fridge, swatted a fly and scratched. "Linnie?"

he called again. "Damned woman." He raised his voice. "All right, fine, don't answer me. You don't answer, and maybe I won't share." He tossed a biscuit to his dog and carried on, garrulous now that he'd traded Bel Air for the more familiar turf of his native East L.A. "You remember that old lady I told you about? The weird old bat who cornered me the other day and told me to stick close to Hollister's house and keep an eye peeled for a certain pretty female? Well, the pretty female showed today. I made five hundred bucks, and all I had to do was close a door and start a car. Hey, Linnie, you listening or what?"

He heard a click in the doorway and, grabbing another dog biscuit, turned. "Your ears plugged or something?" A confused frown wrinkled his thin forehead until he realized that the woman before him was not only not Linnie, but that she was also carrying a gun in her hand.

She smiled broadly at him. "Sorry to barge in, Ace, but the weird old bat almost made a very stupid mistake."

"Hey, wait a minute." Randy backed away, palms up.

"Give the dog a biscuit, Randy, and put him outside."

"Yes, ma'am. You...you can have the money back—"

"I don't care about the money. It's your mouth that concerns me. Stan always did hire poor domestic help. He's a Mickey Mouser, at home and at the studio. Do you know I strolled right into his studio office and not a single soul saw fit to stop me? And there it was, large as life on his desk calendar. 'Call Giancarlo for meeting.'" She took a menacing step closer on the dirty linoleum. "That's when I hired you, Randy, and why. I paid you good money, too. But money doesn't shut mouths anymore, I'm sorry to say."

His Adam's apple went up then down. Sweat beads popped out on his forehead and chest. "I won't talk," he promised. "You don't need to worry about that."

"You were talking a blue streak to Linnie when I got here, and Sam's pretty. Maybe your hormones would tell her something your brain wouldn't. I take risks, Randy. I don't take dumb chances.'' Her smile broadened, lending an eerie, glazed glow to her hazel eyes. Cocking the gun, she chortled, ''Just wait till Tobias hears about this. He was the one who got me thinking. And now here I am, all thought through and itching to use my favorite prop again. Tobias would give his right arm to know where I keep this little beauty stashed.'' She waved the gun, then tipped her head consideringly to the side. ''Would you give your right arm for anything, Randy?'' She steadied the barrel.

Randy went stiff as a board and whiter than the door of his fridge. He had to move. Why couldn't he move?

Teeth bared, she squeezed the trigger. He felt an explosion in his chest, and then pain, waves of fiery hot pain radiating outward from his rib cage. Stunned, he dropped to his knees, and from there facedown onto the floor.

Blackness spiraled in. ''Oh, dear,'' he heard the old woman sigh. ''I seem to have missed his arm completely....''

Chapter Fourteen

"It was awful, Margaret." Sam stood stone-faced at the open French doors and stared out over a sea of flower beds and neatly pruned shrubs. "When we got to the guy's place, his girlfriend was kneeling over the body, crying and shaking his shoulders. She wanted him to wake up."

Margaret made a clucking sound, lit a cigarette and shaded her red-rimmed eyes. "That's dreadful, Sam. No wonder you're so upset. To see a man lying in a pool of his own blood. Where did you say he was shot?"

Sam's gaze moved slowly back to her. "I didn't—say he was shot, I mean. How did you know?"

Margaret moved a negligent shoulder. "It's Mary's style. Look at what happened to Anthea. Mary's always had a penchant for guns. That was one of the reasons she clashed with the writers on *The Three Fates*. She wanted to go after her sister with a .38. They wanted her to use a knife."

Diverted, Sam said, "I thought they were witches. Shouldn't it have been a battle of wills?"

"It would have been, ultimately. To be honest, I'm rather glad we never shot the final scene. I flatter myself that I could have pulled it off. I'm not sure about her."

Sam tried to ignore the twist of—something—in her stomach. Not dislike exactly. Closer to disgust, but that was a terrible feeling to have for one's flesh and blood, especially when that person had done nothing really to arouse it.

Must be an aftereffect of the carbon monoxide, she decided, massaging the back of her neck.

"Where's Aidan?" Margaret inquired as Theo arrived with a tray of coffee and marzipan cakes.

"Still at Randy Paliss's place, I imagine. I took a taxi here. I didn't want to be there with police swarming all around searching for clues."

"Did you tell them about Mary?"

Sam was in no fit state to be tactful. "We had to. She's very likely the one who did it."

Margaret puffed. "You needn't sound so antagonistic, Samantha, it was a fair question. And you're absolutely right. The events of the day as you've described them would lead me to the same conclusion. Mary's always been thorough. A loose end like Mr. Paliss would have cast a pall over her deviant brilliance."

"You sound as though you admire her."

"Good Lord." Margaret pressed a hand to her breastbone, choking on the smoke. "I didn't mean to suggest that. But you must understand, I don't feel toward Mary the same way she feels toward me. That may sound wishy-washy, and possibly it is, but it's also the truth. At any rate—" another deep drag "—Mary's not entirely to blame in this. I could have been nicer at times. When we had our babies for instance. She suffered a terrible loss when her child was stillborn. I think it was the beginning of her troubles. She named Stan as the father, but I doubt it was him."

"Who then?"

"I have no idea. Not with a man who loved me, that's for sure."

"You think Stan loved you?"

Margaret laughed. "Well, no, I don't think he did actually. What I should have said is that the father of Mary's baby would not have been a man who'd been with me first. She would have wanted her own man, if you know what I mean."

Sam wasn't sure she did right then. Her head hurt to the point of nausea. She felt tired and uncharacteristically despondent. She wanted to go home, brew a pot of tea, turn on an old movie, preferably not a Margaret Truesdale, Mary Lamont feature, and curl up in bed. She wanted Aidan to be part of that scene, but he was dealing with other less pleasant matters, specifically the police and Randy Paliss's girlfriend. He might not be feeling very sociable later.

Thinking of Aidan reminded her of something he'd given her. "I found it in a file at Hollister's," he'd told her before she'd left Randy Paliss's East L.A. home. "See if Margaret knows anything about it."

Shivering as the ghostly image of Stan's handyman lying on a bloodstained linoleum floor swam through her head, Sam retrieved the newspaper clipping from her purse and handed it to Margaret. Even swathed in the shadows of the hearth, she saw the old woman's hand tremble as she passed bony fingers over the subjects' faces.

"Is that Frank Durwald standing between Anthea and Margaret?" Sam pointed. "And is that Mary with Dorian Hart?"

"Yes, that's Frank—and Mary, too." She heaved a gusty sigh and reached for a fresh cigarette. Sam, who didn't care for smoke, moved circumspectly away. "I remember that night very well. I'm not sure why. Possibly because it was the first time I met Dorian Hart."

"Had Frank—your husband—met him before?"

"Briefly. I believe Mary introduced them. She'd known Dorian for quite some time, or so the story goes."

"Did she also know that Frank had a problem with gambling?"

Margaret's eyes rose sharply. "What are you saying? That she engineered the meeting?"

"She was a jealous woman, wasn't she? And vindictive and petty and low and—"

"Are you trying to make a point, Sam?"

"If she knew about Frank's gambling addiction, she might have wanted to get him involved with a loan shark like Dorian Hart, knowing full well he'd eventually wind up in over his head. Then she'd have her revenge on Frank Durwald for choosing you over her and on you for all the roles she believed you'd stolen from her over the years."

To Sam's surprise, Margaret chuckled. "What a crafty mind you have, child. I begin to wonder if you might not be Mary's granddaughter instead of mine. Oh, now, don't be insulted. I meant it as a compliment. Mary never did believe her daughter died, you know. The bane of my existence has always been linear thinking. Mary is infinitely more creative than me. You could be right, you certainly could. Frank borrowed a large sum of money from Dorian, and it would seem from Dorian's interest in Anthea that he would like very much to locate me, or rather Frank through me."

Sam's head more than hurt now; it throbbed. She wasn't sure about Margaret's comments. She was even less sure about Margaret.

'Don't be insulted,' Margaret had said when she'd suggested that Sam possessed some of Mary's less-than-desirable personality traits. Sam realized now, and with a faint jolt of surprise, that the prospect didn't particularly disturb her. Then again, why should it? Babies given to the wrong parents had never been a big problem in the U.S. A busy midcity hospital might make such a mistake, but not the quietly overstaffed West Valley Hospital. She was being too sensitive. She needed to distance herself from this nightmare for a while.

"Two people dead in two days," she murmured. "I need a break. Anthea's funeral is the day after tomorrow." She glanced at Margaret's covered legs. "I know you can't go, and shouldn't, but maybe Theo could attend in your place. Incognito, of course. Would anyone there recognize him?"

Margaret tapped an ash into a crystal bowl. "Everyone who knew me also knew him. But a disguise might work. Possibly,

I might even—ah, but no, Mary would be expecting that, wouldn't she? And she seems to be in a killing frame of mind.''

"I'm surprised she hasn't tried harder to—uh, well—to get you."

"Torment," Margaret said simply. "The woman thrives on it."

"So to torment you, she's setting her sights on everyone else first? Why? Because you have a conscience?"

"Does that sound so out of character for her?" Margaret's dark eyes were shrewd as they regarded Sam's face.

Sam made a small movement with her shoulder. "Not really. I'm sure she knows who I am. I suppose she'd think it would hurt you if she murdered me. What I can't figure out is why she sent us those two video clips from *The Three Fates.*"

Margaret's lips thinned. "More torment would be my guess."

"I thought more likely a warning of some sort."

"What kind of warning?" Margaret snapped, then collected herself and passed a weary hand over her eyes. "I'm sorry, child. My nerves are frayed. Mary feels very close to me these days. I can't seem to shed the notion that she's cognizant of my every move."

"You're not implying that Theo or one of us—"

"No, no, nothing like that. Please, ignore my outbursts. I'm upset, and when I get upset I don't think properly. I wouldn't take those clips of *The Three Fates* as a warning, however. A foreboding shadow perhaps, but not a warning."

Sam noticed then that Margaret's knuckles had gone white in her lap. Her fists were clenched into tight little balls, but whether from tension or anger, Sam couldn't say. What she could say was goodbye, and she did so as quickly as possible.

Solemn-faced, Theo removed her jacket from its peg and helped her into it.

"Shall I call a cab, miss?"

"Please…. I still think those clips are a warning," she mumbled to herself. "Theo?"

"Yes, miss?"

"What do you think Mary will do? You knew her, didn't you?"

"I knew her very well." He dialed as he spoke. "I think Madame is right, that she will do her utmost to achieve her goal. I also think that if I were you, I would distance myself from any possible association with her."

Softly, Sam asked, "Why doesn't she just do it? Surely she's tormented Margaret long enough. Why wait?"

"Theo!" Margaret called from the parlor.

"One moment, Madame." Theo ordered the cab, then turned back. "What you fail to comprehend, miss, is the criminally insane mind. Mary is a bold, calculating woman for whom the term 'half measures' has no meaning. She will undertake to kill her old adversary, make no mistake about it. You and I can only do our best to ensure that tragedy never comes about. If you're looking for a warning, that's the one I would give you. Separate yourself from this situation while you still can."

"But she knows where Margaret lives."

Theo raised meaningful brows. "She knows where you live, too, Ms. Giancarlo. You and Mr. Brodie."

"WHAT'S THAT?" Sam stared at the trinket-size object in Aidan's palm.

"A transmitter. I found it on the back of your ficus pot."

"My home's been bugged." Her tone was flat. "Your phone and my home—my potted plant that Aunt Adele gave me as a housewarming gift. That conniving bitch put a listening device in my living room."

The slow rage that started in her stomach burned its way upward into her chest. Her breathing grew slower, deeper, more controlled. Walking over to the him, Sam fixed the device with a cutting glare. "I'm going to catch her, Aidan. Do you hear me, Mary? You won't get away with this."

Aidan seemed to understand that this was not a good time to touch her. He watched her mutinous face for a moment, then placed the bug in her hand. "Crush it," he said simply.

"What?"

"Put it on the floor and smash it with your foot. Or a hammer, or whatever you like. Then go into the bedroom and throw some clothes in a bag. I want you to come back to my place for the night."

"You're all romance, Brodie. Why your place?"

"This has nothing to do with romance. I have better locks than you do, and Theo's right. Mary knows where we live. She's also killed two people. The police are on her trail now. She'll have to move fast to accomplish her goal."

Sam longed to scream. Instead she did as Aidan suggested, took the transmitter onto the porch and whacked it with her baseball bat. The crunch brought a satisfied smile to her lips. It did not erase the frustration she'd been feeling since her visit to Margaret's place from her mind.

Aidan had a point; the police were involved now. Mary might be clever, but her luck couldn't hold out forever. What baffled Sam was that Mary did know where Margaret lived. Why didn't she simply drive over and kill her?

When she put the question to Aidan, he shrugged. "Mental anguish, maybe? An eye for an eye?"

Sam stuck her bat in the closet and headed for the bedroom. Dragging an overnight bag from the shelf, she started pulling open drawers. "That was Margaret's theory, but wouldn't you think Mary'd have had her fill by now? I mean, how much torment can a person inflict and still enjoy it? Not to mention the fact that she's pushing her luck to the breaking point. Unless…" She paused halfway between the dresser and the bed. "Unless Dorian Hart's offering her protection. But that doesn't make sense, does it? If he was helping Mary, he'd expect a favor in return. That is to say, he'd want Frank Dur-

wald's current address. Since Mary could send him straight to
Margaret's door, and he must know that, he'd have had no
need to bug whichever one of us he bugged then send his
grandson out to Anthea's place. Am I making sense here, Brodie?''

"Marginally."

She tossed a dusty pink T-shirt, a white lace bra and matching briefs into the case. "Well, I still think it's odd."

"You think the behavior of a crazy person is odd?"

"You said Thurman called her a smart crazy person. Revenge is her passion, Aidan, her single motivating factor. She
might take a few calculated risks, but I can't see her being
sloppy. Or negligent, either, for that matter." She added a silk
tea rose robe and slammed the lid down. "Who do you think
bugged whom?"

Before she could mangle the locks, Aidan took the suitcase
from her and snapped them in place. "I don't know, Sam, but
one thing I am sure of, my place is more secure than this one."

"Wait a minute." She stopped him. "I have to get Koko.
I'll drop her off at Miss Busby's for the night. And don't be
so smug, Brodie. Your phone's had a problem or two itself as
I recall."

Curling his fingers around her arm, he handed her the birdcage and propelled her toward the door. "Past tense, Sam.
We'll be safe at my apartment."

"What did you do, have a security system installed?"

"In a sense. I dusted off my grandfather's elephant gun—
and loaded both barrels."

ALISTAIR BLUE STOOD shivering outside Sam's apartment. It
wasn't cold; his shaking came from the inside. Dammit, he'd
relished the idea of rough stuff at the start, when he'd thought
it would be up to him to provide it. He hadn't counted on the
direct involvement of a lunatic.

He'd rather be anywhere at this point than here. Home
watching Esther Williams splash around in some ball game

musical with Gene Kelly and Frank Sinatra would be good. This Spy-on-Sam-and-Brodie game was for the birds. If only he hadn't been caught doing those stupid burglaries last year. If only the wrong person hadn't learned about them.

Grinding his teeth, he shrank further into the shadows. Sam's front door had opened. She and Brodie were leaving, really leaving, he realized, swearing at the prospect of a positional change. Muttering to himself, he started for his car.

He hadn't taken a full step when he spied her. He assumed it must be a woman since the black rain cloak where it ended displayed a pair of black tights and sensible shoes. The raised hood allowed no glimpse of her face, but he could visualize the features beneath it, and the image made him feel queasy from crotch to throat. Mary Lamont, in the flesh, and staring. He did not, absolutely did not want to bump into that woman. Not for love, money or threats.

A statue in the darkness, he watched her watch Sam and Aidan as they descended to the street. Silver lamplight gilded the stone stairs and, oddly, the woman in black, as well. Had she moved a muscle? Alistair wondered. His palms grew as clammy as his mouth was dry. Why didn't she just pop them and get it over with?

He didn't realize he'd been holding his breath until Sam and Aidan climbed into his Jeep and left. Then, finally, the woman stirred. Head bowed, cloak clutched tightly around her shoulders, she shuffled away. To where, Alistair didn't know and wasn't the least bit interested in determining. He simply wanted this nightmare finished, the threats hanging over his head put to rest. He was tired of seeing death firsthand. Assuming he survived, he was going to move to Arizona, raise chickens, make clay pots and maybe even resort to weaving straw baskets.

He regarded the woman's retreating form, thought of the handyman at Stan Hollister's who'd been blown away that very afternoon and shuddered right down to his toes. The words became a litany in his head. Assuming he survived.

In the end, he wondered forlornly how many of them actually would.

"THANKS, GUIDO," Sam said into Aidan's cordless phone. "Yes, I'll be careful, I promise. Him, too. Good night." She clicked off, squared her slender shoulders and turned. Marilyn was boop-boop-ee-doing in Billy Wilder's *Some Like It Hot*; the lights were low, and Aidan was pouring hot cocoa from a white carafe. How could those three things smack of romantic ambience? Sam masked a smile.

"Is he okay?" Aidan asked while she wandered about studying the general chaos of the place.

"Fine. Safe. Where's your elephant gun?"

"In the bedroom closet."

She stopped. "You mean you really have one?"

"She's a murderer, Sam. She may be old, but she's no less fatal because of it."

Was there a pun in that wry remark? Sam accepted the cocoa he offered and sank to the carpet in front of the sofa. The smile she could no longer hold back swept across her lips at the sight of Jack Lemmon in drag. He was not a pretty woman. Hilarious but definitely not pretty.

"I asked Guido again about Helen Murdoch," she told him. "He says it's like looking for a needle in a haystack, but he'll keep plugging away."

"That's it for tonight then."

"Is it, Brodie?"

His dark green eyes gave nothing away. "Did you have something else in mind?"

Tension drained from her like floodwater through an open gate. In its wake came a fiery rush of desire. "As a matter of fact," she said, "I do."

Flattening her palm against his chest, she let it slide downward, with just enough pressure to feel every ripple of bone and muscle in his torso. She heard his breath hitch and the groan he tried to suppress deep in his throat.

"Witch," he breathed, bringing his mouth slowly toward hers.

Her hand found the throbbing hard center of him and closed snugly over it. She nipped teasingly at the sides of his mobile mouth. "Well, you know what they say, Brodie," she murmured, sliding herself onto his lap.

His hands circled her waist, moving higher until his thumbs grazed the painfully sensitive nipples. Even through dress and camisole the sensation rocked her. "What do they say, Sam?"

She made a muffled sound of excitement and let out a quick breath. "Like grandmother like granddaughter."

"Uh-huh." Now it was his lips that teased hers. "I think I like the other one better."

"What other one?"

He breathed amusement and fevered desire into her mouth. "Play it, Sam. Play it for me."

LEO ROCKLAND didn't know what his old comrade was talking about. That isn't to say he hadn't known once. He just didn't remember things as well as he used to anymore.

"Think, Leo," Stan commanded. "I knew how to contact Anthea. You must know how to contact, er—" he paused as Leo's housekeeper entered the room "—Helen Murdoch."

Leo blinked. "Helen Murdoch? Yes, I should know, shouldn't I? Don't remember, though."

Stan closed tolerant eyes. "Do you have it written down anywhere?"

"You asked me that this morning on the telephone. I told you I didn't. It's too risky."

"Does Freddie know?"

"Who?"

"Freddie. Your wife, for... Look, Leo, this is important. Anthea's dead, and so's my handyman. The police might not think I'm directly involved, but they're giving me some very strange sideways looks. Go through your files or your safe or whatever other hiding places you've got. You must have an address to go with the name. I want it."

"Here, here," said a voice from the door.

Stan swore. Leo beamed. "Thurman! How wonderful. Sit. Have a drink."

"We were just talking about your wife," Stan put in.

"Ex-wife," Thurman returned, smiling woozily as he doffed his light raincoat. "I'll have sherry," he said to the housekeeper.

"Helen Murdoch, Leo," Stan said again. "Address."

Leo pictured two faces, two beautiful faces. One emerged over the other, dark eyes flashing fire. He chuckled aloud. "My favorite Fate."

Thurman tottered through his line of vision. "Freddie says he's been fuzzier than usual these past few days," he stage whispered. "Keeps calling her Zelda."

"Better than Mary, I suppose."

"Maybe we should have a discreet look around."

"Can you stand upright long enough to do it?"

"If it'll give us Helen Murdoch's address—or whatever she's calling herself these days—I'll make a special point."

Leo jumped slightly as a pair of soft, capable hands descended onto his shoulders. "He burned it," Freddie said quietly from behind.

Stan glared at her. Leo wasn't sure he understood why. Something to do with Helen Murdoch, but he kept forgetting how he knew that name.

"*He* burned it?" Stan challenged Freddie. "Or you did?"

"He's not well," Freddie said, her tone patient. "I'm handling his affairs now. I handled that one, as well, as it happens, but I promise you, it was Leo who did the burning. He's out of it now. So am I. If you take my advice, you'll follow suit. Let Margaret deal with the problem. She's not the helpless female you believe."

Thurman downed a glass of sherry. Amazing, Leo marveled.

"Mary'll kill her," the actor predicted with a hiccup. "And her granddaughter, too. Did you know that Samantha Giancarlo, the stunner we met at your reception, is in fact Margaret's only kith and kin? After Leo's reception I hired a detective to do a little detecting. Tracing these things isn't as difficult as one might think."

Freddie, perched now on the arm of Leo's chair, smiled grimly. "I knew," she said. "Even before I was told, I knew."

Thurman fell heavily into the nearest chair. "Ah, well, maybe it's best to let sleeping dogs lie at that. I told them that Helen Murdoch is no more. Maybe Leo's made that the truth by burning her address and phone number. I don't know about Stanley, but I'm heartily sick of this whole ghastly business."

"That's because it's no longer your concern," Freddie said flatly. She stood, taking Leo's hand in both of hers. "Let it go, all of you. Let the main players take the stage. I spoke to Samantha earlier. She says she and her friend Mr. Brodie have a plan. She wants all of us to be present at Anthea's funeral."

"We intend to be." Thurman sounded miffed.

Leo squeezed Freddie's hand and tried to think. Why had he burned Helen Murdoch's papers? Because Freddie had said she was gone, that's why. But she wasn't really gone, was she? She was only hidden better than before.

His brain moved but refused to clear. This should all make sense to him. Maybe it would straighten itself out if he slept on it.

Blinking his bright blue eyes, he looked over at Stan. "Do you think Mary will go to Anthea's funeral?" he mused aloud.

"I think she might. Unfortunately, I think Margaret might go, too."

"In that case," Thurman remarked blurrily, "we'll have to keep the arrangements low key. The media isn't onto us yet—except for Sam, of course, but she won't tell anyone. No publicity, ergo no showdown." He raised his empty glass. "A single equation, wouldn't you say? Simple as death itself."

Chapter Fifteen

"Traitor," Thurman muttered to Sam as the mourners, several score strong, gathered at the private grave site. "We trusted you to be discreet." He flung an agitated arm. "Do you know how many hundreds of looky-loos are huddled outside the cemetery gates? And every one of them has a camera. What if Mary's here? What if Margaret is? What if Mary brought her gun? What if one of us gets caught in the crossfire?"

"Now, now," Guido consoled, patting the actor's arm. "You're prophesying the worst. It's very unlikely that Margaret will show up today. I can't say about Mary, but if her target's not present, why would she suddenly go on a shooting spree? It makes no sense, my friend."

Aidan listened to both men whose voices, beyond a limited range, simply blended in with the murmurings of the crowd. He swept his gaze over dripping umbrellas and black-hatted heads. Most of the people present at the grave site had worked for the studio at one time or another. Guido, whose eye for aged features was better than his or Sam's, had been rattling off names for the past hour, both in the chapel and here. The mob beyond the gates didn't matter. If Mary was going to show up, she'd be in this smaller group.

With Theo's help, they'd managed to keep the location and time of Anthea's funeral a secret from Margaret. She expected the service to begin at four at a site in Beverly Hills. At two-thirty, Anthea's coffin was currently being lowered into a grave near her home north of Santa Barbara, amid a profusion of trees, rolling hills and quiet country roads.

With Guido distracting Thurman, Sam was able to sidle closer to Aidan. She looked incredible in black; sexy, elegant and beautiful. A hint of red in the band of her hat and the handkerchief she'd tucked into her jacket pocket, provided the perfect contrast. She wore a Ralph Lauren skirt suit, a minimum amount of makeup and a worried expression on her face.

Aidan placed a reassuring hand in the small of her back. He would have liked to do a great deal more, but his primary goal was to keep Mary from harming Sam as an alternate act of retribution against Margaret.

"Do you think we did the right thing?" Sam darted a look around the crowded cemetery. "There must be close to a hundred people here, more than half of them women and most of those, old women. I see a dozen possible Marys every time I lift my head."

Moisture began to seep through Aidan's gray-green raincoat. His hair was wet from the drizzle; his mood was deteriorating rapidly. He'd spotted no less than thirty possible Marys so far and that included a number of short men in shadowy hats.

"We had to try something, Sam," he reminded her, his eyes still scanning. "Making Anthea's death and funeral arrangements headline news seemed the best way to flush Mary out. Guido agreed, and there are several police here."

"Who'll scare her off if she sees one of them."

"They're plainclothes, and that isn't what she's looking for. She wants Margaret."

"Or us," she added, aggravatingly logical. At his tightly leashed look, she blew out a tense breath. "Face it, Brodie, we'll do in a pinch. We know she's on to us, and chances are better than even that she knows I'm Margaret's granddaughter. She might be willing to settle for us temporarily."

Despite the gravity of the situation, Aidan's lips twitched.

"You're a born optimist, Sam. There must be Irish in your ancestry at that."

She made a preoccupied sound and raised her camera, complete with telephoto lens, to her eye. "I wonder. I guess that's a man over there by that tree. Can you see him, Aidan?" She offered the camera to him. "He's dressed like Truman Capote. The brim of his hat covers three-quarters of his face."

Aidan watched him for a moment then allowed a small smile to tug on his lips. "It's a guy, all right. He has a skinny mustache and fat sausage fingers. What about that woman on the fringe?"

Sam zeroed in, sighed and shook her head. "No, Guido already made her. She used to be a dancer at the studio. He said she had the same physical look as Margaret and Mary but not a speck of talent above her ankles." She refocused the lens, her tone amused. "Guido can be brutally honest sometimes."

Aidan caught a jerky movement out of the corner of his eye and moved to block Sam from the hand that would have snared her arm.

Stan's eyes, dark and flashing, bored into hers. "How dare you?" he demanded. "We counted on this being a private ceremony, not a media circus. Have you seen the mob out there?"

Sam stood her ground, head high. "We had to do something, you know we did. Mary's going to show. She won't be able to resist a golden opportunity like this."

"What about Margaret?"

"She won't be here," Aidan told him. He grasped the director's arm when he would have reached again for Sam. "Take our word for it, Hollister."

The other man's glare, suspicious at first, became downright accusing. "Do you mean to tell me that you've known where Margaret Truesdale is all along and you haven't said anything? Why, I ought to..."

"Don't try it." Tightening his grip, Aidan forced the man's hand down.

"You're upset," Sam said in a surprisingly gentle tone. "Please don't be. We only want this to end. And the only way to do that is to try and draw Mary out."

Stan's lips thinned. Snatching his arm free, he straightened his cuff. "Perhaps your intentions were good, but I'd say you failed in your attempt. Anthea's been laid to rest. The crowd's dispersing. In a few minutes we'll have gone our separate ways, and all of this ridiculous hoopla—which, I might add, Anthea would not have appreciated—will have been for nothing."

Sam held his glare with a composed one of her own until he'd stalked off to rejoin his party. Then she made a face. "Spoilsport," she muttered. Lifting her camera, she swept it over the crowd. "They're milling, not dispersing. It'll be another ten minutes yet before…"

Aidan made a full sweep of his own before he realized that she'd stopped speaking. He looked and saw that she'd stopped moving, too. The lens of her camera was focused intently on a huge twisted cedar. Low-hanging limbs obscured Aidan's view but only until the person beneath it shifted and he separated her from the darkened hollows of the trunk.

She wore a hat and veil, probably net, but it was sufficient to conceal her features. Her black coat was shapeless, the hand holding her umbrella gloved. The other hand, he noticed, was buried deep in her coat pocket.

"Is it Mary?" he asked, checking the immediate area. People continued to mill about, some weeping, some showing no emotion, all murmuring as they mingled before the grave.

"I'm not sure. She's an older woman. I can see her throat a little. It's wrinkled." She raised troubled eyes briefly to his. "It feels as though she's staring straight at me, Aidan."

The idea sent a ripple of unease down his spine. He shook it off, at the same time shifting her behind him. "She can't possibly see you from there."

"I said I felt it. That doesn't mean she was— Oh, God, no, don't go!" Bringing the camera down, Sam hooked an urgent hand around his wrist. "She's leaving. We have to follow."

Aidan didn't budge. "Why is she leaving?"

"Maybe because she doesn't see Margaret. Hurry up or we'll loose her."

"Sam! Hello, dear." A blond woman Aidan recognized as Leo Rockland's new wife, bussed her cheeks. "Is everything all right?"

Startled, mistrustful and impatient, Sam pulled back. "I'm—fine, Freddie." She managed a polite smile. "I'm afraid, though, that we have to go."

"Yes, of course... Oh, my!" This as Sam in her haste piled into a slenderly built man with narrow features, hazel eyes and black hair that curled over the nape of his neck. He flashed an apologetic smile, hesitated, then turned and walked swiftly away.

"Are you hurt?" Freddie inquired.

"No. I'm sorry, but we really do have to go. Oh, hello, Ms. Mesmyr."

Enough of this, Aidan decided, and cupped a firm hand around Sam's elbow. "Excuse us," he said before Evelyn Mesmyr could respond.

"She looks like a mannequin," Sam muttered out of earshot. "Freddie looks nice, though. I wonder how much she knows or has guessed. I talked to her— Oh, God, Aidan, Mary's getting into a car!"

The car in question being one of a million similar American cars. Something black by Chevrolet. He couldn't see the make or identify the lines from their present angle.

"What is it?" Guido puffed up behind them. "Mary?"

"She's getting away," Sam panted. Then she skidded to a halt on the grass. "Wait a minute." Whipping up her camera, she adjusted the lens. "Four, three, eight, five...LCS. It's a—" She strained and readjusted. "A Cavalier." Raising anticipatory eyes, she said, "They're California plates, Aidan. If we can trace them, we've got her. We'll have Mary Lamont at last.''

"YOU'RE BEING a regular old stick-in-the-mud, Brodie," Sam accused several hours later at her apartment. She tossed the towel she'd been using to dry her hair onto a kitchen chair, glanced first at the stack of waiting mail and then at Guido, who was calmly spooning coffee into Norman Rockwell mugs. "Don't you think he's being a wet blanket?" she demanded.

Guido shrugged. "You're mixing your metaphors, Minx. He's being cautious as we all should be until those plates can be identified. We'll have an answer as soon as your friend at 'Who's News' calls you back. In the meantime you should sit, calm yourself and eat the sandwich I've prepared for you."

Spiced ham and cheese on San Francisco sourdough. Sam sat, planted her elbows on the table and stared at Aidan through the veil of her lashes. This idea of not telling Margaret about the funeral had been his brainchild. They'd talked about her yesterday at length. They'd even touched on Sam's mixed feelings toward the woman. That had been her big confession, that she wasn't sure she liked Margaret and that it was guilt over the lack rather than affection for her natural grandmother that was driving her to find Mary.

Maybe her feelings would change, she reflected, still staring at him. She wasn't so sure about Aidan's. Oh, they'd made love, all right, several times in the past thirty-six hours, but she didn't sense she'd reached him yet on that deepest of emotional levels.

Demons, she thought, closing her eyes and forcing her thoughts onto another track. Everyone had them. She, Aidan, Margaret and especially Mary Lamont. Mary, whom she was certain had been at the cemetery today.

They'd done the right thing by publicizing Anthea's funeral, but they'd gained the animosity of Stan, Thurman and probably Leo Rockland, as well. Freddie seemed to be on their side. As for Evelyn, she'd shown up in a black limo and stood side by side with the black-haired man Sam had barreled into at the cemetery.

"Could be her grandson, I suppose," she mused aloud.

Aidan, who'd been sifting idly through her mail, offered her a faintly amused smile. "Give us a clue, Sam. Whose grandson?"

"The dark-haired man with hazel eyes at the grave site. I bumped into him. He looked familiar."

Guido snorted. "As well he should. That was Jimmy Visey."

"Dorian Hart's grandson?" Sam's insides tightened as if twisted with wire. "What was he doing there?"

Guido placed a heaping platter on the table. "Same as us, I should think, at the bidding of his grandfather. Which would pretty much cement our theory that Frank Durwald never paid Dorian the debt he owed."

Aidan's brows came together. "Would Dorian Hart be the type to take out his frustration on Margaret if he found her?"

Guido pursed his lips. "Possibly. He was a ruthless bastard in his prime."

"Like Mary." Sam reached for the phone. It shrieked, startling her, just as her hand made contact.

Connie's voice, a soothing balm for her nerves, offered a cheerful, "Got your information, kid, no easy feat on a Sunday with my computer throwing a tantrum. The car's plates are registered to Irene and Fred Heiden. Twelve seventy-three Calvero Boulevard. That's just south of Big Tujunga Canyon, isn't it?"

"I think so." Sam wrote the address down and shoved it across the table to Aidan whose attention was fixed on a package wrapped in plain brown paper. Tapping the paper, she got him to look. He in turn pushed the package over to Guido.

"Remember," Connie warned, "I have dibs on your exclusive. Anything more I can do?"

"Not right now. Thanks, Connie. I won't forget this." She

hit Reset, but kept the phone in her hand. "Well?" she demanded when neither man spoke. "We've got an address."

"And two names," Aidan noted out. "Guido?"

He slit the package tape with a butter knife. "Fred Heiden could be the butler, I suppose. Tobias Lallibertie. He and Mary had a strange sort of love-hate relationship, according to the gossip columns of the day. Nothing physical, you understand. He was more her pillar of support. Two names would be more of a smokescreen than one.... Ah, of course," he exclaimed. "I should have guessed from the shape. Another video."

Sam was more interested in checking out the Tujunga Canyon address than in watching a clip from *The Three Fates*. She gave the tape box a cursory glance, started to argue her point then did a puzzled double take. "What's that picture?"

Guido looked baffled, so Sam reached out a finger to turn the box her way. Aidan's chair scraped as he came to peer over her shoulder.

"X's and O's," she murmured. "It must have been sent with the video." She pointed from left to right. "Margaret, Anthea and Mary."

Guido sighed. "She's put an *X* through Anthea and circled Margaret."

Aidan bent closer. "That's Mary who's circled, Guido."

Sam squinted at the less than clear shot. "He's right. It's Mary, Anthea, Margaret, not the other way around. Why would Mary circle herself?"

"Because she killed Anthea?" Guido suggested.

"What, and she's bragging about it?" She flipped the picture over. "The woman's beyond help." Hitting the Phone button, she pressed Margaret's number. Margaret answered halfway through the second ring.

"You said the funeral was at four," she accused before Sam could say hello. "It's six o'clock now. Why did you lie?"

She must have Call Display, Sam decided. "We had to, Margaret. Knowing you, we thought you'd take the risk and insist on coming. Theo in disguise might have been all right, but Mary would have spotted you for sure.''

''You mean she was there?'' Margaret's voice was low and tremulous.

''I think so, but I'm not a hundred percent sure. We've got an address. We're going to check it out now.''

Margaret managed a shaky laugh. ''You know, for a moment there, I actually felt light-headed. Be very, very careful, child, when you go. Where is it? Here in the city?''

''Near Tujunga Canyon.''

''That close?'' Tension crept in. ''What's the address?''

Sam hesitated, then relented. ''Twelve seventy-three Calvera Boulevard. As I said, though, we're not sure it's her. Lots of women were wearing veils at the funeral.'' None but one, however, had stood apart from the crowd then departed like a shot when she realized she'd been observed.

Margaret drew a deep breath. ''It was her, Sam. Whatever your plan, and I'm shrewd enough to know you have one, it seems to have worked. All that remains now is for someone to return her to Oakhaven. Perhaps I should telephone her doctor and make the arrangements.''

''We haven't even established if this Irene Heiden is Mary,'' Sam reminded her. ''After we're sure we'll call in the authorities.''

Margaret released a gusty breath. ''Very well, but I received another music box today. It came special delivery and contained a most disturbing message.''

''A threatening note?''

''Not exactly. The tune in the box was 'Chopin's Funeral March.'''

THURMAN SAT in Leo's library, his head in his hands, his elbows planted on his knees. ''Farewell, Anthea,'' he said dully. ''Farewell peace and tranquility. Mary's on the prowl and I shall sleep no more.''

''Shut up, Thurman,'' Stan ordered. He tried Leo one last

time. "What can it hurt to give us Margaret's assumed name, Leo? Just her damned name."

"Why?" Freddie wanted to know. "Do you want to see her dead? Perhaps you're in league with that monster, Mary. I wouldn't put it past any of you, especially you, Thurman. You've always felt guilty about having her committed after Margaret disappeared. How do we know you don't want to find Margaret again in order to assuage that guilt by helping Mary to have her revenge?"

Thurman, who wasn't as drunk as he'd like to be, glowered at her. "I may feel guilty, Freddie, but not that guilty. Pick on Stan, if you need to sharpen your tongue. He was the father of Mary's child."

Leo caught bitterness in his tone, but disregarded it. Better to remain a silent spectator while his head was reasonably clear and see what developed next.

Stan's dark eyes gleamed, but he quietly snarled, "I was *named* the father of her child. That doesn't make it so."

"Ha!" Thurman pounced. "Are you denying you slept with her?"

"No, I'm denying paternity. The child was not mine."

"Right, and Eskimos live in grass huts. Peddle your bull to the public, Stan, not to me."

"Thurman does have a point," Freddie said softly. "You were with Mary at the time."

Stan's face turned deep crimson. "I was also..."

"What?" Thurman demanded belligerently. "Seeing someone else? Doing threesomes? What?"

"Don't be crude, Thurman," Freddie admonished. "Go on, Stan."

He looked about to explode. Even his ears were scarlet. "I was—impotent." He stood with a jerk, fists clenched. "I'd been with Margaret before that. When she broke it off, I turned to alcohol."

"Nothing unusual in that," Thurman said.

"Shut up. She..." He ran a hand through his hair. "Oh,

hell, I might as well say it. Margaret's child was mine, not Mary's. So you see, I'm hardly likely to be in league with Mary, am I? Thurman, yes. Me, no.''

"Now wait just a minute..." Thurman blustered.

Leo found himself enjoying this. Still, there were such things as priorities, and Sam and Aidan had taken off hell-for-leather after some veiled shadow of a woman today. Something had to be done about that.

With a barely perceptible nod at Freddie, he cleared his throat. "Gentlemen, please," he said. "Let's be civilized and sensible about this. I suspect none of us really knows what's what here. Perhaps we should, all of us, take a little trip.''

"To see whom?" Stan asked, instantly suspicious. "Margaret or Mary?''

Leo knew how to milk a situation. A crafty little smile played on his lips. "To see a woman named Irene Heiden.''

MARY WAS NOT PLEASED. In fact, her mood bordered on enraged. "You conniving bastard," she shouted at Tobias. "You messed with my parcel, didn't you?''

He stared blank-faced. "Messed with it? I don't understand.''

She jumped up to glare at him. "You took part of it out and did something with it.'' When he didn't react, she stomped her aching foot. "Where's my picture? It should be here. It isn't. What did you do with it?''

"Absolutely nothing,'' he told her calmly.

"What else have you screwed up, you impertinent, interfering butler? I'm warning you, Tobias, you'd better be telling me the truth. That picture was intended for Margaret, not Sam. Aha, that got you, didn't it? You didn't think I'd figure out where you sent it, did you? Well, I did. The only thing I don't know is why.''

"I really don't understand—''

"Go away,'' she snapped.

He bowed his head. "As you wish.''

"As I wish," she muttered after him. "As *I* wish, Tobias, not you." She turned abruptly. "It doesn't matter. It changes nothing. It's too late. *He's* too late."

Hobbling into the hall like a gnome on a mission, she grabbed her coat from the rack. Her plan would work. It *had* worked. All that remained was for her to make more corpses.

"Don't worry your head, Anthea." She pulled the door open with a vengeance. "You'll have company in death soon enough. At least four people." She cast a dark look over her shoulder. "Maybe five."

"I DON'T SEE any lights," Sam whispered at Aidan's elbow.

Neither did he, and that worried him. Not because he expected Mary to be lying in wait, but because they didn't know yet if the woman they'd seen today was Mary. But if it was, and she wasn't here, then where might she be? Watching Sam's place where Guido sat surrounded by files, photos and videotapes, or en route to Margaret's where Theo, capable as he was, could scarcely be deemed a one-man army?

On the other hand, if she was here, he'd been a fool to let Sam come. He'd have had to tie and gag her to keep her away, but at least she'd have been safe.

Crouched low, and cursing himself, he mounted the four steps to the porch.

There were only a handful of homes in the secluded area. People here had large yards, built for privacy and no intrusive neighborhood noise.

"The car's gone," Sam noted as he examined the side windows. "They—she must be out."

He cast her an ironic glance. "Which makes it the perfect time for us to break in, I suppose?"

"Don't give me that look, Brodie. The idea crossed your mind, too, or you wouldn't be peeping in windows. Besides, we're harmless enough as burglars go. We'll slip in, look around and if we don't find anything incriminating, slip right back out again. How many B and E victims are that lucky?"

"Knock off the logic flow, Sam," he said, "and point your flashlight at the door."

Darkness had fallen over L.A. early that night, a result of the late autumn season and the rain that continued to pelt them as Aidan battled the stubborn lock. Boots, jeans and leather jackets gave them the look of bikers on a raid and offered little protection from the elements. But the dark colors provided camouflage, which was the real reason Aidan had chosen them.

The lock clicked beneath the darning needle he'd taken from Sam's for this purpose. Twisting the knob, he let the door swing inward.

No claxons screamed, and he doubted if there was a silent alarm on the premises. He saw no evidence of a security system, and even less of the owners' presence. Pausing to let his eyes adjust, he took Sam's hand, darted a guarded look at the street and stepped across the threshold.

The house smelled of apples, perfume and exotic spices. The entry hall was thickly carpeted, the staircase an elegant curve. The walls were adorned with what appeared to be watercolors and limited edition prints.

"It smells like apple pie," Sam remarked. She frowned. "I can't believe she bakes."

"It's probably potpourri." Aidan ran the flashlight beam over the walls. The living room to their left looked as promising as anything.

"Flowers, too," Sam murmured. "Roses, white orchids and lavender. Oh, and a birdcage."

"With a canary in it."

She left his side to wander over to the hearth. "That isn't potpourri, Aidan, it's apple pie... Oh, damn!" He heard a muffled thud on the carpet and swung around.

"It's all right. I knocked over a photograph. Look." She aimed her smaller beam at the gilt frame. "It's an old...well, elderly—woman—the same woman who was in the picture Anthea was holding when she died. Honey brown hair, plump features.'' Her eyes came up, wide and unbelieving. "It *was* Mary at the cemetery, Aidan. Who else would have a framed picture of her on their coffee table?''

It must have been her excitement infecting him coupled with the fact that she jumped up to throw her arms around his neck. Whatever the cause, Aidan was in no fit frame of mind to notice details right then. The background click barely registered. It wasn't until the hall light flared and he heard a woman's raspy, "Who's there?'' that he realized they were no long alone.

Sam went rigid; Aidan uttered a ripe oath. The woman stood in the doorway, a daunting silhouette dressed in layers of black. Without appearing to move, she took a step forward. "Is that you, Sam?'' Suspicion-laced, her voice dropped to a silky-soft level as she said, "I've been waiting for you.''

Chapter Sixteen

Waiting for her?

Sam's vocal cords refused to cooperate. She could only squeeze the front of Aidan's leather jacket in her fists and pray for a miracle. Or maybe a diversion to remove Mary's attention from them long enough that they could—what? Rush her? Duck? Dive out a window?

Since none of those prospects seemed feasible, Sam tugged on Aidan's jacket and whispered frantically, "Tell her, Brodie."

Or should she do it?

"What did you say?" the woman demanded before Aidan could respond.

"Nothing," Sam said quickly. "I was, uh, wondering how you knew my name."

Lame, she thought, flinching. Mary didn't seem to think so, however. She stopped dead center of the broad doorway. Rain streamed down the outer windows, casting mobile ribbons of light over her shapeless body. Sam recalled every suspense film she'd ever watched, held her breath and ordered herself not to panic as the woman placed both hands in her pockets.

"Did you think I wouldn't know you?" she challenged. "What kind of a person do you take me for?"

"I don't..." Sam swallowed.

"Are you alone?" Aidan asked, rescuing the awkward moment.

"For the present. Is that a worry to you?"

As circumspectly as possible, he pried Sam's fingers from his jacket. She resisted because she knew what he planned to do. Fling her down behind the sofa while he launched himself at Mary.

Fat chance, Sam decided, bracing herself. He was helping a good friend out of a bad situation. She was the one related to Mary's enemy. He'd be taking no bullets on her behalf.

"We're not alone, you know," she lied, pure bravado. "Other people will be here soon."

"Yes, I sensed that might be the case. It doesn't concern me anymore. I've grown rather tired of this charade. It has its pleasant aspects, but as one gets older, the drawbacks begin to outweigh them."

"You have a remarkably cool attitude," Aidan commented. He tried to thrust Sam away but she wouldn't let him.

"Not really." Another step brought the woman to the edge of the sunken living room. "I spend a great deal of time questioning my past, or I should say, certain decisions in my past."

Because he was stronger, Aidan was able to disengage himself from Sam's grip, which had shifted to the bottom of his jacket. Not that that would have deterred her under normal circumstances, but in the pearly shower of light from the entry hall, her sharp eyes picked out a collection of miniature pewter frames, haphazardly strewn about the mantel. The first one contained a photo of a man. Frank Durwald to be precise, much as he'd looked in the newspaper clipping Aidan had found among Stan Hollister's files.

Why Frank Durwald? Sam wondered, edging toward the hearth. Thurman Wells she could understand and maybe Margaret at the height of her career. But Margaret with her first visible wrinkles? And Margaret again, posing with Frank ten or more years after they'd dropped out of sight? That made no sense... Or did it?

Tendrils of nausea began to curl in Sam's stomach. Did her instincts recognize something her brain refused to accept?

Feeling muddy and oddly heavy-limbed, she continued along the mantel. Aidan murmured something. The subtle roar of blood in her ears prevented her from hearing it.

She saw Anthea next, alone in one shot and then with Frank Durwald. Anthea's arms circled Frank's waist. Wrinkles fanned out from her eyes. A spear of light shone directly on that picture, making it clearer than its neighbors. Anthea would have been in her early forties, Frank in his late forties, long after both had dropped out of sight.

The roar in her head faded in and out. This was not possible, her brain insisted. The words became a hammer drum. Not possible. Not possible! *Not possible!*

She felt bloodless and decidedly faint. Her throat had filled with thick cotton. Next to Anthea and Frank stood a picture of Anthea and Margaret. The progression of years was unmistakable. Sam saw it clearly. No great gaps of time. Five years here, seven there. You could follow that kind of aging process with relative ease. Forty years was too much. A computer could do it and maybe Guido, who had an eye for features, but not her.

She knew she was breathing wrong. It surprised her that she was breathing at all. Her chest felt impossibly constricted, like a spring that had been over wound.

This wasn't—this could not be true!

She didn't want to look further. A voice spoke in the background. Was it talking to her? Did it matter?

She'd knocked over a picture similar to the one Anthea had been clutching in death. There were more of those, at least five more. Plump, heathy features. No sign of cosmetic surgery. The subject looked to be a sweet, elderly woman, somewhere in her late seventies. She looked like someone's grandmother. Dear God, she was, she *was* someone's grandmother.

A scream climbed into Sam's throat, a hysterical scream that threatened to dissolve into hysterical laughter.

Far in the distance, the woman's voice reached her, penetrating the din in her head and bringing her shocked eyes into focus.

"Are you ill?" the woman inquired in alarm.

Sam pivoted, very much like Norman Bates's mother in *Psycho*. The revelation scene. Death staring Vera Miles in the face, just as Death had done to her, Sam thought, so numb inside now that she no longer felt the external temperature or the dampness of her clothes.

She knew Aidan was beside her. "What is it?" he asked.

She drew a deep, shuddering breath. Her gaze fastened on the woman in the doorway. She was moving, drifting toward them like a limbless ghost. "I was wrong," Sam whispered. "I got it backward, Aidan, and Anthea knew it. She tried to warn us the day she died. She told us not to be deceived. She warned us."

Aidan caught her by the shoulders when her rubbery knees would have given out. "What are you saying?" he breathed in her ear.

She gained strength if not composure. "I got it reversed, Aidan. Right from the start." Her numbness broke then; her head cleared; her eyes sharpened on the woman before them. "You knew, didn't you?" she said, unbelieving. "You knew and you didn't warn me."

The woman compressed her lips, then murmured, "Sam—"

"No!" She shook Aidan's restraining hands away. Fear, horror and anger melded into a violent ball of emotion. "Tell him who you are. Tell him. Tell me!"

The woman had pressed a gloved hand to her windpipe. She breathed heavily for several seconds, then slowly, haltingly, raised her other hand to her head. Stepping into the light, she removed her hat in a single fluid motion.

Honey brown hair, plump features and dark brown eyes greeted them.

"You thought I was Mary, didn't you?" she said, her tone

as expressionless as Sam's had been earlier. "I'm so sorry I didn't tell you before."

"Tell us what?" Aidan demanded. But he knew. He could see. To Sam's ear, he sounded cross but controlled. Prepared.

"My name." The woman held Sam's unblinking stare. "I call myself Irene Heiden these days. Before that I was Helen Murdoch. In my time, however, I was known as Margaret Truesdale."

SAM LONGED TO SCREAM, to call the woman a deluded liar and send her hurtling back to Oakhaven. But she knew. She could see it. Moreover, she could feel it. This woman was Margaret Truesdale. Which meant that the woman she'd believed to be Margaret Truesdale was really...

Her slender shoulders slumped. "I can't accept this," she murmured.

"But you must." The woman hastened toward her, shedding her black wrappings as she went. "I'm Margaret." Warm, lovely hands reached for Sam's arms. "You must also believe me when I tell you that I was only made aware of your situation the day before yesterday."

"How?" Aidan asked. He was still close enough behind her that Sam could feel his warm body. She did not want him to move away.

At his hard stare, Margaret let her hands drop. "From Freddie—Leo's wife. When we left Hollywood, Anthea and I felt that we should each maintain one outside contact. She chose Stan. I chose Leo. Naturally, when they became involved, Freddie began taking over the bulk of Leo's private affairs. I didn't mind that she found out about me. In fact, I was grateful when she tracked me down and told me about you. But even knowing who you were, I had no idea what you were up to. That you were my daughter Delores's child I had no doubt, especially after I saw your face and delicate bone structure. As for the rest—well, I simply didn't know. Then I discovered that Mary had escaped from Oakhaven, and my mind went blank. She's extremely clever. I couldn't have imagined what she might be planning, though I sensed it would be some grisly scheme to kill me, and perhaps you, as well.''

Aidan regarded her, his eyes half closed. ''So you didn't know that Mary was impersonating you?''

''Good heavens, no. I only guessed that tonight when I realized you thought I was the enemy. Who could that enemy be but Mary? And if you believed I was Mary, it stood to reason she had convinced you that she was me.''

Sam wondered distantly if there really was a Twilight Zone. If so, she'd plunged into it headlong. Through the Zone and straight into the Looking Glass.

Embers of rage glowed hot and bitter in the pit of her stomach. ''She used me,'' Sam said fiercely. ''To get to you, she used me. And I obliged her every step of the way.''

''Now, now, you mustn't blame yourself,'' Margaret consoled.

''I don't.'' Too angry to do anything more temperamental than plant her hands on her hips, she tapped an agitated foot on the carpet.

Rain pounded the roof and walls. The dull roar of blood had returned to her head. Aidan left her then, but only to cross the floor and separate the curtains with his hand.

Sam's spurt of irritation died as swiftly as it had been born, leaving her confused and questioning. ''You really are my natural grandmother, aren't you?'' she said to Margaret. ''That part of Mary's story was true.''

Grim-faced, Margaret nodded. ''She must have gotten hold of my personal files somehow, or photographed them. I don't suppose it would be too difficult. She probably still has Tobias to do her dirty work.''

''Tobias,'' Sam repeated. ''Tobias Lallibertie?''

''That's right.'' Margaret misinterpreted her glance at Aidan. ''He was her butler.''

''He's using the name Theo Larkin these days,'' Aidan told her from the window.

"T.L.," Sam said. "Same initials. That should have been a clue, Aidan."

"Don't be ridiculous." Margaret stroked Sam's dark hair. "You couldn't possibly have known. Mary and I often played sisters in films when we were younger, that's how much alike we looked. I don't know about now...."

Sam pictured Mary's angular face with its fine lines, sagging chin—and large dark eyes. Wrapping her arms around her midsection, she joined Aidan at the bay window. She felt safer next to him than she did anywhere else in the room. "Didn't Mary have hazel eyes?" she asked suddenly.

Margaret ran a finger along the line of pictures. "Yes. Why? Was the color different when you met her?"

"They were brown like yours." Often bloodshot, she reflected, but dark enough to pass.

Aidan let the curtain flutter back into place and with a motion for Sam to stay put, went to check the front door. "Contact lenses," he said over his shoulder. "They come in all colors."

"Naturally." Sighing, Sam plunked herself down on the flowered window seat. Picking up a cushion, she hugged it to her chest. "She always stayed in the shadows. She said she couldn't walk very well. I'll bet that was a lie, too. I guess Alistair must have been working for her."

Margaret's forehead wrinkled. "Who?"

"Alistair Blue. He's been following us all over the city. He said he was working for Thurman Wells originally, but Thurman had never heard of him. He must have been Mary's leg man."

"He didn't kill Anthea." Aidan rejoined them, his eyes flicking from shadow to shadow.

"I know, Anthea said Mary did it, but I still think it's possible that Dorian Hart's grandson might have been involved."

Margaret's eyes widened in alarm. "You met Jimmy?"

"I bumped into him at the cemetery today. He's nice-looking in a cool sort of way."

"No Hart was ever cool," Margaret said fervently. "Ruthless perhaps, but there's a great deal of passion in that family. That's why Frank and I left— Was that you?" she broke off to ask Aidan.

"Was what me?"

"That creak."

He stopped moving. So did Sam. She'd heard the sound as clearly as a rifle crack. It had not come from Aidan's direction.

Feet glued to the carpet, Sam whispered to Margaret, "Where's your husband?"

"Frank? He's visiting a trusted friend of ours. I told him to go, that I'd be fine. He doesn't know..." Another creak halted her. Inching closer to Sam, she found and clasped her hand.

"Don't move," Aidan instructed.

Sam had no intention of it. Not until she had determined the source of the creaks. One thing penetrated, however; Margaret and Frank Durwald were still married. Mary must have wanted her to track Margaret down through Frank. Then again, Mary had provided numerous routes by which she could conceivably have located Margaret. One, apparently, being the name Helen Murdoch.

God knew Mary was an extremely clever woman. But had she followed them here? Or come on her own perhaps? With a start, Sam recalled that she'd given Mary this address on Calvera Boulevard.

The lights gave a barely perceptible flicker, then settled. The rain made a plopping sound where it landed in the flower beds. The seconds crawled by, until finally, Margaret released a strained breath.

"It must have been the house shifting. It does from time to time."

"Maybe." Aidan touched Sam's cheek in passing, a casual, loving gesture that brought a lump of emotion to her throat.

Which was precisely where it solidified three seconds later.

The quicksilver shadow could have been caused by a gust of wind through an open window. It could have been a cat or the rain coming down at a different angle. It could have been many things, but somehow, instinctively, Sam knew it wasn't. She suspended her breathing as Mary, not bothering with melodrama, hobbled out of the shadows and into the lighted hallway, a black .38 caliber gun held fast in her gloved hand.

"Hello, Margaret," she greeted, her tone nothing short of gleeful. "Hello, Sam and Aidan. Hello, one and all. I've been waiting for this moment for more than forty years."

Hazel eyes glinting in the glow of rain-washed light, she raised the gun and cocked the hammer with her thumbs. "Hello, goodbye, Margaret Truesdale. It's time to meet your ultimate Fate."

SAM WAS THE FIRST to react. "Mary, don't!" she screamed, then jumped as the gun turned in her direction. "You'll—uh…" She glanced at Aidan, who was torn between tackling her and strangling her. She moistened her lips. "If you kill Margaret, who will you have left to hate?"

"No one," Mary chortled. "It'll be delicious. Oh, good Lord, do get that wooden expression off your face, Margaret. You're as spontaneous as a coat of paint. Do you see?" she demanded, waving the gun in agitation. "Do you see what I had to spend my entire career playing second fiddle to? A third-rate stage actress from—" she stuck out a contemptuous tongue "—Duluth. A farmer's daughter. A pig farmer at that. My parents were of bold military stock. My first words were 'Yes, sir' not 'Here, suey, suey.'" She swung the gun abruptly in Aidan's direction. "Touch that poker, buster, and they'll be scraping your remains off the wall."

Margaret swallowed shakily. "*Gangland Grace,* nineteen forty-nine. You played Bedelia Grace."

"And you played Angelina Grace, opposite Thurman. He only took that part to get back at me, you know. All because my baby didn't also happen to be his baby. Men are such egotistical jackasses."

"Can't imagine why," Aidan muttered in an undertone.

"Sam." He motioned to her, relieved when she gave a quick terrified nod. He was less worried about having his remains scraped off the wall than he was about losing Sam to this raving lunatic. Mary was only watching him peripherally. She wanted to see Margaret suffer. Shooting Sam would fit that bill perfectly. First the granddaughter, then quickly him, then Margaret. From her knees up, he suspected, with the process drawn out as painfully as possible.

He tried to work his way in front of Sam, but she was having none of it. The little idiot. Didn't she realize that he loved her? Maybe, he thought grimly, gnashing his back teeth, he should have mentioned it before now. He absorbed the icy shaft of guilt that stabbed him midchest. Maybe he should have acknowledged the truth himself. Mary made one valid point. Men really could be egotistical jackasses.

Mary bared her teeth, spewing daggers from her eyes. "I couldn't even have a healthy baby. You had to beat me in that, as well, didn't you, Margaret?"

"I gave my child up for adoption," Margaret reminded her in a choked voice. "How can you consider that a victory for me?"

"Because you had a choice, that's why. No pasty-faced doctor came in and told you your kid had been stillborn. You didn't have to go to its father and tell him you'd failed."

Sam slid an apprehensive glance in Aidan's direction. "Who was the father, Mary? Stan Hollister?"

"No. And not Thurman, either." Her expression grew smug. "So I guess I've one-upped old Margie in at least one thing. I have a secret to take to the grave. She'll have nothing but the grave itself. Cold and empty and dull as mud."

Without removing his gaze from her, Aidan edged sideways toward the bookshelves. He was a dead aim with a cricket ball. A paperweight shouldn't be all that different.

Catching the movement, Sam moved to Margaret's other side, drawing Mary's attention as she did. "You stole the film canisters of *The Three Fates,* didn't you? Why?"

Mary gave a rusty laugh. "Because I wanted them. Actually, Tobias did the dirty deed. He does have his good points."

Like a witch's familiar, Aidan reflected darkly. Seven feet to go.

"Why would you want an incomplete movie?" Margaret asked steadily, but she seemed to recognize Aidan's intent and did her best to keep Mary diverted.

Mary's mouth trembled. "Because then I could give it the ending I chose, the ending that should have been, and would have if that idiot writer and all the other idiots in power at the studio hadn't nixed the idea of you dying in the final scene."

"Really? Margaret was really supposed to die?" Sam sounded genuinely surprised. Jittery but surprised. "Guido said that, but I thought it was just studio hype."

"That's exactly what it turned out to be," Mary snapped. "But it had been fact at the start. I have a copy of the original script. Margaret was to die and I was to 'replace' her, so to speak. Didn't you watch the last clip that traitor Tobias sent you?"

"Tobias sent the videos?" Shock replaced surprise as Sam drew Margaret farther to the left. "I don't...why?"

"You said it yourself. A warning. You had to see the last clip to understand. I realized you were right when I looked at that piece. All the others made sense then."

"It was the part where you impersonated me in front of our lawyer, wasn't it?" Margaret said softly.

Mary made a face. "You always were sharp as a tack after the fact. Tobias was trying to tell them, in a roundabout way, of course, that I was impersonating you. The man's as subtle as a brick wall, but give him credit, he took his best shot. He was never more than half a step ahead of me, even when he enlisted that cocksure grandson of his to deter you."

"Alistair?" Sam exclaimed weakly. "He's your butler's grandson?"

Aidan continued to edge toward the paperweight.

"Lucky Tobias, huh?" Mary made an impatient gesture.

"But forget them. I handled that problem. I couldn't get a damned thing through the heads of those studio nitwits. *The Three Fates* was supposed to end with the ultimate impersonation. I was going to *become* my sister, take her place, her name and all her power. That's how it should have been. But no, Margaret couldn't die. That wouldn't work. And God knows, I could never take her place."

A wicked smile appeared on her lips, giving her the look of a spiteful goblin. "That's where I got my idea for this masquerade originally. It came to me years ago, but preparation takes time. First I had to pick up Delores's trail, then Sam's. Then I had to lay a trail of my own for her to follow—several of them, actually. I didn't care how you found Margaret, only that I didn't get 'made' in the process. So I started with the name Helen Murdoch. I weaseled it out of Thurman on one of his visits. I had to get him drunk to do it, mind you, but he's always been a sucker for the bottle."

Margaret, playing for time, cleared her throat. "I sensed that Thurman knew the name Helen Murdoch. That's why I changed it to Irene Heiden. I don't understand how he got it, though. I only ever gave that name to Leo."

"Who kept it on file and more than once sitting plain as you please on his writing desk. During a party, too," Mary tutted. "Thurman had no trouble finding it. Of course, you couldn't know that poor Leo's mind was going to slip away, could you? One day sharp, the next day fuzzy. Soon they all knew about Helen Murdoch. I trust you were a bit more circumspect about Irene Heiden. Only told Freddie?" she speculated.

"She'd been with Leo for a long time. We'd also been friends. I knew I could trust her."

Mary's eyes flashed, gold and loathing. "Trust or not, Margaret, I've got you now. You and your so-beautiful granddaughter who looks like you and whom I just know you do not want to see die. Well, tough luck, baby, because that's exactly what you're going to do. See her die. Followed by the man she loves. Followed finally, pleasurably, by you.''

Her muscles trembled visibly. Whether from anticipation or the strain of standing for so long, Aidan couldn't be sure. He *was* sure that the paperweight was mere inches out of reach.

''Hello, over there. Are you home, ma'am?'' A feeble voice crackled over the wall intercom.

Margaret jumped and spun. Her eyes locked on Aidan within range of the bookcase. She said nothing, simply raised the gun and pointed the barrel at his face. No fool, Aidan let his hand fall away.

''Who's that?'' Mary demanded of her old rival.

Margaret's fingers bit into Sam's arm. ''It's Jenny. My maid. Please, Mary, she's old and unwell. She lives in the cottage behind—''

''Tell her to go to bed.''

At Sam's nod of encouragement, Margaret steadied herself and, while Mary held the call button down, said, ''Yes, it's me, Jenny. Everything's fine. Go to bed.''

''Are you sure, ma'am?''

''Positive. Don't fret. Just go to bed. Frank—Frank and I want to be alone tonight.''

Mary made an unpleasant sound as she released the button. ''You stayed with that loser, Frank, all these years? My God, what a martyr you are. Although I have to admit I was pleased that my little introduction to Dorian Hart should actually cause the pair of you to drop out of sight. Maybe they wouldn't let me take over from you, but at least you were out of my face.'' She grunted, stomping an angry foot. ''If you move one more muscle, Aidan Brodie, I'll plug you. Or...no.'' The gun whipped from his face to Sam's. ''I'll plug her instead. That ought to keep the pair of you in line. Get away from her, Margaret.''

To Aidan's astonishment, Margaret's body tensed. He saw the frustration clearly, coupled with the sudden need to retaliate. He doubted that Mary saw much of anything right then.

Swearing to himself, he snatched up the paperweight. "Move, Sam," he shouted.

Yet even as he did, Margaret was snarling, "You won't shoot her, Mary. Not my granddaughter!" and rushing toward her enemy.

The gun went off. Rain hammered the roof, muffling the sound. Mary looked at once outraged, shocked and resolute. The paperweight struck her outstretched arm hard, but as if fixed with glue the gun stuck fast in her hands.

Aidan had heard of cases where crazy people displayed incredible bursts of strength, but he'd never heard anything like Mary in the next instant. The growl that emerged from her throat could only be termed feral, and her eyes, those large, impassioned eyes of hers, took on a sheen that transformed them from flashing hazel to fiery red in the space of a single second.

She fired once, then again, and again. Aidan dove for Sam who was clawing frantically at Margaret's hand.

"Margaret, no," she pleaded, but Margaret was already sinking to her knees.

A blast of wind pummeled the walls and had tree branches slapping the windowpanes.

Pain ricocheted through Aidan's head where it impacted on the edge of the coffee table to his shoulder where it slammed into the floor. A prisoner beneath him, Sam twined her fingers around the ends of his hair and breathed, "Don't move, Brodie."

A delighted cackle started low then rose to a hysterical crescendo. "I did it!" Mary exclaimed, exultant. "I got 'em all. Every last one of them."

What the hell was going on? Was Sam hurt? Was Margaret? Was he? Through half closed eyes, Aidan watched Mary scurry over and nudge Margaret's unmoving shoulder with her toe.

"Dead as a doornail." She stopped suddenly and stared down at the three of them, close together on the rose colored

carpet. "Dead as three doornails. Just like that. Just like…"
Her triumphant words slowed. Her body began to quiver. A
light of fury appeared in her eyes. She seemed not to notice
that the lights had dimmed, throwing the entire room into
shadow. The sagging skin around her throat shimmered, and
her face crumpled as she rasped, "I didn't want it like this.
It's no fun. She's dead. They're all dead, and I didn't get to
savor the moment." She gave Aidan's leg a vicious kick. "It's
no *fun!*"

Sam's fingers tightened on his jacket. Her breathing,
though, fast, seemed strong enough. And hard as it was now
to see, he thought, he felt certain he'd seen Margaret's head
shift.

Infuriated, Mary stomped both feet on the carpet. "I had it
all planned. The music boxes, the names, the adoption papers.
All according to plan. I even found Anthea." Bending with
difficulty, she shook Margaret's shadow-swathed shoulder. "I
killed her, Margaret. I was going to send you—well, me, but
they thought I was you—a picture of the three of us, from *The
Three Fates.* I put an *X* through Anthea to show you I'd killed
her. Just like I was supposed to kill her in the movie. Except
that Tobias got into my last package—the music box that
played 'The Funeral March'—and he took the picture out. I
think he must have sent it to Sam with that last videotape. He
wanted to stop me from killing you, but I wouldn't let him. I
had to get you. You know I did. But I wanted Sam to go first.
Every time I looked at her, I saw you. Every damned time.
She even sounded like you."

She shook Margaret again, harder. The silhouette on the
carpet remained limp and lifeless. "I don't know how Dorian
got wind of my plan. Didn't your idiot husband ever pay him
back? My God, how much stupid pride can one man have?
Margaret? Margaret!"

Unable to lie still and watch her wrench Margaret's arm
from its socket, Aidan started to rise. Sam made no attempt

to stop him at first, then, "Aidan!" she whispered. Her fingernails dug into his wrist. "It's Tobias."

He snapped his eyes around. From the deeper shadows near the staircase the man they'd known as Theo Larkin emerged and walked to where Mary knelt, head downbent. With a motion to Aidan and Sam not to move, he took Mary by the arms and drew her kindly to her feet.

"I did it, Tobias," she croaked brokenly. "I killed them all."

"Yes, you did." Sadness threaded his voice.

"They knew who Sam was, all of them—Stan, Leo, Thurman. But they didn't know what to do about it. They're ostriches, every last one of them. Except maybe Stan."

"Yes, he might have said something eventually," Tobias agreed.

Mary's face lit up in triumph. "That's why I hired his handyman to lock them in the garage. I had to divert their attention, stall for time, shake them up." Her squawk of laughter reverberated through the darkened living room. "That's the ironic part of it, Tobias. At first you wanted your grandson to scare them away, but then it occurred to me that I should be doing that. I, Mary, not I, Margaret. Mary would have wanted them off the scent, so I did things to try and deter them. Not anything that actually *would* deter them, but…things."

"You did what you've wanted to do for close to fifty years," Tobias said somberly. "You should be happy now."

"Damned right." She stared numbly up at him. Rain streaming down the window seemed to wash all the vibrancy from her body. "It's over, Tobias, I know it is. I beat you and them and her." She hesitated, then in a raw tremulous whisper, asked, "What do I do now?"

Chapter Seventeen

Sam couldn't have explained why that pathetic last question affected her so deeply. She only knew it did, despite the fact that she had no real idea what had just happened or why Margaret had signaled her to play dead.

Well, no, the play dead part was clear, as was Mary's state of mental deterioration. Wresting herself from Tobias's grip, she went to her knees in the spreading shadows and began shaking her three "dead" victims. Weakly at first, then as her energy returned, with greater force.

"No, no, *no!*" she declared, and poked Aidan hard with her knobby fingers. "You did it wrong, all of you. Get up, Brodie. You, too, Samantha." She jiggled Sam's shoulder. "Margaret, for heaven's sake, you stupid woman. You missed your cue completely. You were supposed to die after Sam. My pleasure was in your pain when she went down. Brodie's pain was in seeing his lover shot like a dog. Can't anyone take direction anymore?" Her head came up and twisted around. "Lights up," she ordered. "Can't film in the damned dark. Get away from the camera, Tobias. Retake. Retake! Stan, get everyone back to their marks…"

Reaching down, Tobias drew her upward. "They're dead, Mary. It's over. You've killed Margaret and those who led you to her. Be happy now. You've succeeded."

"I *am* happy," she shouted. "Of course, I am, you old fool. It just wasn't right, is all. They—she didn't do it right."

"Nevertheless, it's done." As he spoke, Tobias wrapped her cloak around her thin shoulders. "Margaret Truesdale is gone. You're number one now. You can relax at last, Mary. Relax and start to heal."

Sam saw her head come up, her chin jut at a regal angle. "Don't be an ass, Tobias," she said haughtily. "You're the one who needs to heal. You and your crazy schemes to undermine my plans. Ha! You thought you could fool me, didn't you? But I'm the best. I've always been the best, and soon the world will know it. I'll make them rewrite *The Three Fates,* and do it my way, the proper way. We'll shoot around Margaret. I'll take her place, the way I was supposed to originally. I'll play both parts. Or they can make it *The Two Fates.* Yes, omit Margaret entirely. Let her crawl into hiding with her gambler husband. Dorian's got enough clout to keep them under a rock for years. Forever, maybe." She blinked owlishly at Tobias as he began to lead her out. "Did I ever mention my friend Dorian Hart? I've known him for years. I think he likes me. He says a dame with balls is hard to find. He did, Tobias, he really did. Are we going to do a retake now or not?"

"Tomorrow," Tobias assured her. "Open the door," he said to some person Sam couldn't see.

She waited until they'd exited the living room before cautiously raising her head. "Aidan?" she whispered, fearful that he alone had been hit. "Are you okay?"

"Fine." He sounded disgruntled, a good sign, she thought with a relieved grin.

The grin faded as her anxious eyes fell on the woman in front of her. "Margaret?" she asked tentatively.

The woman stirred. "I'm fine, dear, just a bit creaky. Aidan, do you think you could... Thank you. Are we all intact? Oh, no, Aidan, Sam, don't go there. She'll see you."

But Aidan had already drawn Sam to her feet and started

for the door. Just inside, looking guilty and conspicuous, stood Alistair Blue, shoulders hunched as his sullen gaze darted from Tobias and Mary on the sidewalk to the pair in the hall.

"The old goat made me do it," he defended, pouting.

Sam watched Mary being led away by a solicitous Tobias and set her hand on the door frame. "What did he make you do, Alistair?" she asked, her tone distracted.

"Scare you at first, then when Mary started in with her own scare tactics, follow you and make sure none of them backfired." His hands balled in defense of his actions. "No one wanted you dead, you know. Granddad was just being an old fusspot. He said my broken brake line tactics were too rough that first time, but I knew you'd bail out. And Mary didn't really want you dead, either, did she? You had to find Margaret for her. So you see, everything was under control. Well, until Granddad got sloppy and Mary got hold of the paper where he'd written how to get to Anthea's place."

A right cross to the jaw sent him staggering into the papered wall. Mouth gaping, he slid down until he was seated straight-legged on the floor. Eyes wide and unbelieving, he stared at Aidan who was rubbing his knuckles.

"You're nuts," he said, his tone awed. Then he scrambled to his feet, backed away and shouted, "My God, you're a bigger loon than Mary Lamont." Rounding his shoulders, he dismissed them both. "Forget it. I'm outta here. If he asks, tell my grandfather I've gone to Arizona. Better rattlesnakes and scorpions to the weirdos in this phony town."

Sam watched him half swagger, half scurry down the sidewalk, then she shifted her attention to Tobias who was in the process of bundling Mary into a car across the street.

She touched the hand Aidan had laid across her shoulders. "Should we follow them?"

He kissed her temple, a small but infinitely tender gesture. "He'll take her to Oakhaven. I think it's what he wanted to do from the start."

"But she murdered Anthea Pennant. And Randy Paliss. She needs more than Oakhaven."

"John's no fool," he assured her. "She won't be there for long. The story's bound to break wide open. He didn't want that, but he'll deal with it. If we both call in a few favors, maybe we can keep Oakhaven from coming out of this too badly." He turned her gently to face him. "I do have a question for you, though."

She hesitated, then because she was so happy that he was alive, hooked her arms around his neck. "Shoot, Brodie."

His green eyes narrowed in mistrust. "What the hell just happened here?"

"THE BULLETS WERE BLANKS," Margaret explained, though not till forty minutes and several arrivals later. "Tobias must have replaced the real bullets with fakes so she'd believe she killed us. You see, I knew Mary was a crack shot, and the way that gun was pointed, she couldn't have missed me. So I did what any actress responding to her cue would have done. I 'died.' I'm so pleased, dear," she added to Sam, "that you're such a quick study. It's in your blood. You should consider acting. You, as well, Aidan. Matters could have gotten much uglier had we not reacted as we did. And of course, Tobias helped greatly by turning down the lights. No blood is a sure sign of no death where gunshot wounds are concerned."

"Too damned close if you ask me," Stan grumbled from the sofa.

He'd shown up shortly after Tobias had driven Mary away, squealing his BMW to a halt at the curb. Barely in Park, he'd piled out along with Freddie, Leo and a tipsy Thurman.

"Ah, Glenlivet," the actor had exclaimed after staring goggle-eyed at Margaret for five minutes. "Don't mind me, people."

Now, on the sidelines of the tearful reunion, Sam leaned her back to Aidan's front and drank in the happy scene. Margaret had made her revelation about the bullets, but she and

Aidan had had it all figured out anyway—or most of it at any rate.

"Tobias really does love Mary, poor man," Margaret sympathized, patting Sam's cheek en route to the old-fashioned radio. She switched it on, gave the rounded top a thump with her palm and heaved a sad sigh. "Perhaps he was the father of her child. Ah, well, I suppose we'll never know, will we? What were you saying earlier, Sam?"

"Asking actually," she said, blushing a little at the inanity of her question. "I was just wondering who, uh, was locked in the attic in *The Three Fates*."

Margaret smiled. "Oh, that. It was our leader. Our mentor, if you prefer. The idea was that we all knew he held the key to great powers and each of us wanted that key. But it was really nothing more than a test on his part. I was going to pass. Mary was going to fail. And Anthea, who was to have died midpicture, was going to remain a question mark."

"That was the revised version," Stan put in gruffly. "Originally, their prisoner was supposed to die along with Margaret and Anthea. Only Mary was to have survived and she was going to pretend to be Margaret's character."

"It would have made for an interesting ending," Aidan remarked. The hand circling Sam's waist stroked her midriff in such a natural, easy fashion that it felt suspiciously like a gesture of affection. Sam smiled and settled more securely into him.

Her gaze on Stan across the room must have transmitted a silent message for he held his glass of sherry up to her and offered a brief acknowledging smile. Her family ties still firmly intact, Sam nodded at her blood grandfather, then placed him into the same mental niche as Margaret. Blood, to her, was far from being the only tie that binds.

The radio crackled as the volume came up. The announcer's voice proclaimed two hours of comedy, drama and science fiction with "Suspense Theatre," "X Minus One," "The Shadow" and "The Jack Benny Show."

"Nostalgia," Freddie said, hugging her old friend. "I love it."

As Margaret turned to beam at the young pair, Aidan arched a polite inquiring brow. "Tell me, Margaret. Did your husband ever pay Dorian Hart the money he owed?"

The old radio broadcast music played above the storm. Margaret dipped her head. "Not all of it, I'm afraid. It was a very large sum with high interest. We did try, but we became fearful of giving ourselves away."

"Fear not, fair lady," Thurman called from the bar. "Your old friends will help you pay your debt. We'd have done it forty years ago if you'd let us. But then we males have pride, not to mention egos the size of New York. No doubt Frank wouldn't have heard of it."

"No doubt," Aidan murmured. A pair of headlights swept ghostly white through the room. Most of the occupants huddled around the radio chatting didn't notice. "Looks like more company," he observed.

"Or Margaret's husband," Sam suggested.

Thirty seconds later, the doorbell rang. Aidan frowned into the shadows to their left. "What now, I wonder?"

Curious, Sam took his hand and approached the door. The dark-haired man who stood there dripping on the welcome mat was the same one she'd banged into at the cemetery.

"It's, uh, Jimmy Visey," Margaret announced, her trepidation apparent. "Dorian Hart's grandson. I— Come in, won't you, Jimmy?"

"Don't mind if I do," said a female behind him. Pushing past the man's arm, Evelyn Mesmyr marched in and shook her umbrella vigorously. "Don't look so shell-shocked," she said to Margaret. "He isn't here to collect."

"You're not?" Sam echoed, surprised.

Jimmy shook his head. "It's an old debt, more than paid to my satisfaction. Grandfather's very old, and unfortunately very sick. He feels, and so do I, responsible to a degree for Mary Lamont's mental condition. That in turn led to the attack on

Miss Truesdale and yourselves. We're not murderers in my family, Ms. Giancarlo. We do only what we must when we must.''

"I knew that, of course,'' Evelyn remarked, checking her makeup in the hall mirror. "So when Mr. Hart contacted me via Jimmy here, I figured it couldn't hurt to try and help them track Mary down.''

"Track Mary down?'' Sam repeated. When Margaret and Aidan both gave her uncomprehending looks, she summoned a small smile and said, "Would someone mind explaining what's going on here, please?''

Jimmy dipped his head. "Yes, I'm sure you must all be rather confused at this stage. The straight truth is that my grandfather, and laterally myself, as well, wanted to insure that Mary was returned to Oakhaven unharmed. Ms. Mesmyr and I followed her butler here tonight. By the way, Ms. Giancarlo, it was me who bugged your home. I'm sorry, but Grandfather was insistent. He wanted Mary caught before she could cause any real trouble. We arrived, I regret to say, too late to save Anthea Pennant's life and, too late, as well, to capture Mary.''

"But why?'' Sam asked.

"Because my grandfather wants her safe. He also wants to see her again before he dies. I must admit, I'm rather curious myself, in light of what he told me recently.''

"Which was?'' Aidan asked when no one else did.

Jimmy's hazel eyes glinted. "Apparently Mary's child, the one everybody, including she believed had been stillborn, was very much alive after birth. My grandfather, er, took her. He'd always wanted a child. He would have wanted Mary if it hadn't been for her consuming hatred of you, Miss Truesdale. So, as I said, he took the child and paid the doctors to tell her it had been stillborn.''

"Terrific doctors,'' Sam muttered. Aidan nudged her into silence and Jimmy continued.

"That was the point when her decline into madness became apparent. I suppose, now, being so close to his Maker, whatever guilt Grandfather felt over that act has grown to rather large proportions in his conscience. He says it should end, now, all of it. Your husband's debt is canceled, Miss Truesdale, and Mary will be well taken care of.''

"Mary's child was also your grandfather's child then," Aidan clarified. "He didn't just take it because he wanted an heir.''

"Not at all," Jimmy assured. "The baby's name was Maria. She was my mother. I'm Mary Lamont's grandson.''

"It gets curiouser and curiouser all the time, don't you think?"

A quick smile crossed Sam's mouth as Aidan replied, "I'm trying not to think at all right now.''

The others were well out of earshot. For all intents and purposes Sam and Aidan were alone in their little corner of Margaret's living room.

"What?" he asked at her stare.

"Nothing. Just looking. I thought you were hurt earlier. I'm glad you weren't.''

"Yes, well, a similar thought crossed my mind." His thumbs slid upward to caress her collarbone. "It was the longest few minutes of my life.''

Her gaze steady, she asked, "Long enough to exorcise your demons?"

He gave his head a slight shake. "I don't know, Sam. It scares the hell out of me to love someone as much as I love you. I'm not sure I'm up to the responsibility.''

The fear and tension in her mind might never have existed so swiftly did they evaporate. A delighted smile lit her face. "An interesting choice of words, Brodie. I don't think I've ever been called a responsibility before. A liability once or twice when I was a bratty kid, but otherwise I've strived for independence. I think—" she snuggled suggestively closer, drawing his forehead to hers "—that you should say to hell with your reservations and admit that you're crazy about me.''

She saw him fight his amusement. Fight and lose. "All right, I give up. I'm crazy about you. Are you happy now?"

"I will be." She rocked her hips into his more rigid ones and had the satisfaction of hearing his quick hiss of reaction. She glanced at the gathering on the far side of the room. "I think we can leave here, now, don't you? I love you, you love me—and they'll never miss us. I vote we make a toast to our happiness, and theirs, at your place."

"Why mine?"

Eyes sparkling, she raised challenging brows. "Because I don't have any elderberry wine, that's why." And before he could respond, she set her hungry mouth on his.

Epilogue

She glided through the lavish common rooms at Oakhaven like a queen, elegant and regal. A celebrity. A star. Her comeback was imminent, her place in Hollywood history assured. There was that one nagging concern, of course, but she could deal with it. She'd dealt with far worse in her life, had she not?

They were waiting for her in the lobby, half a dozen of them at least. Well, she was famous, after all. She deserved the very best protection. And there were so many unstable people on the loose these days.

In her mind, she played *The Three Fates* to its conclusion. A bit cloudy, but her character had survived. It always did. It always would.

The voices on the outside jarred but didn't intrude. She would let nothing intrude on the grand finale.

"This way, Mary," an elderly man dressed like a butler bade her. "Doctor?"

"The papers will be forwarded, Tobias. Take care of her, gentlemen."

A white-suited attendant placed her arms into a ridiculous jacket with sleeves that went on forever. She sighed. The indignities one had to suffer for a role. He tied the sleeves behind her and stood back.

"Ready, Lieutenant."

"Take her out."

Mary blinked, roused. "Take who out? Not me, surely. That's not in the script, young man. Who do you think you are? You can't ad-lib. I won't allow it. I wouldn't let Mary do it. Why should I let you?"

The lieutenant's brows went up. "Excuse me, ma'am?"

"It's all right," John Christian promised. "These men will take good care of you." To the lieutenant, he added, "She's a little confused."

Her head came up at an imperious angle. "I am not confused. And they had better take care of me. I'm a priceless commodity. Ask anyone at the studio. No one's as valuable as me."

The lieutenant shuffled his feet. "Yes, well, let's go then, Ms. Lamont."

She stopped dead, nostrils flared, chin thrust out in anger. "How dare you call me that, young man."

"Call you what?"

"That name. I despise that name. Despise it, do you hear me? I'll eradicate it one day, see if I don't."

"What's she talking about, Doc?"

"Don't ask him," she snapped. "Ask me. What I'm talking about is that name. I am not Mary Lamont. My name is, and always has been, Margaret Truesdale."

KEY TO MY HEART

Unlock the secrets of romance just in time for the most romantic day of the year— Valentine's Day!

Key to My Heart
features three of your favorite authors,

**Kasey Michaels,
Rebecca York
and Muriel Jensen,**

to bring you wonderful tales of romance and Valentine's Day dreams come true.

As an added bonus you can receive Harlequin's special Valentine's Day necklace. FREE with the purchase of every *Key to My Heart* collection.

Available in January,
wherever Harlequin books are sold.

Take 4 bestselling love stories FREE

Plus get a FREE surprise gift!

Special Limited-time Offer

Mail to Harlequin Reader Service®

3010 Walden Avenue
P.O. Box 1867
Buffalo, N.Y. 14240-1867

YES! Please send me 4 free Harlequin Intrigue® novels and my free surprise gift. Then send me 4 brand-new novels every month. Bill me at the low price of $2.94 each plus 25¢ delivery and applicable sales tax, if any.* That's the complete price and a savings of over 10% off the cover prices—quite a bargain! I understand that accepting the books and gift places me under no obligation ever to buy any books. I can always return a shipment and cancel at any time. Even if I never buy another book from Harlequin, the 4 free books and the surprise gift are mine to keep forever.

181 BPA A3UQ

Name	(PLEASE PRINT)	
Address		Apt. No.
City	State	Zip

This offer is limited to one order per household and not valid to present Harlequin Intrigue® subscribers. *Terms and prices are subject to change without notice. Sales tax applicable in N.Y.

UINT-696

©1990 Harlequin Enterprises Limited

When little Adam Kingsley was taken from his nursery in the Kingsley mansion, the Memphis family used all their power and prestige to punish the kidnapper. They believed the crime was solved and the villain condemned...though the boy was never returned. But now, new evidence comes to light that may reveal the truth about...

The Kingsley Baby

Amanda Stevens is at her best for this powerful trilogy of a sensational crime and the three couples whose love lights the way to the truth. Don't miss:

#453 THE HERO'S SON (February)

#458 THE BROTHER'S WIFE (March)

#462 THE LONG-LOST HEIR (April)

What *really* happened that night in the
Kingsley nursery?